DEVON C. FORD

GENESIS

DEFIANCE BOOK ONE

GENESIS

©2019 DEVON C. FORD

Print and eBook formatting, and cover design by Steve Beaulieu.

Published by Aethon Books LLC. 2019

All characters in this book are fictitious. Any resemblance to actual persons, living or dead, is purely coincidental.

Dedicated to you.

You're awesome, keep that shit up.

PREFACE

All spelling and grammar in this book is UK English except for proper nouns and those American terms which just don't anglicize.

PROLOGUE

Years of training, his whole life, had led to this. Still, he wasn't quite prepared for the adrenaline; for the fear he felt before he suppressed it.

The guard lay dead at his feet, the last twitches and heaves of his chest both fascinating and terrible to watch. It had been easy; he had been training with knives for as long as he had memories. The guard hadn't stood a chance. A quick distraction and two fast strikes had opened up first the femoral artery of his left leg, and then the carotid on the right side of his neck as he spun in uncomprehending pain.

He hadn't uttered a word, just the strangled cry of sudden agony and shock before he was silenced forever. Quickly, he remembered himself and dragged the body back into the shadows out of sight. The guard's death would invite a strong response very rapidly. They were all tracked and monitored, and the failing life-signs of this unnamed and faceless number would be setting off alarms in The Citadel's huge control room; a mythical and terrible place he had been told stories of, but had never seen. They would know exactly where to go, and would be there all too quickly. He had stalked the helmeted, faceless soldier from the shadows and low rooftops to make sure he was alone, and now he had to find another one quickly to keep to the timeline.

Everything had to be memorised and all contingencies remembered in detail. They couldn't be in contact by radio; the government could track all communications just like they could identify all the people by the chips inserted in their necks.

But not him.

He didn't have one. He had been born free, not that he felt it was any kind of freedom, and in secret eighteen years ago, and kept hidden in the dark until he was old enough and well trained enough to fight.

He crept away in silence, ignoring the rifle and sidearm his victim carried; they were all tracked too. He made his way across the rooftops as the overwhelming strength of the response was laid out for him below. No fewer than four dull grey vans burst into the area with their near-silent hydrogen-electric engines, and spilled their contents of armed men and women to search for the dead guard.

Well trained, well drilled, lethal and unforgiving.

He leaned back from the parapet and moved on. He had a schedule to stick to. Other guards would be on high alert now, aware of the murder.

He found another victim patrolling alone, stalking them as he had done with the first guard minutes before.

Something was different, something *off*, about the way this one moved. Realising that this lone soldier would be aware of the death of a comrade, and feel isolated and scared, he dismissed the feeling and continued.

He dropped to the ground silently and rose, drawing both wickedly sharp blades from his lower back where they were sheathed. The slight whisper of steel on worn black leather made the guard stiffen.

Too late; he drove both blades into the ribcage under the armpits where the protective armour offered nothing to the wearer but vulnerability. The involuntary gasp that came from the guard's mouth behind the anonymous face covering was unmistakably female, but he felt no shame or regret.

With her heart punctured from both sides by the long blades, she fell lifeless in his arms where he lowered her gently to the ground. They were the enemy. They had chosen their side, just as his had been chosen for him.

He slipped away; conscious that the response to this new death would be as rapid and likely far more intense. Within minutes he had made his careful way back through the warm June night and was safely underground, away from the guards and their CCTV and their drones scouring the skyline.

The year was 2551. His name was Adam, and he had been raised to lead the resistance.

CHAPTER ONE

ANCIENT HISTORY

Adam's education had been something of great debate. Eventually he was told everything that was known about the life they now lived, and about how it had been before the wars. Not that anyone still alive remembered a time before, but the resistance had kept those memories alive like a race-memory. A genetic history of their own self-destruction.

His mother, a painfully thin woman often racked with illness, had insisted she be involved in his upbringing. She argued that there was no point in raising a leader with no concept of love or compassion.

His tutor, Mark, had a different view but he was over-ridden. He was there to train him, not to concern himself with the boy's emotional state, unless it impacted on his efficiency. He was a wiry, unsmiling man, but he was a fast and capable fighter, something he had taught Adam well. He also taught Adam how to listen and take in every detail, though not through the compassionate means his mother employed.

He still vividly remembered her telling him how the

DEVON C FORD

world came to be, reciting the story of the first people from the wafer-thin and battered pages of an ancient bible, copied by hand by someone long forgotten.

With the theology confusing his young brain, the more recent facts were explained to him.

In the early 21st Century, a small migration of refugees from war-torn regions became a tide.

The tide became a flood, and the flood became a relentless and crushing tsunami which washed north through Europe and almost collapsed the systems of the compassionate and accepting societies it flowed into. Extremism and terrorism rocked the continent, with mass shootings, suicide bombings and other barbaric acts of murder. The trend seemed to take on a grass-roots appeal, and the UK saw domestic terror attacks which were both laughable in their amateurish simplicity, and horrifying in their brutal effectiveness.

Not a day went by without a major city suffering an explosion, or even a small village seeing a lone knifeman reduce the local population by half, before the impossibly under-staffed police arrived to render them safe.

Parts of the world were at breaking point; torn between being humanitarian and maintaining a viable and safe infrastructure. The less discerning of governments made decisions to close borders, not that that stopped the flow, but the automatic gunfire and summary executions of illegals found crossing the borders went a long way to dissuading the majority.

The channel tunnel was eventually collapsed by the British, even though they denied it to the rest of the world and blamed the refugees for overloading the structure.

Countless people were walking through it in desperation when it imploded under the crushing weight of the English Channel. British warships, the few which remained in service due to the decimated Ministry of Defence budgetary cuts, abandoned their postings abroad and sailed home with orders to once more defend their island, whatever the cost may be.

Intentionally marooned, fighting one-sided battles with unarmed refugees to drive them away from the shores of the UK, the naval forces worked themselves to exhaustion to maintain the dwindling sovereignty of their home.

When the last of the nuclear powered Astute-class submarines still in working order suffered a catastrophic fire through lack of maintenance, it seemed almost to signal the end. Almost all hope was lost as the recordings of the trapped sailors, banging tools on pipes in desperate morse code whilst stranded at the bottom of the North Sea, played on every working television screen.

Then there had been a war.

"What's a war?" asked a young Adam from the depths of his memory, the boy's scruffy hair sticking up randomly above the questioning face.

"War is when countries fight each other," Mark began before he was interrupted again.

"Like Scotland fighting the Party?" he asked, leaning forward in his chair as though eager for the answer.

"Not exactly," Mark said carefully, hoping to avoid confusion, "that was a *civil* war, where different parts of the same country fight each other..."

"But Scotland *is* a different country," Adam interjected, annoyed that the facts in his head were being contradicted, "so is Wales..."

Mark sighed, closing the book he was reading from, and sitting next to his ward. The boy instinctively moved up closer to him, as though he thought the man was reading a bedtime story to him like his mother did.

"They are," Mark said patiently, "but they're also part of the same place. The United Kingdom."

Adam's face screwed up, trying to make sense of this new information before finally deciding to accept it.

"Okay," he said, "so other countries fought with us?"

"Yes, a long time ago," Mark explained.

"Why?" Adam interrupted again, prompting Mark to reach over and lightly jab the boy in his ribs to elicit a squeal.

"Stop interrupting, boy... Territory. Resources. Ideals. Religion," he listed tiredly, "Any excuse for people to kill each other, basically. But this war was the worst ever. This ended everything..." he trailed off, unconsciously smoothing down the boy's unruly hair.

It had truly been a global war of such huge proportions that there were still vast areas of the world which went uninhabited.

Countries in the Middle East had deployed nuclear weapons against countries who had been their allies before. The neighbouring countries responded and only some parts of the world had avoided the radioactive explosions.

Thousands of years of social evolution, of rich and developed culture, were destroyed in a few short months of intractable positions.

Adam was told that countries had designed and maintained these weapons as something they called a deterrent; as a bigger stick with which to threaten their enemies.

They were never supposed to be used, but they were. And now half of their planet lay in radioactive ruins as a result of simple human egotism. The snap decisions of insulted, narcissistic politicians reduced the lives of millions to a matter of statistics in mere seconds. Britain, more through inability to get in the fight than indecision, stayed mostly out of it. Her armed forces were stretched as woefully thinly as the police and security services were, and for a once great empire nation, they were largely overlooked by the huge superpowers intent on annihilating the competition.

They were reduced to insignificance, and they had enough troubles of their own after years of a failing economy, when the rich got richer and the poor became a threat to them.

From the ashes of the war rose a political power in Britain which dedicated itself to the protection of the island they lived on. They spoke of solidarity. Of perseverance. Of making their country strong again. Of that stiff upper lip which got them through the Blitz.

Studying the faded map he had been given, he saw the United Kingdom marked clearly, only it wasn't called that any more. That political power which emerged to protect the people had utilised the remnants of the military forces to enforce their rule, and they had become all but unopposed overnight. They now declared the larger island on his map to be "The Republic of Britain". The survivors of the war had been herded into camps for their protection, resulting in their effective imprisonment and work allocation.

He was told of concentration camps like in the wars from six hundred years ago; that time fought over ideals and land, instead of the last drops of oil on the planet.

Now everything was controlled by the Republic's governing body which was referred to only as *The Party*.

The Party was the true enemy, he had been told; the ones who lived in relative luxury and bore the fruits of the labours of their subjects. They had gone by another name when they were foolishly, legitimately, voted into power by the terrified and ignorant alike, but that had long since been eroded, along with any possible opposition.

Adam had been raised on various dilutions of vitriol about the enemy; each word or phrase he didn't understand went in his small notebook for reference later. He spent hours looking up the terms in an Oxford dictionary, a relic from an old world, as everything he had was.

Communism. Dictatorship. Fascist regime. Police state. Ethnic Cleansing.

There were other references he couldn't find, and asked his mother when she visited to teach him more history and English. She explained what 'Big Brother' meant, telling him of the drones and the cameras on every street.

"It's a term from long ago when people volunteered to be locked into a building with each other, and their every move, every word was recorded," she told him. "Like now, they watch everything we do," she said with an almost undetectable hint of fear and awe "and they know who we all are because of these."

She turned and lifted her greying hair from her neck to show him a much faded inch-long scar.

"They put them in all the babies," she said, ever showing her kind but sad smile. He felt his own neck, searching for his own badge of society. He didn't have one. His mother, Jean, had kept her pregnancy concealed, with great risk to her and Adam.

She had given birth in silent secrecy to prevent any citizens from hearing the sounds of labour and reporting her to the authorities for the reward of extra food credits.

He survived on the food brought to him, taken from the rations of those in the resistance.

They were all thin, the Party providing a calorie controlled diet to prevent obesity in its subjects.

He was left alone for hours on end, as the others had to attend the large factories and build whatever they were told. They weren't paid, they were given everything they needed by the government.

Everything they needed - the bare minimum - and nothing they wanted.

He was to help put an end to that, he was often told. He had learned not to cry; to keep silent, keep studying, training and waiting.

The large room next to his small sleeping quarters had padded floors and carefully crafted apparatus to help him learn to climb and be strong. He was five years old when he reached ten pull-ups each morning.

He could do over a hundred now, followed by the same in press-ups and sit ups. He copied the poses in a faded book marked 'yoga' and held the difficult ones for minutes on end. He became strong and flexible.

He was skilled - lethally - with knives in his hands. He practised for hours, cutting and thrusting and throwing them into a foam padded target as he rolled around the room.

He was just as dangerous with his bare hands.

One of the most important subjects he had studied was anatomy; he knew every artery his blades could reach and could even disrupt a target's blood flow by striking with his hands like a snake.

Arguments raged about when to let him out. Mark argued that he was ready and had been for years, but Command - the mysterious controlling element of the resistance - said that the Genesis program wasn't ready. Mark knew things like that. He used to be a Party soldier of the Republic, but got injured in a training accident, so he was sent to the general population away from The Citadel, his usefulness discarded.

Eventually circumstances finally dictated his unleashing, and he was given the job of creating a distraction whilst a cyber attack was made on a Party building. He knew nothing of the wider plan, other than his own, compartmentalised part.

On the first night he was allowed out into the world, he pulled on the black suit which masked his body heat from the prying eyes in the sky, sheathed his razor sharp knives behind his back and went topside.

CHAPTER TWO

COG IN THE MACHINE

Whilst Adam was creeping over the rooftops to find the first of two victims, other 'free-born' of the resistance were making their underground journey to their target near to The Citadel.

They were all thin and dirty, the signs of malnourished life in the dark showing on their spare frames and gaunt faces. They were born into secrecy and silence like Adam, kept and cared for in the same ways. Unlike Adam, they were bred and trained for different roles in life.

The resistance had been doing this for generations; maintaining a covert guerrilla force. They had been overwhelmingly beaten in the civil war, which raged for almost fifty years after the end of the global conflict, forced underground whilst their members hid in plain sight of the Republic's armed forces. Fed by them. Shepherded into their work placements by them.

Four other Pure Born found the first marker, as their nominal leader, first among equals, crouched while he checked his stopwatch. He was a computer expert, trained as the others had been, in secret. Practising on a keyboard plugged into nothing, memorising operating systems and code in the dark.

He was a genius with a photographic memory, but his abilities were offset by his habit of never making eye contact, as he twitched and felt awkward around others.

He had small, pointy features and squinted constantly, earning him the unkind nickname of Mouse. The unkind name stuck, not that Mouse seemed to mind, and it became a codename.

With Mouse went Fly; another ferrety-looking young man five years Mouse's junior, who could open any door with his small leather roll of picks and probes. Manual locks were still everywhere, but the closer they got to The Citadel, they found retinal scanners, swipe card access and fingerprint readers. There was precious little he could do with the retinal and biometric scanners, other than to burn the lock away and leave evidence. Or remove someone's eye.

The two lookouts were the twins, Jenna and Jonah. They were the back-up. The utility players. Both could open a door and both could work a computer, although neither was even remotely as accomplished as Mouse or Fly. The twins could also fight, and both carried hidden whispers of steel capable of cutting an enemy open with ease.

Jonah stayed put to keep their escape route open as Jenna led the other two up an access ladder to their target.

Mouse again checked his stopwatch, knowing that the planned diversion should be in play by now, and if it wasn't, then they could all be running for their lives soon.

They didn't know who provided their diversion, which was necessary in case they were taken.

They didn't exist officially, so the authorities would torture them and kill them with impunity, not that they didn't already do that to their citizens, but at least they had to offer some explanation for that.

Eventually one of them would give away something, so the less they knew, the better for everyone.

Fly made short work of the locked metal door barring their way, then crouched in the shadows and waited to be needed again. Jenna stalked in, masculine in many ways, with a strong body and short, fair hair, checking for any sign of enemies. That masculinity evaporated when she smiled, but she didn't often smile. The small substation was a metal shed; it wasn't seen as tactically important and they weren't expecting to have to deal with guards. As planned, all the patrols in the area which could detect them by pure chance were rushing to the other side of the city to whatever Command had planned to distract them.

Mouse worked fast, a small torch between his teeth as he sorted wires and chased a fibre optic cable back to its source. He connected a small box of his own design, hiding the wireless signal mimic device behind the mess of cabling.

He was careful to make it neat and straight; seeing something out of alignment attracted attention when it came to wires.

"Done," came the low reply to an unanswered question as he shut the cabinet with barely a sound. Silently they retreated, slipping back below ground undetected and showing no visible trace that they had been there.

CHAPTER THREE

PRIDE

Adam slipped silently into his quarters, peeling off the black hood and upper body of his suit. Pulling a small chain made his reflection flicker in front of him as a light stuttered on, making visible the dark brown of the dried blood on his hands and arms.

He drew his knives from behind his back and cleaned them thoroughly in a bowl of water before scrubbing the blood from his skin without emotion. He carefully dried, sharpened and oiled his blades before returning them to their worn sheathes.

A ritual.

A resetting process.

A return to his state of impatient rest.

He changed into loose clothing, relishing the freedom from the restriction he felt in the suit. He sat, but couldn't rest. He wanted to know what had happened, what his distraction had made possible, whether it had worked.

He waited, and waited. He lay on the bed and tried to close his eyes to will the time to pass until he was told more. By the time his door creaked open, his excitement had turned to annoyance. He leapt from the bed, lithe and taut. It was Mark.

"What happened?" blurted out Adam in his curiously quiet voice. Mark held up two hands to stop the onslaught of questions which he couldn't or wouldn't answer anyway.

"You tell me first. From the beginning."

Adam closed his eyes, partially miming his story to the older man. He described how he had crept along the rooftops, how he had stalked the first guard before dropping to ground level and assassinating him with ease. He turned, still with his eyes closed, and recounted how he had got back to the rooftops and moved away after pausing to count how many more soldiers responded to his first kill.

Mark fired off a series of questions about the number of vehicles, number of soldiers, how quickly they got there, what equipment they carried. Adam answered them all after a slight pause, giving the answers from the memories he replayed in his head. Satisfied that the hours, days and years playing memory games with the boy had borne fruit, Mark asked him to continue.

Adam told him of how he found another soldier alone and ended her life, miming the violent two handed thrust of the blades into her heart. He told Mark how he climbed again and disappeared over the buildings, once more recounting the numbers and speed of the reaction.

"Another three carriers, four each in the back, standard equipment," he said quietly, with his eyes closed.

"Drivers stayed in the vans," he said "I heard the drones coming but didn't see them."

Mark nodded to himself. The drones were everywhere, and unless you knew what to listen for, you wouldn't know one was hovering ten feet above your head, recording everything you said and did.

He had seen it himself; ranks upon ranks of Party

soldiers sitting in bucket chairs with virtual reality visors pulled low over their eyes, piloting the small drones all over the cities to observe the 'safety' of their subjects.

Adam continued with how he had dropped from the rooftops when the soft buzzing sounds reached his highly attuned ears, making his way back to his quarters unseen. The drones' heat-sensing imagery wouldn't detect him thanks to his suit, but a sharp-eyed operator could still have seen movement and located him.

Finished, Adam opened his eyes and stood up straight again, released from the spell of his re-enactment. He saw Mark deep in thought. His impatience allowed him to stay still and silent for only a few heartbeats.

"So what happened?" he asked, figuring he had waited long enough for his turn.

Mark seemed to consider telling him for a few seconds, weighing the risk of operational security against the likelihood of Adam being taken.

"It worked. Your diversion took most of the soldiers in the city away for almost an hour. The drones were scattered to keep watch after a while, but it was long enough."

"Long enough for what?" Adam hissed excitedly.

Again Mark paused, before allowing a small smile to creep onto the corner of his mouth.

"Long enough for us to piggy-back their network. We can see what they see now, and we can hear what they say to each other."

CHAPTER FOUR

COMMAND

It was far more than just that, really.

The device Mouse had connected to an ancillary subsystem had cleverly infected the wider network. Slowly creeping through wires and into databases, it left no trace of its presence as it ghosted along, gifting the Resistance access to systems as it went. CCTV, drones, communications, shift rotations of soldiers, personnel files, medical records, intelligence databases bearing information reports on citizens. Piece by piece, all of The Citadel's computerised material became available to them. Mouse explained what he had done, and what he could do with the access, to the shadowy figures sitting opposite him in the gloom.

"It's more of an intrusive surveillance thing," he explained as he fidgeted and looked to the ground "I can change stuff, but that might alert them to the compromise. I've only managed to change one thing that they shouldn't notice, to cover our tracks, but if I covered up the explosion then they would know we've hacked them."

He had been summoned to Command to report on the mission, and tried to warn them of the dangers of showing their hand. He reasoned that small victories using this information would be safer than trying for a big result and losing their covert advantage.

The half dozen members of Command listened, occasionally interjecting with a question or two. They didn't need the advice of this awkward young man, but none of them could deny the success of his genius.

Already their new information had saved lives; a message was intercepted giving the details of a suspected Resistance operative, and the crucial timing allowed the operative to be spirited away and removed from the grid, before the soldiers blew in the door to her quarters to find an abandoned living space. More importantly, it gave the identity of the subject who had reported her suspicious activity to Party officials in reward for additional food credits. What happened to them was not openly discussed.

They thanked him, inviting him to leave. Mouse was relieved at the dismissal, eager to return to his underground sanctuary and dive headlong into the lake of information he now had access to.

Command sat in the same gloom and discussed their plans long after Mouse had gone.

"Project Adam seems to be on course. Reports of his performance tonight show great promise" said one faceless voice from the shadows.

Murmurs of agreement from others, and pointed silence from some.

"And the other, the Genesis girl? How has she progressed?" asked the same voice to one particular shadow.

The shape of a person shifted in their seat before a soft female voice responded.

"She has made progress," she said almost reluctantly.

"But?" came the prompt from her left.

"But she is overly inquisitive," came the answer in a snap of annoyance, "she wants to know more than her part, and to give her the information she wants is to compromise everyone if she is taken. I do not propose to utilise her yet."

With that, the members of Command were dismissed, and they melted away to their own hiding spots scattered over the city. To their everyday *normal* lives. To meet all together was risky, but now much less so as they effectively knew what the enemy were saying to each other.

Only two shadowy figures remained, both understanding that they needed a more frank conversation about the other project.

"Cohen. Tell me about Eve," said the man, leaning into the light and showing a tired, pale face.

The woman named Cohen relaxed, but in an exhausted way as though she were dropping her public face.

"She just makes things… *difficult*," she said, "Her training is complete, but everything she is told gets a *'Why?'* in response. She is impossible at times and I worry that she won't be able to follow orders."

The man leaned back and steepled his fingers under his chin. He stayed like that for a few seconds in thought.

"Keep trying," he said, rising abruptly and leaving the room. Cohen sat with her head in her hands, tired.

CHAPTER FIVE

CONSEQUENCES

The Captain of the watch sat in uncomfortable silence. His dress uniform was cut intentionally tight, which made sitting down for any length of time painful. He had known this moment was coming as soon as the readouts of the soldier on the large screen went red and flashed, only to be followed minutes later by another on a different screen behind him.

Being Captain of the watch during the night was usually an easy task; he had teams of soldiers on a dedicated patrol route to enforce the curfew, drones in the sky and closed circuit video on all major areas. When the first soldier died, he followed protocol and deployed the nearest reactionary force units to converge and search. They found nothing but a butchered soldier, and followed the given orders to search for the killer. When the second soldier went down in a different sector, the Captain panicked and deployed everything he had to the area.

In retrospect, leaving most of the city unpatrolled and unwatched for a time was a mistake, and now he was being called to answer for the loss and damage suffered.

Whilst all the drones and soldiers were searching for an assassin whose disappearance underground was unknown to him, no fewer than twenty of the surveillance cameras were destroyed.

Then, to his horror, a bomb was exploded at the door of a military storeroom.

He recalled his panic with a cold shiver at how different screens went blank within minutes of each other.

He realised he had lost control of the situation, but still intended to report his success to his superiors.

It was a success, if looked at in a different light. The bomb had failed to breach the door of the storeroom and no weapons or equipment were stolen. The damaged cameras were all repaired now, but he had no idea how he would account for the death of two soldiers and the complete lack of information on their killer. He sat in his uncomfortable silence and waited for the reckoning.

"The Chairman will see you now," announced the attending adjutant confidently. The Captain stood, smoothed down his tight black uniform and donned his cap. Satisfied with his appearance, he turned and nodded to his Lieutenant to follow him, for there was no way he would be taking the entire blame for this; hence the summons for the commander of the troops deployed to find the killer.

The two junior officers marched smartly in, stamped to attention noisily and fired off simultaneous salutes with such crisp tension that their bodies quivered. Their taught muscles held the pose in front of the high-backed leather chair, waiting for the occupant to slowly spin the chair and look at them.

"At ease," came a husky growl from behind them. Both officers fought to control their involuntary jolt, but relaxed their arms to their sides as a taller man stalked forward.

The Chairman was, in truth, actually the Vice Chairman. He was named Nathaniel, like his father and his father before him. His father was the Chairman, but for the last five years all duties had been abdicated to his son piece by piece.

The older man was only Chairman in name, and his son was treated by everyone as though he held the title.

The Vice Chairman encouraged his subjects to call him Chairman. He had greedily climbed the military ranks and been given preferential positions of great influence and power by his father. He made no secret of his intentions, and made no friends on the way up.

What he did have was a reputation as a savage but intelligent military commander. He was feared, which had always been his intention. He was a tall man, well-built and strong, but he moved with a disturbing grace which caught people off guard. He glided like a predator.

He glided close to the two terrified officers and stood directly behind them.

"I've read your reports, so spare me any more excuses," he said in his quiet growl of a voice. "Tell me who is to blame."

CHAPTER SIX

HIDING IN PLAIN SIGHT

Mark got up, despite only having had two hours of fitful sleep, and prepared for his day job. He washed, dressed, ate a hurried breakfast and left the tower block for his work allocation.

High-rise buildings had been erected years before, and now covered the majority of the civilian subjects' residential areas. Dark and gloomy, the blocks were host to all types of illegal activity, only it was conducted in absolute secrecy to prevent a desperate occupant from selling out their fellow human being for a measly meal credit.

Mark was expert at using the shadowed stairwells to access the basement and labyrinth of tunnels beneath. Party soldiers made random inspections of the block, swarming in en masse and forcing terrified subjects to scatter like insects. Sometimes they came in fast, blew open a door and carried out the occupants, hooded and bound. Sometimes they made sweeps of the floors and just intimidated anyone unlucky enough not to have gone to ground, other times they came in secret to skulk and listen.

Mark joined the flow of subjects lining up to enter one

of the huge factories under the watchful eyes of soldiers on raised sentry platforms, their matte black uniforms and visored helmets rendering them asexual and almost inhuman. He filed into the huge building, waiting for the scanner in the doorway to register his thumbprint and flash a green light in acknowledgment.

He joined his place in line, waited for the loud klaxon to sound, and began the first of his two five-hour-long shifts on the factory conveyor making the drones which littered the skies of The Citadel's streets to keep them all under constant surveillance.

No talking was permitted, and the Party propaganda played on a seventeen-minute loop throughout the day. Mark could recite the words perfectly within a week of the footage being updated every month. He mimed along to the words as he worked automatically.

"The Party works tirelessly to keep you safe. You, the rightful inhabitants of the Republic of Britain, are bound by duty to report any wrongdoing you witness," came the smooth tones from the speaker over his left shoulder.

The propaganda continued for another sixteen minutes, going on to spew more hatred and intolerance. Mark was unaffected by the brainwashing, but he was one of the minority who was exposed to the deeper truth and an education in history, which many didn't possess.

He could see how others had been so saturated by the words; day after day, week after week and so on to the extent that they no longer even heard the words in their heads, but accepted them into their very DNA without question.

The indoctrination wasn't entirely wasted on him, however; he knew what words to use when spoken to by the factory overseers and guards. He could regurgitate the vitriol with such believable gusto that his loyalty to The

Party was never in doubt, but it took away a slice of his soul every time.

The message ended by strongly urging the loyal citizens of The Republic to be ever-vigilant in their daily activities and reminded them once again to report all suspected transgressions to The Party. Such loyalty would be rewarded, it said, and that was the key message. Human nature dictated that a person would seek the path of least resistance, to be selfish at their very core, and in a world where people survived on the bare minimum, such bounties were too often worth another person's life.

Mark's hands moved in practised grace, as muscle memory did the work for him while his mind was elsewhere. He thought over plans and targets, pondered over the goals of Command, and only stopped when the klaxon sounded again to signify the end of the first shift.

Again, he shuffled along in line to receive food and water. He sat in silence as others around him talked about the film shown the previous night on The Party television channel, or gossiped about other residents in their blocks.

He listened as he ate, disgusted at the careless nature of the sheep surrounding him, and returned to his place on the conveyor again after the third klaxon of the day rang loud through the factory.

Mark's mind wandered to the history lessons given to Adam, and the boy's annoyingly insatiable quest for knowledge. He could still see his face of almost ten years previously as the explanation for the world they now lived in was given.

The global war had brought about great change in their country. There had been dissident factions of society already; groups described as 'right wing' who wanted different people to leave the country.

The migration crisis in the middle of the 21st century

had seen these militant groups take to the streets and mercilessly beat people they believed were illegal immigrants.

Most of the time they weren't, and the government of that time had no answers to stop the vigilanteism becoming disorder and riot. There were far-right political parties who held a shred of eligibility then, and in the face of a crippled, dying economy and an influx of hundreds of thousands of mouths to feed, all coming with open hands, they grew stronger.

The riots blew through the cities, and emergency measures taken by the remnants of the existing government had ended with the military maintaining order on the streets, as the vastly depleted national police force had practically crumbled in the first few days of disorder. Years of budgetary cuts and reductions in recruitment had all but finished them, even before the violence stretched their thin lines to snapping point. The anti-immigration faction of government rapidly gained support, and in an unprecedented measure, the country saw its first hostile takeover of modern ruling. A truly 21st century coup. The successful party never took the military from the streets after a semblance of order was returned. Adam was told this was what a great leader of one of the world's largest empires had once done. Then the party's ideas suddenly took a trend more in line with the right-wing elements.

Nobody was prepared for the 'Britain Act'; the first official legislation since the Party seized power.

It was when he read this part of their history that Adam finally understood what the term *ethnic cleansing* meant.

The Party was publicly adamant that it wasn't a racist organisation.

An official census was taken, and those who could not

prove that their parents had been born in the country were deported by force to their country of origin; the difficulty being that many of their countries of origin were wastelands incapable of supporting life.

The military had to work around the clock to enforce the laws, ripping families apart and throwing screaming people into transport trucks, never to be seen again. Many of the soldiers refused to carry out their orders in those first weeks, which is when summary execution was reintroduced. After that first wave, compliance became more commonplace.

Huge detention centres were erected and policed, with planes leaving constantly for different countries. The passengers were bound and in many cases had hoods over their heads. Plane by plane, the country became predominantly white and irreparably poorer in moral stakes. It was during these mass deportations that civil war broke out.

The war was still being fought today, only by a tiny minority and in total secret. There were eyes and ears everywhere, and the general population was enticed with food credits and other luxuries to report any wrongdoing to the authorities immediately.

The legislation came thick and fast, totally unopposed. As time went by, the people were catalogued, microchipped and monitored twenty-four-seven. They became cattle. Cogs in the machine. After the wars came the diseases, and nobody knew if the raft of fatal illnesses was an intentional release of a weapon or a by-product of the planet's inhabitants tearing each other apart.

Nobody in the Resistance ever found out, and Mark suspected that any truth would be buried deep in secret archives controlled by the Party.

Their island was reduced to a population of under five million from the almost seventy million it had been before, and those survivors were clustered in a few large cities nestled amongst the ruins of history. After that, the racial purity of their home became less of an issue than the survival of their species was.

Mark continued his work, standing not ten paces away from Jean, and ever conscious not to allow his face to betray any signs of recognition. He returned to his endless plans of how to bring low the mighty machine which encompassed them all. He kept his face neutral as always, as deep inside he planned how to help burn it all to the ground.

CHAPTER SEVEN

DERELICTION

Neither of the nervous junior officers spoke.

"I shall ask again," said the Vice Chairman dangerously, "who is to blame?"

"Sir, Mr Chairman," stuttered the Captain, eager to throw any other victims in front of him for self-preservation, "I followed protocol when our soldier was killed and redeployed all nearby resources to…"

"I told you already," interrupted the Chairman with a quiet fury, "I've read your reports. I asked who was to blame."

The Captain's mouth opened and closed, but his courage escaped him and he said nothing. The Chairman turned on his heel and stepped quickly behind the large desk where he sat. His own closely tailored jacket kept him sitting up tall and stiff. He stared at both of them until their fear was palpable; he could almost taste their anticipation of punishment.

"Very well," he said, breaking his gaze away, "I shall tell you who is to blame. I am."

He left the words hanging heavy, enjoying his moment

as he saw both men shrink slightly as they relaxed. He did not let them enjoy that relaxation for long.

"I am to blame for allowing either of you to command anything more than a security barrier," he snarled at them, rising from his chair and placing both hands on the desk as he leaned across at them.

"*You*," he snapped, pointing at the Captain, "should never have left the rest of this city unguarded whilst you deployed everyone you had to chase their tails. *You*," his voice rose as he jabbed the finger towards him again, "should have realised that these terrorists operate such diversionary tactics in order to avert your eyes away from their real goal. *You*, should consider yourself lucky that they failed to breach the stores and get their filthy hands on weapons," he finished, maintaining eye contact with the petrified man before turning his attentions to the younger of the two.

"You," he said in gentler tones "simply failed to find a murderer with over a dozen trained soldiers. You have a lesson to learn from this."

The mood in the room relaxed again slightly, as both now believed that they would survive the meeting.

"Had the stores been breached, then I would likely have both of you executed for your incompetence. Think yourselves lucky that I am merely redeploying you to the frontier. Dismissed."

With that, he sat and turned his chair to show them the back. Uncertainly, they both stood to attention, saluted the high-backed chair and marched from the room. They were met by a group of adjutant officers outside and given their new assignments, effective immediately.

CHAPTER EIGHT

THE FORMATION OF THE FRONTIER

As history went, during the civil war there were factions of Britons who objected to Party rule. Ireland, long at odds with the mainland through some deeply ingrained genetic memory, rebelled with a united front of both north and south.

Weeks of relentless bombing runs brought that uprising to its knees and eventually scrubbed it from the face of the earth. A desperate mass migration from the west coast across the Atlantic in forlorn search of land not irradiated, left the country a cratered pile of rubble. For over fifty years the Party sent work teams over the Irish Sea to establish supply routes and to plunder what resources there were. Now the emerald isle was a ruined, pillaged, uninhabited wasteland.

Wales made little or no play to resist occupation and a change of government, and instead they obediently shuffled their collective way into the camps where the population was cleansed and the remainder set to work. The majority were kept in the lush valleys of the midlands, to farm and grow the supplies to feed the surviving inner-city areas, after the old capital and other big cities had long been abandoned for habitation.

Scotland was another matter entirely. Something fiercely ancestral was awoken, even more dangerous and rebellious than in Ireland, and the battles raged for over two decades until the overwhelming force and air superiority reigned supreme.

It was said that necessity was the mother of invention, but in truth it is conflict.

Domestic toys were weaponised and deployed as surveillance tools. The development of the drone program was largely responsible for the Party's superiority, and that development had continued to grow at an exponential rate.

Huge swathes of the borderlands were reduced to scorched ash, creating an endless stretch of no-man's-land. It was believed that some elements of resistance still existed in the highlands, but they were too few, too poorly equipped, and too far away to be considered a credible threat. The Party captured—they called it *liberated*—many of the population and killed anyone who offered resistance, before retreating back to the lower ground south of the vast lochs and mountain ranges.

That left the Party in total control of the most viable and fertile parts of the island, with the sole exception of the south west.

As with many invasions of Britain throughout history, geography was key to the success of military strategy; if you could not march your army somewhere and keep them fed and suitably equipped throughout the changing seasons, then you were destined to fail.

When the civil war began, the harsh terrain of the moors and the flow of water kept the soldiers out again.

Some form of leadership must have emerged rapidly, as by the time the soldiers spread out across the land to bring the subjects under their protection, all the roadways and bridges had been irreparably severed, creating a peninsular of isolation.

Attempts by sea were made by the fleet protecting the English Channel, but with so few viable ports to make landings, and the subsequent guerrilla tactics employed by mining the deep water approaches, it made the area simply more trouble than it was worth. That and the fact that the body count rose unacceptably. The plan to eradicate the problem by the tried and tested method of carpet bombing was mired by the ghost-like ability of the dissident factions to seek underground cover in their multitude of disused mines.

The option of a nuclear attack was overruled by the then Chairman, and that decision had never been revisited; as dangerous as Nathaniel seemed, even he would not poison the earth of his own island. After years of the two sides pretending the other didn't exist, the Party's newest drone program was rolled out in full, and manufacturing still continued.

In the first week alone, over four thousand drones went offline in the south west, their remotely operated cameras picking up nothing of their destruction.

Now the frontier was manned by what was effectively a penal battalion, and commanded by either disgraced officers who would never see promotion, or brave young officers seeking reputation.

Unlike in the far north, the lines could not be withdrawn as any territory yielded would be instantly reclaimed and mined with an array of savage traps.

Losses were often high on the frontier, and sentry duty at night was not a task to be taken lightly.

By sundown that first evening, Captain Smith and Lieutenant Shaw walked into the officers' mess. They were regarded coldly, and no greetings were offered. Fresh meat.

All the other officers in the room had suffered the same degrading walk when their own humiliation was raw, and none would offer solace to the two newest embarrassments to The Party.

Although few in the room expected to survive their deployment, many clung on to the hope that an act of bravery or the capture of a prisoner would allow them to regain their honour and return to the relative safety of their former units.

The two newest recruits sat apart from the others in silence, trying to ignore the looks and bursts of laughter at their expense.

A Major walked towards them and stood unnervingly close to their table.

"You two are to report to the quartermaster and draw equipment for tonight's sentry duty. You will shadow the officers in command, and take responsibility for one section of the lines for the rest of this rotation."

With that he turned and walked away. Neither the Captain nor his Lieutenant knew where the quartermaster was, or how long a rotation lasted. They stood and left the room with the sound of laughter rising when they were outside, and went to find a junior rank to intimidate into giving them the information they needed. Two hours later they were transported to the forward operations base, paired off with the officers they were to replace, and sent into the uncertain dark.

CHAPTER NINE

GAME ON

The Chairman sat in his chair long after the two terrified incompetents had been removed. He thought hard, playing out a scenario in his head until it reached a conclusion he found undesirable, then he retraced his mental steps and made different theoretical decisions until he found outcomes he could work with.

He sat like this for hours, until his thoughts returned to the present and he realised the sky outside had darkened. He spun his chair and pressed the buzzer by the telephone, causing a harsh noise to sound muffled through the door of his office. At once an immaculately uniformed assistant appeared.

"Yes, Sir?" she said, exuding efficiency whilst attempting to sound seductive at the same time.

"Coffee," he growled in response, totally aware of, but utterly immune to the clumsy effort to charm. With a silent nod, the assistant retreated from the doorway to return shortly afterwards with a tray bearing a pot and a glass. He nodded with almost reluctant manners as it was laid gently on his desk.

"Summon the duty guard commander, the chief of drones and someone who knows about where our stores are located," he said, offering no names or further assistance. Again the adjutant nodded in silence and retreated with demure deference.

The deference was a false front, disguising the fear she felt in his presence.

He insisted on having a female adjutant on duty twenty four hours a day, and she had known several of her peers be reassigned to menial or dangerous roles without any known cause. She returned to her desk, and began making phone calls.

Thirty minutes later, five assembled men sat uncomfortably on the metal bench opposite her desk. She pressed the buzzer, returning the two-way harsh noise to the office behind her.

"Are they here?" came the response.

"Yes, Sir. I have Colonel…" she stopped as the door burst open and The Chairman strode out.

"Walk with me," he commanded, prompting the five men to leap to their feet and scurry after their leader. He said nothing as he walked, but entered a briefing room and sat at the head. The small following clustered uncertainly, not sure if they should sit uninvited.

The Colonel, nominally in overall charge of the guard, and the most senior officer present amongst the summoned men, sat and the others followed suit timidly. Silence reigned for almost a minute as the Chairman remained still in thought.

Without preamble, he launched into verbalising his thoughts for the others to catch up with.

"Colonel," he said, not turning to look at the man "the attacks of last night appear to me to be connected in such a way as to appear like an attempt on a weapons cache."

The Colonel said nothing, waiting for a direct question to be asked of him as his attending assistant fidgeted next to him.

"Major," he said, addressing the duty chief in control of the drone program, "I know our drones saw nothing of the attacks as they were redeployed, but I want all footage of everything within a two mile radius of all incidents last night checked again. Thoroughly. Including all CCTV footage."

"Sir," said the Major, nodding. His Captain sat beside him tapping away on a tablet.

"You," he said, finally switching his gaze away from emptiness and looking directly at the man who was clearly roused from the logistics corps. The man froze when fixed by the cold, grey eyes and swallowed hard.

"Sir?" he managed, quieter than he intended.

"Why that store? There are a dozen like it all over the city so why that one?" he demanded. The man hoped the question was rhetorical, as he had no clue how to answer. Luckily, the rhetoric continued.

"It occurred to me," said Nathaniel as he stood to his full height and towered over the seated assembly, "that our assumption that these terrorists were after weapons was too easily come by."

He began to pace around the table slowly, lingering behind the seated men and making their very souls go cold at his presence. He stopped behind the Captain who was still flicking through files on the device, leaning down to look over his shoulder. Of all the people present, the young officer was the only one who seemed not to exude a palpable fear.

"What do you have?" he said.

"A working theory," came the confident reply. No fear. No 'Sir'.

Nathaniel felt a touch of respect for the young man for having the self-assurance not to revert to being a scared child in his presence. No other explanation was offered as he continued to work. Nathaniel waited patiently, watching deft fingers flick over the screen.

"Gotcha," the man said to himself with relish, before turning to the large screen in the room and flicking his finger up the face of the tablet towards the wall.

The screen came to life, showing a still shot of a poorly lit street at night. The footage played through, frame by frame in slow-motion. Silence in the room prompted him to rewind and play it again at normal speed. Still nothing from the seated officers.

"I see it," said Nathaniel "Where?"

"Nowhere near the attacks," replied the Captain, "Sir" he added hurriedly, remembering the company he was in.

None of the other assembled men were willing to display their ignorance at seeing nothing of note in the few seconds of footage, so they said nothing. The Chairman stalked back to his seat and sat in silence. His eyes were vacant, like his mind was deeply immersed in his thoughts.

"Colonel," he said, fixing the man with a direct stare, "you will organise a detailed search of that area at first light. All Party buildings within a mile radius, and if you find nothing, then extend the cordon until you do."

"You," he said, pointing a finger once more at the logistics corps man, who bore no insignia and hence was referred to simply as *you,* "will provide a full complement of engineers to assist and check that all equipment and systems in that area are uncompromised."

"Major," he switched his gaze "call in all relief drone operators and increase our coverage by fifty percent for the next week. Focus on Party assets in the city."

"Captain, your name?" he said, looking directly at the

young man, without waiting for confirmation of his last orders.

"Stanley, Sir" he replied, making unafraid eye contact.

"Captain Stanley, you will report to me directly in the morning."

He moved back to the Colonel without waiting for any answers.

"In the meantime, deploy units to round up any wrong-doers. I want public executions in the morning to send a message that we will not be mocked like this."

With that, he stood and left the room without another word. He returned to his office to find that the shift had changed and a different adjutant was now sitting in place of the clumsy girl he had suffered already. Stopping to pause in the doorway, he glanced back at the desk and saw the replacement pretending to be busy and failing.

Picking up the phone, he satisfied some tiny part of the urge to be cruel. He informed the person on the other end of the line that he would prefer it if the adjutant on duty that morning found herself on guard duty in a residence detail.

"And Captain Stanley, assigned to the drone control commander?" he waited for records to be checked before receiving confirmation that they knew to whom the Chairman referred, "Send me his full personnel file imme-diately."

CHAPTER TEN

INFORMATION SUPERHIGHWAY

Mouse sat squinting at the bank of screens in front of him while a member of Command looked over his shoulder. He was never alone with the information, but at least now the older man behind him had learned to stop asking questions. Sometimes a runner came in to whisper in the ear of his watcher, and he would be asked to mine the systems for a specific piece of information. Mouse was uncomfortable, not because of the poor light or the uncomfortable chair, but because he was never truly relaxed unless he was alone; other people expected things from him, and he never knew the right way to respond.

One such request came now, and he dutifully accessed the sub-systems to review communications traffic between The Citadel and the frontier. He found the correct files and brought them up one by one as the resistance administrators copied the text. Annoyed at the inactivity, he turned to another screen and transferred his attention to supply route information and locations of food caches, daydreaming of having more food than he could eat.

His wandering mind played out through his fingertips;

simple gestures and minor movements of his fingertips navigating him to more recent Party activity.

A massive increase in drone coverage, all relief operators activated and shifts increased to twelve-hour duties. The Citadel guards the same. Threat level increased to 'critical' rating.

A Captain Sterling promoted to Major and reassigned to Special Operations: Project Erebus. Peculiar, that order was signed by the Vice Chairman himself. He had never heard of Special Operations, or Erebus, and made a scribbled note on a scrap of paper to be passed up to Command.

The things he didn't know far outweighed the things he did, and he didn't like not knowing anything. Ignorance offended him, it kept him awake at night until he found the answers to his questions. As a child, he would fly into a rage when he didn't understand what he was told, which prompted a harsh response as his noise placed everyone in danger. He had learned to control his outbursts from a young age, but still the burning need to consume information raged on inside him. He didn't know if he was anti-social because of this, or if the two were inextricably linked.

He had to fight to control his annoyance when another member of the resistance was brought in to relieve him. He refused to leave, and moved to another screen, again to research Erebus until he found out what it meant.

CHAPTER ELEVEN

HOW TO FIGHT AN IDEA

The Chairman stood in his office, immaculately uniformed with his trademark revolver holstered on his left leg. His face and stance did not betray the fact that he had slept only for a few hours after his long night spent mentally running through the corridors of the maze in his mind, figuring out the best response to the latest acts of terrorism.

He had risen at dawn, exercised rigorously, showered and dressed. He stood rigid, sipping his coffee. Right on cue, the buzzer sounded.

"Captain Sterling, Sir," came the voice of the day shift female adjutant. He made no response, and there was a loud knock on the door.

"Come," he announced loudly, walking behind his desk and opening a drawer. Sterling marched in confidently and saluted. His drill was precise, respectful, but Nathaniel saw that this was one of the few men who did not seem terrified in his presence. For that reason, he sketched an uncommon salute in return and gestured for the younger man to sit.

He slid his hand into the drawer and brought out a set

of braided epaulettes and collar badges bearing a cluster of four stars.

"Major," he said, sliding them across the table.

Sterling stared at the symbol of his sudden and unexpected promotion for a brief second, before removing the single bar epaulettes and the more plain three-star badges from his collar.

He replaced them with his new rank in silence, smoothed his uniform and sat back with a small smile of satisfaction. A promotion from company rank to field rank was huge, he was young for a Captain and now probably one of the youngest Majors since Nathaniel himself.

He had no family ties to thank for his ascent; he possessed a razor-sharp intelligence and a confidence which senior men either despised or respected.

"I've searched the rest of the footage of where the movement was seen," he said without a trace of fear or awe at his current company, "I'm positive there was terrorist activity in that area, but no signs of any attempt or attack is evident. Either they didn't do anything, for whatever reason, or they did and we haven't found it."

"The search will carry on until I am given a definitive answer," growled Nathaniel in response. "Now, what do you know of Special Operations?" he asked.

A crooked smile appeared at the younger man's mouth.

"Nothing, Sir, officially. Only rumours of covert units and research projects. Genetic testing and the like," he answered.

"All true, and more," said Nathaniel "I promoted you for multiple reasons, one of which was to give you the prerequisite authority to access the program. Your official posting is as adjutant to a certain project, but your privileges have been greatly extended. Come," he said, rising suddenly and stalking from the room.

Sterling fell in step behind him and kept pace as Nathaniel went through secure door after secure door, until they reached a retinal-scan operated lift at the very heart of The Citadel. The Chairman stood aside and invited Sterling to access the control panel.

He placed his right hand on the scanner and saw it turn green as his newly-acquired access levels dawned on him. The retinal scanner blinked red lights at him, and he leaned in to allow his eyeball to be scrutinised. Again the lights turned green and the big steel door clunked and hissed as it opened.

They travelled down for an impossibly long time as Sterling tried his hardest not to betray his excitement with a smile; a Major with Special Operations access should not walk around smiling. Eventually the lift stopped, the scrolling red readout showing sub-level 11. The doors opened again, revealing a room the size of an aircraft hangar.

He could no longer contain his awe, and wandered into the expanse like a child marvelling at a grand sight for the first time.

To his right were glass-fronted cells, he walked towards them and saw that a few were occupied; muscled young men were sitting still, and the blank looks on their faces registered no interest in the visitors.

Sterling wandered to a rack of equipment, running his hands over a lightweight armoured uniform of a design he had never seen before. Beside the suit which resembled a cat, a big cat, a predator and not a pet, were various weapons which were new to him too. Blades, telescopic batons which he suspected were electrified, and other things, the functions of which he could only imagine.

"Major," came the voice from behind him, startling him back to the present "welcome to Project Erebus."

CHAPTER TWELVE

THE FRONTIER

Smith and Shaw were equipped and deployed. They shadowed their respective ranks to learn the individualities and peculiarities of the command for the stretch of frontier which was due to become their own in twenty-four hours.

Their new home was ten miles of Devonshire countryside, and in front of them in the darkness was the inhospitable expanse of Dartmoor. The winter weather alone could kill them if they walked southwest of their position, not that they would live long enough to succumb to exposure.

The bulky optics on their rifles pointed to the wilderness from their fortified positions, seeing nothing in any of the wide spectrum of vision modes available. Every noise was amplified by fear into an impending attack, the stress evident on the faces of the soldiers shivering throughout their night duty. The eerie green glow of enhanced night vision showed nothing, nor did the alien glow of the heat-detecting mode.

This was them now, for the foreseeable future and

beyond, unless they did something spectacular which could be reported as a success.

As they sat in the back of the command vehicle moving between the foxholes, Shaw leaned in to whisper to his senior officer.

"I'm not staying here," he said, receiving a skeptical and quizzical look in return.

"We'll die here," Smith responded, making the junior man unsure whether he was unsupportive of the veiled suggestion, or simply resigned to his fate.

CHAPTER THIRTEEN

CAGED ANIMALS

Adam paced his room. He had trained vigorously for hours to try and ease the feeling of claustrophobia.

He had been outside. He had fought the enemy, and he wanted more. His mother came to him with food and he took it ungratefully and sat to eat, wolfing it down so fast that he could not have tasted it, not that it tasted of much.

"Where's Mark? Is there another mission?" he asked through mouthfuls of food. Jean said she didn't know, and that he should be patient.

"I've been patient for years," he whined, "I want to go out again!"

"Patience," she soothed him, pointlessly, his indignation at feeling useless outweighing his maturity.

———

"The assets have been modified from birth," explained the Chairman "genetic enhancements, intense training and psychological conditioning…"

He stopped, regarding one of the three perfect specimens closely.

"There were twelve initially," he went on, "three did not survive their infancy; some subtle congenital defect which caused the enhancements to be rejected, I am told," he said dismissively.

"The nine who survived came under my control when they were almost ten years old. I was a young Major, younger than you even," he gave a curious small smile which put Sterling in mind of a boa constrictor. The smile evaporated as soon as it came.

"Their training was… *thorough*. Two died in the space of a year, sparring with the others. Another was killed in his sleep shortly after I took command of the frontier; his killer had to be euthanased to prevent further losses. His psychological conditioning appeared to have pushed him too far to the upper end of the spectrum. Of the remaining five, one died in another training mishap, and another took his own life after going on a rampage and killing half of the science staff on this level. The three you see here represent the pinnacle of our technological know-how." He paused, regarding the trio of killers.

"They have been kept separate from each other for years, but their conditioning allows us to exert total control over them." He nodded to a chinless man in glasses and a lab coat, who stepped forward, lifting up the black frames over his eyes and activated the retinal scanner on one of the glass cells.

The door slid open, and the occupant showed no sign of seeking freedom.

"SHADOW. REPORT," barked Nathaniel. The supine figure rose from the bed as effortlessly as a bird of prey changing direction on a thermal of wind; powerful and lithe.

He walked out of the open doorway, wearing only crisp white linen trousers. He had broad shoulders, was heavily developed but not muscle-bound, he had rigid abdominals and he moved with a lethal grace. He stood in front of the Chairman and stared into his face with dull eyes.

Nathaniel paced slowly around him, assessing the evident peak of physical capability, before stepping back a distance. He looked at Sterling, clearly anticipating the demonstration.

"TRAIN," he snapped, prompting the subject to tense and run towards the framework in the centre of the large room. His pace gathered easily until he was sprinting like a predator. He sprang through the air, catching a bar easily ten feet from the ground and swinging himself up onto a large frame. He leapt across the apparatus, before backflipping to the ground with a perfect landing. He attacked a piece of moving equipment with deadly accuracy; slamming hands, elbows, knees and feet into pads which caused a responding arm to spin back and pose a threat. Each threat was easily avoided or nullified with a strong counter.

The subject kept this up, increasing the intensity and effort for an impossibly long time until eventually one extravagant flying back-kick shattered the wooden bar coming fast at his head.

"FATHER," shouted Nathaniel, prompting the subject to step smartly back from the next attack and stand still, sweating but only slightly out of breath.

"HOME," he said again, and the subject walked past them without a glance, went through the open door to his cell and lay down on the bed again.

"Shadow," Nathaniel said. He indicated the next two cells in turn and said, "Host, Reaper."

In awe, Sterling walked forwards as the scientist locked the cell again. He could see that the glass was thick.

Shadow lay on the bed, his chest now heaving to repay the oxygen debt of his demonstration.

He walked sideways, tearing his gaze from the glistening torso of one subject to the next. He was identically built; muscled but flexible with an essence of resting murder. The last cell contained the only subject not to be bare chested.

"Reaper," he whispered to himself, unable to take his eyes from the dangerous looking young woman. She was the only one to respond to his presence; the only one to look at him.

She fixed him with a stare that burned through him, seeing through his skin and into his soul. He marvelled at the frightening beauty of the girl, the power in her limbs and the bright eyes. He felt cold, violated, and very grateful for the three inches of glass separating them.

———

Cohen finished her shift in the medical unit. The population of their city was not large, her hidden knowledge of the history of their country told her that the island hosted less than ten per cent of what it had done before. Back then it had been war, crime, disease and starvation which had lowered the numbers. Now it was industrial accidents, seeing that The Party regarded productivity over safety, and the occasional case of malnutrition.

Cohen did her best to keep people healthy, as she had done for years since she was allocated the job at the age of fifteen. She swept and mopped floors, wiped down switches and door handles with disinfectant from one end of the floor she worked on to the other, then she went back to the beginning and did it all over again.

She was careful to work slowly and methodically, yet

appearing to be putting in a sustained level of effort so that none of the supervisors or Party soldiers assigned to guard the unit decided she was slacking and chose to review her status.

In the almost three decades since she had first been given a mop and shown what to do, she had repeated the task twice daily, six days of every week, year after year.

Her cleaning tasks were carried out robotically, but her mind was always alert.

She listened to the doctors and nurses, watched their procedures and paid attention to their discussions when diagnosing complaints.

At great risk, she smuggled remnants of usable medical supplies from the bags marked for the incinerators every day. A bandage here, a suture needle and some thread there, and over the course of her years she had amassed an in-depth knowledge of medical practices and equipment.

She had delivered four babies in secret, Adam being one of them, even though she hadn't seen him since before he could walk. The last baby she had delivered, the youngest of the pure-born, had been given to her as her assignment, but she saw it more as a reward. She had a bright-eyed, mischievous little girl who she spent every evening and every Sunday with. Tutors spent the days with the girl as Cohen worked, and when she was only small a tiny, blunt sword was placed in her hand for the first time.

Of late, the girl's company felt less like a reward or even an assignment, and more like a burden of ingratitude. She was argumentative, and stubborn.

She was aggressive and reckless.

She was also lethally skilled and dangerous should she feel the urge, and when this was combined with the attitude she displayed, Cohen felt a sense of fear.

As much as the thought repelled her, she had found

herself an advocate of utilising the pure-born children at younger ages than she had originally thought was right. Even though she had only just turned sixteen, Eve was a competent killer, and Cohen worried that her immaturity would be their downfall.

Other projects under the banner of the Genesis program were already activated, but Eve was the youngest. Not that her age was an issue, but her childish temper was, and Cohen fought against Command every time they wanted to activate her.

Tidying up around the overweight overseer of the floor, she hid her feelings behind a neutral expression as the braying, obnoxious woman spoke on the telephone. She wedged the receiver between one flabby jowl and her shoulder, clearly discussing the previous night's televised entertainment and not engaging herself in important Party business. Cohen heard an electronic whirring noise. Eyes flickering towards the source of the noise, she saw that the woman needed both hands to work the small contraption she held. Placing a fingernail inside the end of a tube, she depressed a button with her other hand as he spoke loudly into the receiver and gave her opinion on something Cohen didn't care about. When the fingernail came out of the tube it was covered in a shiny red gloss.

The woman became aware of Cohen's attention and loudly declared into the phone that she had to deal with something, and would call back soon.

"Have you finished?" she demanded of the small cleaner rudely. Cohen didn't answer aloud, merely nodded and walked away only to return minutes later to empty the bin under the woman's fat elbow, without drawing attention to herself. She took the rubbish bags to the chute and deposited them inside.

Finishing her shift, she returned her equipment to the

store cupboard and hung her overalls neatly next to her mop and broom. The mop was beginning to feel a little threadbare, and she mused that she would give it another ten days before submitting the requisition to her supervisor. Hearing a commotion as she prepared to leave, she found herself ordered to stand still by a guard. She complied, finding her body and pockets searched roughly before being ordered on her way.

"It was here, somebody took it!" shrieked the voice of the floor supervisor behind her. Cohen smiled to herself as she took the stairs down to ground level and stopped briefly by the large metal dumpster to reach gingerly into the small rubbish bag on the top.

Using her fingers to separate a hole in the thin material, she quickly retrieved a small, black item and pocketed it as she barely broke step.

Keeping her head down and her posture small and unthreatening, her feet moved fast back towards her residence. Living on the fourth floor of the most southern tower block, block six, in the city limits had some perks but the downside was the twenty-minute walk to and from her work placement.

She made it back unmolested by either citizens or soldiers, ate a small and hurried meal more out of habit than hunger, then made her careful way to the basement where she navigated a labyrinth of dark tunnels to find her girl.

Opening the door to the hide, she scanned her eyes left and right to see where the child was hiding this time. Each night the girl must have sensed her coming. Either that or she waited for hours for the opportunity to scare the woman who had cared for her since birth.

As Cohen let the door close silently behind her and she took a few tentative steps into the gloom, a streak of long, dark hair descended behind her. The hair was followed by a pale face with large, wide eyes set like gems in a smooth stone. Like a cat stalking prey, the head flipped from upside down as the bright eyes momentarily closed and a small body dressed in black followed to drop to the ground with a ghostly absence of sound.

Cohen froze, an imperceptible sense warning her of the proximity alarm.

"Nice try," she said aloud, prompting the figure hunting her to leap forward and plant a kiss on her cheek before spinning away with a giggle.

"How did you know?" asked the girl in a small voice which seemed to hold its own slight echo.

"Eve," Cohen said seriously, the corner of her mouth curling into a small smile as she handed over the fascinating bauble to the girl and delighted in her expression, "you've only learned to do that recently. I've been invisible my entire life."

CHAPTER FOURTEEN

JUSTICE

Nathaniel sat alone in his office, having left his newly promoted Major in the depths of The Citadel, combing the archives and likely learning more truths about the history of the Republic than he had ever known. He perused the reports from the duty guard commander, as well as two from the intelligence cell assigned to sniffing out dissidents.

He had asked for the raw materials to furnish a display of power, and he had been given dregs.

Wrongdoers, he thought to himself, *I asked for wrongdoers. Not this rabble.*

He dropped the papers onto his desk and rubbed his face, feeling the tiredness for the first time since his long days after the recent attacks. Forgetting the tiredness as rapidly as he had allowed it to affect him, he sniffed hard and hit the intercom buzzer.

"How can I help, Sir?" came a voice dripping with such insincere allure that he almost recoiled.

"Coffee," he snapped, releasing the button so as not to hear any response. The silver tray arrived less than a minute later, brought in by a uniformed adjutant with an overly exaggerated swing of her hips. Nathaniel opened his mouth to dismiss her, until he caught sight of her face. He assessed, considered and decided within a split second.

He did not dismiss the girl, and he abandoned any thought of having her reassigned to some menial task, but felt that he still had to address the behaviour which had irked him.

"Corporal..." he said, eyeing the girl he had not seen in his office before.

"Nadeem, Sir", she said, looking him directly in the eye, "Samaira Nadeem". He caught a vague hint of an accent in her voice and was temporarily stunned by the sight of her pale brown skin, big eyes and jet black hair. Now that he saw her face to face he knew that the allure she had exuded through the intercom was not a ploy or an attempt to curry favour with him. Even though he was the most powerful man on the island, he found himself believing implicitly that the playfulness in the woman's voice was totally genuine, and utterly enchanting.

Then he remembered himself.

"Thank you, Nadeem," he said, nodding towards the door and casting his eyes to the tray to pour his own coffee. His eyes wandered up just in time to see his newest adjutant's full hips swing from the doorway like some form of weaponised hypnosis.

Sipping his coffee, he realised that he had just, for the first time, learned the name of a female adjutant. Picking up the phone he dialed the five numbers from memory for the head of resources and staffing.

The line was answered within three rings with obvious deference and the head of resources and staffing asked how they could assist the Chairman.

"The new adjutant you sent me," he growled, "Nadeem?"

Hesitation reigned momentarily on the other end of the line before the repsonse came, "Yes, Mr Chairman?" came the nervous reply, "Shall I reassign her?"

Hesitation came from the other end of the line this time.

"Yes. No," came the response, "give her primacy as my adjutant, and send me her personnel file," before the line went dead.

———

Having experienced some strange reaction to human contact, Nathaniel returned his full attention to the collection of suspected wrongdoers which had answered his summons for people to punish. He liked to keep things simple for the citizens; imprisonment, pain and death. These were the three levels of punishment he dispensed under the banner of justice. He decided on two of each.

A man and a woman had been found with stockpiled food supplies. In the eyes of the Party, this could only be seen as treason, as the couple refused to say during questioning what the food was for.

Their silence would meet a firing squad.

A teenager had refused their work placement, and had kicked a Party soldier in the leg.

They would be paraded alongside a man who defied an order from his work supervisor and both would receive ten doses of non-lethal electricity for the assembled crowds to witness.

The final two would receive thirty days imprisonment for minor contraband infractions found on routine residence searches. The truth was that 'contraband' had become such an ambiguous term that it was widely viewed as a reason to punish a citizen for anything.

He signed the orders, and summoned the adjutant to take the orders away for actioning.

As she stood in his office waiting for further instruction or dismissal, Nathaniel was rescued from further interaction by the return of Major Stanley.

"Stanley, come in," he said, waving a hand at Nadeem without looking at her as he sat. Stanley came in, eyes slightly reddened from hours spent staring at information on screens without a break. His eyes weren't so tired as to not notice the cut of the Corporal's uniform as Nathaniel asked her to bring more coffee.

"Sir," Stanley said with a smile, taking a seat without being offered one.

Nathaniel stiffened on impulse, but relaxed as he recalled this was the precise reason he had first considered bringing the young man in closer; he wasn't afraid of him.

"Archives give you much?" Nathaniel asked him dryly.

"Much?" Stanley asked with wide eyes, "They've given me more than I learned in school and since. I have some ideas…"

Nathaniel cut him off with a raised hand, "I'll tell you some of what *isn't* in the archives…" he stopped as the door opened again and Nadeem brought in a fresh pot of coffee with two glasses. She placed it gently on the desk, then retrieved a file from behind her back where she had tucked it into her figure-hugging skirt and rested it gently in front of the chairman. The file clearly bore the printed legend, "Nadeem, Samaira. CPL. Adj:54894" and she retreated from the office wearing a ghost of a smile.

Nathaniel experienced a new sensation at that moment, and covered what he felt was embarrassment by tossing the file to let it skid across the desk towards Stanley.

"The new adjutant," he said in a voice which he hoped was nonchalant, "I reassigned the last one because she annoyed me. Look into her for me?" he asked, hoping that his casual explanation would cover the redness of his cheeks.

Stanley swept up the file and put it on the pile of paperwork in his lap without another word. Nathaniel would have to read up on Samaira's life after Stanley had perused the file.

"You were saying, Sir?" he asked, deftly changing the subject. "Oh yes," replied the Chairman as he leaned back in his chair with a fresh coffee, "the things you don't know."

CHAPTER FIFTEEN

OLD-FASHIONED FUTURE

Stanley's eyes grew wide at intervals, and Nathaniel noticed the curious way he puffed his cheeks out and gently blew out a breath of air when he didn't believe something he heard.

Not that he didn't believe it, just more that he was incredulous about the facts, or simply the fact that those facts had been buried.

"So this thing," he asked as he leaned forward, "what was it called again?"

"The *in-ter-net,*" Nathaniel said carefully, rolling the alien word over his tongue.

"Right," Stanley said, "this internet thing really held all the information that was in our sealed archives?"

"That and more, apparently," Nathaniel answered, rising from his chair and removing the heavy leather uniform coat he habitually wore, and rolled up his sleeves before sitting down and steepling his fingers, "people used to be able to speak to each other, anywhere on the planet, via this internet. Knowledge was transferred instantly, and it was as though everyone had access to a global communication network as well as archives from everywhere."

Stanley's eyebrows went up again, indicating that he thought that level of access was astounding. And dangerous. "So how did governments control the flow of information to citizens?" he asked naively.

"They didn't," Nathaniel said with an internal shudder as he stretched his arms up.

Stanley's eyes flicked to the Chairman's forearms, and his gaze rested on the ugly, puckered patch of skin which looked rough and hairless. Nathaniel's own eyes followed the line of Stanley's, resting on his disfigurement, but he didn't move to cover the scars.

"That serves as a reminder of what people do when given freedom of choice," he said simply, offering nothing more on the subject. Stanley's sharp, investigative mind would usually have followed the interest to conclusion and discovered the story behind the injury, but his mind was on bigger things.

"So, after the wars...?" he prompted, waiting for the rest of the facts.

"Nuclear strikes in other countries damaged a lot of the industrial infrastructure, and the internet got shut down. Seems like they never turned it back on," Nathaniel smiled to himself, eyes seeing past Stanley into some other thought. "Good thing really. Can you imagine what the rabble would do if they could find out more than what we tell them?"

Stanley thought about that.

Being a person who loved to find out new things, he enjoyed his new and unprecedented access to the very inner sanctum of knowledge, and thanked whatever divine chance had led him to be be born on the right side of the fence.

Stanley was the son of a drone design engineer and his wife, a senior adjutant in charge of guard rotations, so he had the benefit of a more thorough education and a chance to train for the Party's military program.

Had fate dictated that he be born of a factory worker or a cleaner, then he would have been allocated a work assignment at fifteen and would still be doing that job now.

If he still lived.

A knock at the door interrupted the two men in their private revelries.

"Come," snapped Nathaniel as he pulled down the sleeves of his shirt and began to button the cuffs.

"Sirs," Nadeem said smoothly from just inside the threshold, "the punishment parade is due to start in twenty minutes." With that, she left the office, no trace of approval or disapproval in her tone or mannerism.

Nathaniel stood and buttoned the stiff leather uniform coat before fixing Stanley in the eye, who had risen and was similarly straightening himself.

"Don't forget to look over her file," he reminded his junior adjutant "now let's give them a lesson in power."

———

The fourth klaxon of the day sounded and Mark rushed to finish the remaining fixing of the drone motor.

Everyone else downed tools and materials where they lay, but Mark could never leave something unfinished. It stopped him sleeping.

"Move along, citizen," came the muffled voice of the Party soldier, who was probably as eager to finish his own shift as the unprivileged workers were who he was nominally there to protect.

"One second," Mark said, fixing the final small set of

rotor blades to the fourth and unfinished arm of the matte black drone.

"*Now,* citizen," snarled the faceless soldier, stepping close and putting the reflective, black visor of his helmet directly in Mark's face. Mark turned to him, smiling.

Luckily he remembered himself quickly and dropped the smile, cowering away from the bullying behaviour and apologising.

Little prick, he thought to himself as he shuffled out of the factory in line with the other cattle. *If you were any good you wouldn't be watching people put drones together.*

Trying to put the annoying confrontation out of his mind, along with the drone which would have taken him less than twenty seconds to complete, he turned his attention to the exit, which made him squint as the sunlight hurt his eyes after another day spent in gloom.

Something was different.

Something was off.

He spotted it instantly; far more guards than normal. Either this was a spot-check, where they would all be searched before being sent away to the residential blocks, or one of his mindless co-workers was about to be arrested.

It was neither. They were herded together by the additional guards, these ones carrying rifles in addition to the usual batons and sidearms, and marched awkwardly as a group towards the centre of the city instead.

Mark could have walked the distance in a few minutes, but the ungainly and halting progress of so many people forced to act as one made the journey twice as long as it needed to be. They arrived under the wide steps of The Citadel where other similar groups were huddled in confusion. They were shepherded into large pens, where they muttered quiet conversations to each other to pass the time and hopefully not attract the attention of the guards, who prowled around the peripheries looking for opportunities to haul out any suspected wrongdoer.

Mark knew what they were there for, even if most of the senseless, broken people surrounding him possessed insufficient capability for independent thought to care.

Twenty minutes later, the guards began to stiffen and seem more alert and professional.

As soon as that happened, the public address system crackled into life with an ear-splitting, high pitched shriek.

"Citizens of the Republic," boomed a gravelly voice which Mark recognised instantly, "You are here to bear witness to what happens when rules are disobeyed."

Even from the great distance, he could clearly make out the stone-faced Chairman. *Vice* Chairman he reminded himself, eyeballing the massed crowds as though he could beat each one into submission with just the power of his eyes.

"Rules are for your protection." he boomed through the speakers, making the staggered echo from distant speakers reverberate around the open, concrete arena.

"Rules are for order. Rules are for safety. Rules are for our security," he finished, reining in his anger and passion.

Your protection. Your order. Your safety and security, Mark thought to himself, wondering how anyone still believed the bullshit he had been fed since birth. He hadn't been born to the right family, but his physical attributes in school had been noticed and his parents had simply been told that he had been selected for Party military training. That was the last time he saw them alive. His attention was brought back to the steps above him in the near distance.

"These people are guilty of crimes against the Republic," Nathaniel said, annoyed as he always was that he had to wait for the echoes to die down before he could speak again. It forced him to speak slowly, which he hated because he didn't waste any time on anything.

He turned to the six people atop the steps not in party uniform. Two were bound at the wrists, two were strapped into metal frames with their hands and feet lashed tight to the four corners to stretch them upwards and outwards, and two were tied to metal posts the height of a man, their arms bound behind them. All were flanked by faceless soldiers, their anonymity seemingly giving them a sense of power without fear of accountability or retribution.

An adjutant stepped forward and read the charges against the two with tied hands. They were summarily sentenced to imprisonment, which meant imprisonment and forced labour, and led away to be transported north to the mines, where they would likely die or have their spirits broken beyond repair.

The two bound to the frames were dealt their punishments, as soldiers stepped forwards to drive stun-batons into their flesh ten times over, as their bodies arched and went rigid with each unimaginable dose of pain.

Even from a distance Mark could clearly make out blood running from the mouth of the younger and smaller of the two, and he suspected that the boy had likely bitten his tongue off.

Nathaniel stepped forwards after the charges against the final pair were read aloud. He sentenced them to death in as few words as possible, then smartly stepped backwards into the line of four soldiers bearing rifles. He reached over with his right hand and drew the large, silver coloured revolver from the holster on his left thigh.

Mark had heard stories about that weapon, and had even seen it once many years ago. It was a brute; ugly and heavy. It was rumoured to be the only weapon which wasn't controlled by the microchips implanted in them all, almost as if Nathaniel was personally inviting anyone to come and take a gun from him, if they felt up to the task.

The Chairman thumbed back the hammer on the gun and called the commands out himself.

"Ready," the soldiers chambered rounds into the breeches of their rifles in synchronised unison.

"Aim," the soldiers raised their rifles as one, the gloss-black visors lending them an ethereal status and somehow dehumanising them.

"Fire!"

CHAPTER SIXTEEN

THE APPROPRIATE RESPONSE

"We need to strike back," fired an angry voice from the shadows.

"We need to wait," said another, before being cut off by the first speaker.

"We need to strike back, and we need to do it now so they know they can no longer treat us like cattle…"

"And how do you propose that we respond?" asked a quiet voice from across the dimly lit underground room.

The owner of that quiet voice pushed her small frame off the pipes she was leaning against and walked to the centre of the room to stand under the single, weak bulb which cast the only illumination on the secret Command meeting.

"Well," started the angry voice, faltering, "we should hit a supply convoy or blow something else up," he finished lamely.

"James," Cohen said as she dropped her head slightly to one side as though disappointed, "if we destroy a supply convoy, then we will just end up with less food and more punishments." She raised her head again, gathering a momentum far bigger than her physical presence. "And blowing something up?" she said in a louder voice, "Isn't that a little beneath us?"

James deflated, dropping his shoulders and standing up. He walked around the small room, rubbing his hands through his hair.

Cohen knew that he was reacting emotionally, knew that the old couple storing food had been among the many people doing so in order to feed those members of the resistance who weren't on any food ration database, and she knew that James also had a problem when it came to accepting criticism.

"I'm not against you," she said, heading off that avenue of retort from him, "and we do need to respond but *not* like this. *Not* a knee-jerk reaction that will put more of us in danger."

Silence reigned briefly, as though the tense conversation was holding its breath. Cohen scanned the gloom and only met a few eyes which weren't either watching James Phillips—their de facto leader by nothing but seniority—or simply averting their gaze from her.

"They will be watching closely for our response," she said more gently, "and we need to wait so we don't get drawn into a trap."

"Fine," James answered irritably as though he realised his emotions were ruling him. All but one of the leaders had borne witness to the Party's vulgar display of power as they were herded from their work placements to The Citadel.

"What would you suggest we do?" he said, the challenge overt and implicit in his acidic words. He smiled wolfishly, yielding the floor to Cohen to provide him with the answers he couldn't arrive at by himself.

Cohen smiled back, knowing that she was being called out; either her idea would be slapped down as too weak or stupid, or hijacked and used as James' own.

"We go slow," she started, raising her voice over the snorts of derision which answered her opening gambit, "we go slow, and we hit hard. They are trying to evoke a violent reaction from us, so we must respond in a way that they wouldn't expect."

The snorting stopped and the eyes watched her from the gloom.

"We go into their home," she said, holding the silence, "we undermine their assumption of safety, and we show them we can strike accurately at their hearts and all they can do is punish us as a whole."

Eyes glanced between the shadows, unsure about the unexpected change of pace she suggested. Maintaining her momentum, Cohen dragged her stool towards the centre of the room, the metal legs scraping loudly on the bare concrete and punctuating the meeting with an obvious switch in supremacy. Cohen knew that one wrong word or badly phrased suggestion would rob her of her audience, so she sat and carefully explained what she had in mind.

"This will not be quick, but it will be quiet" she began.

———

James rubbed his eyes and continued the movement over his thinning, greasy hair. He walked tiredly to the small room where he found the nominal guard asleep on an old chair tipped back against the wall. He stopped in front of the man and watched him, waiting for any sense of awareness to puncture his sleep. Nothing. No response to one of the Command elders watching him sleep on sentry duty.

James sighed, walked past the man in his deep sleep

and pulled up a wobbling wheeled chair to sit just behind the left shoulder of Mouse. The small young man flinched involuntarily as another human being encroached on his personal space without warning, but righted himself. He recognised James, but that recognition earned no change in response from him. He tapped away at the keyboards, eyes darting between the two screens in front of him and mentally tutting every time the information he wanted to see scrolled over the line of distortion, created by some old damage he didn't know the cause of.

His annoyance wasn't caused so much by the fact that one of the monitors was damaged, but more because he didn't know what had caused it. He liked to know things.

He ignored the man behind him who watched as he typed, looked, and intermittently snatched up an old nub of a pencil to scribble a note on a pad of paper for later reference.

The man obviously wanted something from him, but he would get to it in time. That time came less than a minute later when he cleared his throat.

"I need a list of senior Party personnel," he began, "and their residences," he swallowed audibly, "and their families."

Mouse kept his eyes on the screen but nodded his understanding and assent. His fingertips spoke for him, as he closed windows off; white, red and green text scrolling through black boxes on the screens. He brought up new windows, going from link to link as he descended further down the maze of computerised hallways and corridors.

Often, he found a dead end or worse, a location which held nothing interesting, and then he retraced his digital steps, recalling the lefts and the rights and the ups and the downs of his reverse course. James watched on, but all he saw was someone typing impossibly fast and lines of text coming up on both screens.

"I'm in," Mouse said after a few minutes silence, "how senior do you want them?"

"Start with the Chairman," James said before correcting himself, "the Vice Chairman that is."

"One and the same," Mouse said absent-mindedly, "at least some of the time anyway."

"What?" James said, annoyed at the young man's strange habits and unsure if he was even addressing him.

Mouse seemed to snap out of his computer-guided wanderings and half-turned to address the troublesome human.

"I mean that the Vice Chairman has a residence with the Chairman, but he also has quarters at The Citadel." he mumbled in an embarrassed voice.

"Just say that then," James snapped at him, completely unaware of the fact that he was affecting the mood, and ultimately the efficiency of the task. Mouse sighed in obvious discomfort and annoyance and resumed mining the information.

"Get the details and have them sent to me," James said as he rose and left the room, disappointed that he didn't understand the process he had instigated.

He walked towards the exit, Mouse ignoring his exit as it bore no more interest to him than his entry had.

James didn't break step as he passed the sleeping guard, merely exaggerated the forward motion of his left boot and added some power to the swing. The guard jolted awake with wide eyes as whatever internal gyroscope registered the momentary weightlessness.

He crashed to the floor and gained enough sense of his surroundings in time to recognise the retreating back of

James. Sitting on his backside on the rough concrete floor with the upturned chair tangled in his legs, he blinked at Mouse, who stared resolutely at his screens wearing the smallest of smiles.

CHAPTER SEVENTEEN

THE WAY OF THINGS

Contact with the enemy was a weekly occurrence, not that anyone knew in the city surrounding The Citadel at its nucleus, or in the outlying industrial districts.

Or the farming districts in the west.

Or the mining districts in the north.

That the Party was still effectively at war was a state secret, which was easily kept, as few soldiers returned from the frontier battalions and those who did counted themselves so lucky to have returned whole that they kept their mouths tightly shut.

Captain Smith had been formally handed command of a twenty-mile stretch of barren landscape, and his bitterness and anger were no longer masked by his presence at The Citadel, so he delegated almost every unsafe or unpopular task to his Lieutenant, Shaw.

Shaw, in turn, showed equal cowardice and disdain and passed those orders on to their company Sergeant. Owen Du Bois had arrived at the frontier as a private soldier who had been disciplined twice for showing excessive leniency to the farm workers under his protection. On the third occasion, he had been caught issuing extra rations which he had marked as spoiled, his commanding officer had placed him under arrest and he had found himself court-martialled within a day.

His transfer to the penal battalion had come a day later, and there he had stayed. He had let his beard grow on the front line, and now the fearsome and large ginger foliage had become his trademark.

It itched him terribly when he had to wear the helmet and visor when deployed, but he refused to trim it.

He was a capable soldier, and his easy authoritative manner with the other soldiers made him a useful man to his superiors. Effectively, Du Bois ran the company of soldiers; disciplined them when required and ensured they carried out the orders given by the officers.

Only the rank and file stayed together as a unit, even though each company would expect to lose one or two men every few months. The officers were rotated among units, to ensure that they never felt comfortable or grew attached to the men under their command.

So, on their fifth and last consecutive night of their deployment, Smith and Shaw cowered in the command bunker with a guard of four soldiers acting as their personal sentries, weakening the front-line defences by doing so, yet lacking the tactical awareness or bravery to deploy soldiers otherwise. They had the remainder of that night to survive before they were rotated back from the front line by five miles for three nights of rest in relative safety, before returning to spend a further five consecutive days in the cold sunshine overlooking the same barren landscape.

The enemy usually came at night, in silence and shrouded in the invisibility of the darkness. The use of lights was a foolish invitation of an attack, so the Party soldiers huddled in the darkness of their entrenched positions and kept nervous eyes on the ground ahead. Complacency was often rewarded with a lonely death, and the horror stories passed on between rotating soldiers of different companies grew in horror with each telling.

Reports of the enemy had been embellished in this manner over many years until each man serving on the frontier genuinely believed that they were fighting against mutated monsters, more animal than human, who lived in burrows and could see in the dark.

They could see in the dark too, the precious optics issued to each soldier allowing them to see in a myriad of spectrums. None of these, however, had ever detected the enemy, at least not by any surviving soldier.

"I heard they eat parts of the soldiers they kill," came the wavering whisper from the young soldier to Owen's left in the dark bunker.

"Don't be so stupid, boy," he growled back in a low voice, which he had perfected to not carry in the darkness, "why would anyone want to eat us?"

Owen saw the funny side of the outrageous stories, but the newest 'recruit' to his unit clearly still believed the hype.

"Because they're not human," came the hoarse reply, clearly believing the rumours and nearing the point of tears.

Du Bois turned and put a firm hand on the shoulder of the boy. He couldn't remember his name, and had a vague notion that he had been sent to the frontier as his previous commanding officer feared he was too nervous for guard duty. If he survived the year he had been posted to serve in Du Bois' company, then the boy would likely be cured of that nervousness; if he survived.

"They are human," he said as he squeezed hard to get

the boy's full attention, "they are just different. They're our enemy, and we're theirs. That's just the way of things," he finished, almost kindly. Then the squeeze shot through the boy's shoulder much harder and made him wince.

At least he didn't cry out, Du Bois thought, *maybe he does want to live.*

"Now stop crying like a little girl, and keep your fucking eyes pointed towards the dangerous bit."

Two hundred metres behind him, Smith and Shaw were in a sunken hide, set eight feet deep in the earth and the lumps of hard granite. There was just a small patch of moonlit earth visible through the firing port. The two officers in command of the company waited for the last few hours of their first deployment to end as their bodyguards shivered outside, exposed to the elements. They would have to face the nightmare of the long nights again in twelve days' time, but that was twelve days of relative safety in comparison to the terror they were currently experiencing. They too believed the stories of the inhuman ghouls who stalked them using their unearthly powers of invisibility, but neither would demean himself by displaying this in front of these hard-bitten soldiers who had spent days, weeks and months on the threshold between their worlds.

Du Bois forced himself to concentrate. He was due to be returned to The Citadel for reassignment, having completed his three-year long 'developmental' posting to the frontier, and getting killed now would just annoy him.

———

Mouse worked without any meaningful connection to the world outside of his own mental creation. In the safety of his mind, his fingertips walked him through the maze of rooms and corridors he navigated, his eyes translating the code on the screens into a physical construct with colours and textures.

He imagined himself walking along the hallway now. Brushing his fingertips along the brilliant white paint of the wall on his right, he felt the smooth coldness of the surface until the wooden doorframe disturbed the path. He turned to regard the door, seeing that it looked out of place and not like the others in the corridor.

His fingertips flashed and his imagination took a step back to regard the door. The wood looked unpainted and seemed in some way tainted in the sterile environment he was navigating.

He tried the door handle and found it locked. Taking a step back again he looked to the left of the doorframe and waited until his fingertips created an opening in the wall. Reaching through he opened the door from the inside and watched as it swung inwards.

Mouse smiled as he found himself looking at a room filled with information. He liked information, it made him feel complete. His smile faded slightly when he saw what the information was, opening an encrypted file to make another box pop into life and begin playing a video clip. Mouse quickly killed the screen, upset and angry at what he saw, but the knowledge gave him exactly what he wanted.

He had found the perfect person to exploit, but he realised he needed more materials to make any mission a survivable one.

———

"I get to go out?" Eve shrieked at Cohen, earning a two-handed shake of the girl's shoulders to remind her to keep quiet.

"Yes," replied Cohen cautiously, resignedly, "but you are to do exactly what you are told. Adam will…"

"Who is Adam?" the girl interrupted her, "Is he like me too?"

Cohen held up both hands and fixed the girl with a look of stern temper. She deflated, dropped her shoulders, and placed a sullen finger to her lips.

Cohen could almost feel the electricity course through the girl as though she were fully charged and in desperate need of action.

"Adam is like you," she told her, "and the others who will get you where you need to be are like you too, only they have been trained to do different things. Your job— your *only* job—is to keep watch and help if something goes wrong."

Eve nodded seriously, even that gesture making Cohen fear that the girl was too immature to understand what was at stake on her first mission. The girl glided to the low wooden table in the room and picked up the matt-black stick resting on two hand-carved brackets. She snatched up the stick, and the way she carried it made it obvious that it was more than just a piece of wood, as the weight and balance were alien.

Eve closed her eyes and let her fingertips play over the stick as she held it out in front of her in both hands. Tensing her shoulders, her arms, and then her whole body as though the power rippled through her, she snatched her hands apart and the stick broke away with three quarters of the black sheath whipping away in her left hand.

The last black section stayed in her right hand and, as the two parts separated, a bright streak of silver erupted in the gloom.

Eve kept the sheath in her left hand and tucked it vertically behind her back as her right hand twirled the long, slim blade with a murderous and practised ease.

She cut the air as her eyes stayed closed, with her feet effortlessly running through one of the sword-dances she had been practising since she could first walk.

Finishing a flourish of blade twirls, Eve flicked her right wrist to spin the blade once more, raising her right hand and pointing the tip of the long blade vertically down, snapping the two parts in her hands together. Cohen heard the hissing slide of the sword returning home into its sheath, and then the heavy snap as it clicked safely in.

Eve's eyes opened as the black stick twirled back around her waist to be held still at her left hip. As her head raised, the bright eyes locked onto Cohen's and a small chill ran down the spine of the older woman.

"I'm ready," Eve declared in a low voice.

Cohen believed her, but she wasn't sure the world was ready for Eve.

CHAPTER EIGHTEEN

WEAK LINK

Professor Michael Winslow was a lucky man. He was lucky in where he was born, and he was lucky that he possessed an intelligence that made him very valuable.

He was also unlucky. Unlucky in that he had remained perpetually thin and weak his entire life, and unlucky that his almost complete lack of a chin, combined with such a pronounced overbite, lent him an impossibly awkward appearance.

That appearance made him unattractive to women, repulsive even, which in turn rendered him sullen and resentful and perpetually unlikely to ever attract a member of the opposite sex.

He had excelled in school, earning himself graduation in the educational proficiency tests at the age of eleven, and he had been selected to undergo further training as an apprentice in the science labs of The Citadel. Now, decades later, he enjoyed an unprecedented level of access. The genius son of an engineer, he was raised in safety away from the regular citizens, and attended school with the other children of Party soldiers and scientists. He had never married, despite the unrequited advances to each and every female he had ever worked alongside, and had appropriately earned the nickname muttered behind his back of Professor Weasel.

Winslow's high level of access had been earned by his advances in research into behavioural science and neuro-programming.

He had been assigned to a top-secret project over twenty years before, codenamed Erebus, and had found his office being moved deep underground. His own lab was one level above the area where the successful subjects were housed, and his experiments on the citizens had been something of an underground ghost story for years.

The Party often removed citizens from the population for days or weeks at a time at his request, usually female and young, and they had mostly been returned to their homes with little or no idea of what had happened during their internment. Some had memories, all had nightmares, and none were ever the same after their abduction.

Winslow held his thumb over the reader on the secure elevator from the western edge of the large underground labs deep below The Citadel, making a disgusted noise of annoyance as it beeped at him in response. The beep was only a small noise, but its connotation was obvious and negative. Huffing to himself, Winslow wiped his greasy thumb on the lab coat he wore and tried once more, this time earning a positive noise after a second's pause.

Leaning down, he removed his glasses and opened his right eye wide for the retinal scanner to perform the second phase of the security procedure for escape.

The doors opened, Winslow stepped inside, the doors closed and he then reached out to input his personal six-digit code into the keypad.

This was the third phase of the security protocol, and

was unique, as far as he knew, to this level of the underground lab complex. Even if he was killed and his still-warm thumb was placed on the scanner, then his eye removed to access the elevator, his killer would not know of the security code and would be trapped.

If the keypad was inside the lab, any would-be escapee would know to torture him for the code first.

The security procedure was designed with the sole intention of preventing a subject from escaping, not to safeguard the lives of the scientists.

Winslow knew this, and every time he accessed the elevator to eat or return to his own bed, he hated the world for it.

As he walked out of The Citadel, his right hand was clamped around the flash drive in his pocket, the very thing which was making his right thumb too sweaty to activate the biometric security scanners. He walked briskly down the gargantuan expanse of the grey concrete steps, hurried through the failing light to get to his residence, which he had specifically requested be chosen as close to The Citadel as possible, without being an apartment inside the building itself.

He walked through his front door mere minutes later, again cursing his clammy hands for its not recognising his thumbprint, threw down his bag and opened the terminal on his desk.

As it whirred into life, he snatched shut the blinds over the two windows and threw off his lab coat, fumbling to retrieve the flash drive from the pocket as he did so. Extending the plug and fitting it into to the port on his monitor, his breathing grew more rapid in anticipation.

He had removed the classified material from The Citadel, stored in an encrypted file and well disguised so as not to be accessed via The Citadel's mainframe.

He knew the removal of such material would earn him severe punishment if caught, but he doubted it could ever result in anything which would prevent him from continuing his work. He believed himself invaluable, irreplaceable, which made him arrogant and utterly deluded.

He gasped aloud as he saw the first image on the screen pop up before his eyes, and reaching out, he pressed a sweaty fingertip to the play icon. As the video began, he turned down the volume so that the sobs and screams could not be heard by anyone but him, and he unzipped his trousers without taking his eyes off the video of his most recent examinations of a detained citizen.

———

Adam was excited, but tried his hardest to remain calm and appear in control. The others gathered were like him, yet different at the same time.

They were all thin; but where he was slim, the others seemed as if their build was not through physical training but malnourishment. He had seen the nervous young man standing at the front of the dingy subterranean room before, when he was first unleashed, but none of the others except Mark were familiar to him. They seemed to be waiting for something or someone before the speaking started, so Adam stayed quiet and still in the shadows beside Mark.

Another door at the rear of the chamber opened, and through the gloom, his accustomed eyes saw an older woman of small stature walk in, followed by a petite but lean shape, seemingly tall but made of just limbs.

Something in the way she—it had to be a she, he thought—moved suggested a predatory nature. In the darkness Adam could make out large eyes scanning the room nervously until they met his and stopped roving.

The big, wide eyes locked onto his and stayed exactly where they were. Her body still moved as it followed the smaller woman, but the eyes stayed stuck on his without narrowing or widening at all.

The nervous man at the front of the room coughed to clear his throat, but Adam couldn't tear his gaze away from the girl.

Mark's elbow found his lowest rib, perilously close to the axilla nerve cluster which he had been taught to exploit in hand to hand combat, with just enough force to make his body jolt in response. He turned away to face the front, trying to sense more about the girl behind him.

"We have a mission," mumbled the man at the front, eyes cast down to the ground, "we need to get…"

"Speak up, please," said the small, older woman at the back of the room. Adam swore he could hear the tiniest of whispered giggles after she spoke.

"We have a mission," said the man again, evidently uncomfortable at speaking to an assembled crowd, even if that crowd was very small and shrouded mostly in darkness, "We need to get two pieces of Party security hardware from a storeroom."

With that, he stopped, leaving others looking around as though someone else would fill in the rest. Mouse then understood that they expected more from him, so he added the only other information he was willing to divulge.

"I need to be escorted there, and let in, and I will do the rest. That way only I can give up the plan if captured."

Nods rippled slowly around the congregation. They all understood the dangers of knowing too much.

"Okay," said Mouse as he raised his face to risk eye contact, "let's go."

CHAPTER NINETEEN

THE GREAT OUTDOORS

"Stay close to the others," Cohen said, her hands clamped on Eve's cheeks, "and stay silent and hidden unless you need to act. Remember," she snapped as she increased the pressure on the girl's face to make her point, "do *nothing* to get detected."

"You said that already," Eve complained quietly. Cohen let out a sigh of exasperation and let her go. She had argued against Eve being used, but she suspected that James was insistent simply because she was opposed to him. At least this way she would be sent out with others who could get her back safely.

"When you get there, you and Adam stay out of sight to protect the others inside," she said again. Eve didn't respond, as she had acknowledged that instruction four times already.

Eve kept shooting glances to Adam, as though she were looking at the male counterpart of herself. She was, precisely, but the two had woven an almost mesmerising spell over each other. Both tall and lean, both carrying bladed weapons and dressed in the skin-tight black suits which masked their body heat from the persistent threat of the sensors of overhead drones.

Mouse had selected the softest target he could, given the massive increase in The Citadel surveillance, but that meant that their team had to begin the long underground journey as soon as the sun set, but whilst most residents of The Citadel were still awake.

The six of them crept along in silence; at least, two of them moved in silence but to them, the other four crashed around like drunken infants. They hadn't been raised as shadows, and although they carried weapons, they weren't the fine-tuned killers that the two dressed in the rippling black material were. Mouse and Fly had their specialist fields, and Adam regarded the twins and briefly marvelled at their similarities.

It took an impossibly long time to reach their destination, with Mouse calling left and right turns out in the forgotten tunnels as though he had a map inside his head.

He did, in a way, and was referring to the photographic image in his brain of the route sketched on a drawn map. To take the map with them would be to risk the Party following the breadcrumbs back to their underground lairs, but Mouse's uncanny ability rendered that possibility void.

Stopping underneath a metal ladder, Mouse stepped back and another man stepped forward. Fly scaled the ladder with ease and used a thin tool to probe all around the edges of the metal hatch above.

"It's clear," he whispered down as he slipped the tool into his coat and took another step up the ladder to place his shoulder to the metal. Slowly inching his body upwards, his eye broke the horizon at street level, to be met with darkness. He slowly lowered himself, switched sides and did the same to look in the opposite direction.

He paused for a heartbeat, then pushed on upwards

until the metal lid could be slid away and he could expose the outside world.

Fly slipped out onto the street, followed by the others. Mouse went last and restored the metal grate with as little noise as possible as the other five melted into the shadows.

Sticking to the darkness of the alleyways between the large buildings, they moved cautiously. Only once did Adam's keen ears detect the almost imperceptible hissing, shrieking whine of an approaching drone. He snapped his fingers and spun a digit over his head to signal to the others in the low light of the threat.

As one, they all sought cover from sight, masking their body heat and movement from the invisible eye in the sky.

"It's gone," Adam said in a low voice as he pushed away from the wall. The others unfolded themselves from their hiding positions, including the tall girl wearing the same suit as he had.

"We don't need to hide from them," he told her quietly, "but you need to stay still so they can't detect you. If we do that, then we are invisible," he said as he plucked at the black suit. The head inside the hood nodded once, and the hands adjusted the long, black stick strapped to her back and protruding over her right shoulder.

A few minutes later Mouse declared that they had found their target. He turned and nodded to Adam, who returned the gesture and cast his eyes upwards. Finding the best way skyward, he stood and took a short run up.

Jumping from the ground to run three quick steps along the concrete block wall, he sprang diagonally away to spin and catch a ledge of a first-floor window. Raising his feet and bunching his legs, Adam released the power in his long limbs and launched himself backwards and up, spinning around above their heads to catch the opposite edge of a low roof, where he hauled himself up and disappeared from view. His head reappeared and a hand was visible in the gathering dark, gesturing for Eve to follow.

Smiling to herself inside the thin fabric covering her face, she turned her gaze to the other male in their group, who was never far away from the female who looked like him. She nodded down to him, and he took a second to understand. Bracing his feet wide and cupping his hands in front of him, he nodded back.

Eve took two long, light steps forward and leapt lithely to plant her right foot in his hands. Bending her leg to build up the power as Jonah heaved her skyward, she uncoiled vertically and sailed directly upwards to land her hands and her right foot on the ledge where Adam peered down at them.

She winked at him, not that he could see through the material, and carried on bringing her left leg up where she crouched like a gargoyle before slipping onto the roof.

Below them Jonah smiled, which was mirrored by his twin sister. Mouse moved away to a doorway set opposite them in the alleyway. Fly knelt in the doorway and unrolled a leather bundle he had produced from a pocket. The smallest of metallic tinkling noises drifted up to the low rooftops as he scraped and probed the lock before it yielded to his delicate touches. The door creaked as it began to swing inwards, but Mouse grabbed the handle and lifted it to take pressure from the hinges, and returned them to the relative safety of silence.

The four of them drifted inside and closed the door quietly behind them. Adam began subconsciously counting, keeping track of their exposure time. He wanted to speak to the girl fifteen feet to his right who kept her eyes on the end of the alleyway.

He even considered sliding towards her so they could speak in soft voices whilst still maintaining the security of the team inside. Just as he was considering this, voices found their way to his ears and his whole body tensed.

Turning his head to find the source of the interruption, he found himself directing his eyes in the exact same direction as Eve, towards her end of the alley, just as a pair of armed Party soldiers came into view. They sauntered around the corner, totally unaware that they were about to interrupt the covert activities of people whose capture would elevate them greatly in the eyes of their leaders.

CHAPTER TWENTY

FEAR OF THE FUTURE

Nathaniel left The Citadel and waved away the two soldiers who fell in step behind and either side of him. The soldiers assigned to protective detail were accustomed to the Chairman dismissing them. They would still follow him at a very respectful distance, if only to be in the same area should anything untoward happen, but they were happy to let the man wander the capital alone. He was, after all, a big man who carried a gun and had proven himself in combat.

Nathaniel walked briskly, aware that the two guards he had summarily dismissed would still try to keep their eyes in his general direction. He put distance between himself and the huge building which embodied the seat of his power, not ashamed of where he was going, but mindful that he didn't want too many others to know about it.

Making turns between the neat rows of uniformed residences, built to strict specifications depending on the occupants allocated family size, he found his way mechanically to the building which was designated for five people even though it technically housed only one. Climbing the steps, he opened the front door without breaking stride and was removing his leather coat even before the door had swung closed behind him.

"Why is this door unlocked?" he demanded of the man who burst upwards from a comfortable seat and snatched up the rifle propped against a low table.

"Sir," stammered the man, "the last shift must have left it unlocked when they left just now," he said lamely.

"Inexcusable," said the Chairman as he carried on through the open-plan living area to the foot of the staircase. Dropping his coat on the bannister, he took the stairs two at a time until he reached the landing.

Opening a door to a bedroom, he strode in and picked up a folder from the foot of the bed where it rested in a plastic bracket, to leaf through the most recent pages.

"He is doing well today, Sir," said the nurse in the room, "he hasn't had any outbursts."

Nathaniel grunted a neutral noise in response, snapping shut the folder and regarding the elderly man in the bed.

The man stared back at him, a sullen hostility in his eyes and evident in the upturned sneer of his top lip.

"What do you want?" asked the old man in a slurred voice, caused largely by the left side of his face hanging slack and lifeless. "Who do you think you are, bursting into my office like this? I'll have you lashed on the steps of The Citadel."

Nathaniel said nothing, prompting the old man to use his right hand to push himself further up the bed and draw himself up taller.

"Answer me, or I'll have you arrested," snarled the old man, his voice growing louder and more forceful.

Still Nathaniel said nothing, merely regarded the old man with a disappointed amusement.

"Guards!" bawled the old man, spittle running frothily from the drooping side of his mouth, and prompting the nurse to step forward.

"Ok, Sir, that's enough now," she said, reaching out a hand to him. He slapped her hand away and turned to issue an animalistic growl at her.

"None of that!" she said, whipping her hand first away from the swipe of the old man, then back to his thigh where she stuck him with a small syringe filled with a sedative. She stepped smartly back again as the old man swiped to hit out at her once more, but harder. Already he was growing lethargic in response to the fast-acting medicine, and he slurred the word, "Bitch," at her before turning his eyes back to the intruder.

"I'll have you all executed, all of you, traitors…" he said in a voice growing quieter with each breath. Nathaniel let out a sigh and put the folder back down gently just as the old man's eyes went as slack as the partially paralysed side of his body.

"Correction," he said as he turned to face the nurse, "*now* he's had an outburst."

"If you knocked before walking in, perhaps he might not get angry?" the nurse gently chided him, one of the few people alive who could speak to him like that, but then her long years of service and silence had earned her that right to speak to him as an equal, at least in the house where they both now stood alone in each other's company.

Nathaniel said nothing, merely stared long and hard at his father. The man had been such a symbol of unwavering strength for all of his life until the sudden affliction took him four years ago. The doctors, all now either dead or sworn to trusted secrecy, had told Nathaniel that a blood clot had become stuck in his brain, and that was the cause of his lunacy.

Nathaniel suspected that the truth was something more sinister, and he had demanded more tests be conducted.

He knew, even if the doctors and research scientists could not say for certain, that his father's affliction would be his own fate in the future; a final legacy to the holders of the crown, and the very reason he had never fathered any offspring.

Every time he visited the Chairman he felt as though he were watching a premonition of his own painful death, and he vowed that if he ever felt the first slipping of his mind into madness, then he would stand down from office and lead a huge offensive into the Badlands in the south west.

Better to be butchered in glorious battle against a worthy enemy, than to die in bed as others watched you pissing your own pants.

————

Adam froze, locking his body into stillness whilst still allowing the breath to seep in and out of his lungs without shifting his profile at all. He knew the others inside would soon be still and silent, because whoever was guarding their exit would alert them to the danger. The chances that the two guards were heading to an obscure storeroom, for he thought that was surely what the poorly secured building must be, were so slim they were impossible.

The pair would pass by, totally unaware that they were walking through the jaws of a dangerous beast and would survive only because they didn't pose a significant enough threat. Adam's eyes tracked their ponderous movement, and they made it evident that they were a lowly patrol, acting on orders no more specific than to wander around and be seen.

A low-level deterrent. Not worth the risk of discovery just to remove to minor pawns from the board in a big game.

Eve evidently didn't see it that way.

Adam almost cried out to stop her as she rose fluidly to her feet and turned her back to the deeper darkness of the alleyway below. Arching her back lazily, she spun away to the ground below and landed with barely a sound.

But the small sound she did make was enough to alert one of the soldiers, who stopped talking and half turned to glance behind him.

The darkness in front of him morphed into a darker shadow taking the shape of a person. His hand flew up to the switch on the right side of his visored helmet to activate a bright light. The cone of brilliant white illuminated the drab, empty ground in front of them and was reflected back painfully from a long slither of silver metal. A scraping noise hissed and whispered as the rest of the sword appeared in the light with the eerie black shape wielding it, shifting almost unnaturally behind the bright steel.

Eve kept her eyes shut to preserve her vision, and swung the sword gracefully from the snapshot of memory where she had seen the two men before her.

Her first swipe cleanly removed the head of the soldier who had turned on his flashlight, making insane shadows spin around the alleyway as head and helmet pirouetted to the ground. The punctuation of the headless soldier falling first to his knees, then forwards where his chest impacted the concrete sounded flat and loud in the confined space.

The second guard babbled incoherently and raised the rifle into his shoulder to squeeze it tight. Before he could apply pressure to the trigger, the sword whipped and hissed again, cutting through flesh, bone, sinew and the metals and polymers of the gun with a ghostly ease.

The two halves of the rifle fell to the ground, one severed hand still gripping the handle and spasming on the trigger to no effect, the safety catch still being engaged. The other disconnected hand, complete with most of the forearm still attached, bounced off the front part of the destroyed gun and flopped, fingers pointing upwards, at Eve's feet.

Reversing her grip, she slid the blade point-first into the crease where the collar of the uniform met the bottom of the helmet. The screaming stopped, replaced by a few seconds of gargling and choking.

Leaning down, she wiped the long blade on both sides against the dead man's uniform before sliding the long steel back into the wooden sheath and looking upwards.

Instead of awe and praise, Adam dropped down to the alley and glared at her from behind his mask, furious that she had exposed them for no good reason.

The other four burst from the door of the storeroom, having seen the death of the two guards, but not yet fully comprehending that the terrible interruption was unnecessary. Mouse reached down to the dead soldier with blood still oozing from both wrist stumps, to snatch a small box from the side of his helmet.

Taking three steps to the other side of the alley he bent and did the same to the other helmet, stifling the vomit which threatened to erupt from his mouth as he retched in response to the grotesque cross-section of bones, muscles and tubes protruding from the helmet.

"Quickly," Mouse said quietly, "this way."

Without waiting for an answer, he ran on further into

the maze of alleyways and away from their exit back to the tunnels beneath the city.

They followed, knowing that a force had likely already been dispatched to investigate the sudden disappearance of the patrol's life-signs.

Eve was bundled along with them, unsure why nobody had congratulated her and scared that they were now running. Adam was furious with the girl, but at the same time mesmerised by the speed and grace she had employed to dispatch the guards.

She had demonstrated a lethalness equal to his own, appearing untouchable by the slow soldiers.

Yet somehow the skill in the killings seemed more frightening coming from her than it did from him.

He ran along with the others, abandoning stealth for speed, as Mouse kept glancing up whenever a patch of exposed sky showed itself.

"Here," he said finally, rummaging in his bag for an item among the tricks he carried. Bringing out a bundle which was unmistakably an explosive, he turned a dial and stood to lob the device over a metal fence.

"Go," he snapped, leading them in a new direction with his eyes glued to the ground this time.

Finding what he wanted after almost half a minute, he dropped to the ground as Fly ran his hands over the grate to check for wires or devices. The grate was lifted, and the six of them dropped into the tunnels just as the crunch of tyres on concrete sounded.

Mouse was at the foot of the ladder as the grate overhead closed, holding a weak flashlight to throw insane shadows along the abandoned tunnel.

"Seven, six, five," he counted down, "four, thr—"

He was interrupted by a sound which felt like a *'crump'*. His flashlight flickered out, plunging them back into darkness. Rustling sounded in the inky black, followed by a crack preceding the dull green glow which grew brighter as the chemicals mixed together in the plastic tube Mouse held.

He glanced left and right before announcing, "This way," and leading them back to safety.

CHAPTER TWENTY-ONE

UNACCEPTABLE

The commander of the guard on duty that night was, by random happenstance, the newly promoted replacement for the disgraced Captain Smith.

Captain Parker was only too aware of the mistakes that had been made that night, and was eager not to follow directly in his predecessor's footsteps.

He had deployed the reactionary force held in reserve to the last known location of the foot patrol, but he sent them via three different routes in the three troop carrier vans at their immediate disposal. He knew the likelihood of his forces catching any culprits were infinitesimally small, but hopefully he could demonstrate through his understanding of tactical awareness that his actions were carefully planned and not merely panicked reactions. All other units were ordered to hold firm at their current positions and to engage anyone and anything moving that didn't identify as the reactionary force.

As the first units reported that they had boots on the ground, his initial wave of standby drones converged on the area. No sooner did they receive their orders, than every drone inside a two hundred metre radius dropped from the sky.

"QRF one, Command, come in," he said into the radio microphone in front of him, hailing the senior officer on scene. No reply.

"QRF one, QRF one, this is Command, over," he said again, a glimmer of panic rising from his chest to affect his voice.

"Radio is dead, Sir," said the woman sitting to his left as she frantically tapped at a keyboard. "Going to broad spectrum bandwidth." A few more seconds of tapping and she turned to nod to him.

"QRF one, QRF one, this is Command," he tried again, this time receiving a squelch of static preceding the answer on the reduced clarity of the new bandwidth.

"QRF one, go ahead," came the response.

"QRF, Command. Drone coverage is down on scene and we are on backup comms. Situation report, over."

"Drones just dropped from the sky," came the reply, "We detected something like an explosion when we got here."

Captain Parker bit his retort about poor radio discipline to the Lieutenant on the ground. He knew the man was likely frightened and full of adrenaline. Precious few of the Party soldiers had actually seen anything resembling combat, other than the simulated battles of training. They were more accustomed to bullying an unarmed populace, in Parker's opinion.

"Lieutenant," Parker said carefully, "deploy your forces and report."

No acknowledgement came, but Parker turned to see the area where the two life-signs disappeared on a large screen, the area magnified and showing red icons bearing numbers moving.

There was a time delay of a few seconds, between five and ten seconds if he were forced to guess, which made the icons leap from point to point. It annoyed him that one of those soldiers could be killed and he would not know for a handful of precious heartbeats.

"Command, QRF," came the loud, wavering shout of the ground commander over the speakers. Parker snatched up a headset and nestled it over his ears, indicating to the woman sitting beside him to cut the feed to the speakers by motioning a finger across his throat.

"Command, go," Parker said, his voice even, controlled and steady.

"Oh my God... they... they..."

"QRF one, Command," said Parker sternly into the boom mic protruding from the headphones. His voice now held an edge like a sharpened blade, "Sort your shit out, Lieutenant, and report."

"Sir," came the response. Parker swore he could hear the sound of someone vomiting behind the voice.

"We've found the patrol, they've been..." Parker didn't cut the young man off, "they've been cut up. Butchered. Oh, Christ, his fucking *head's* gone..."

Parker hit the transmit button to cut the hysterical rantings of the junior officer off from the airways. Parker knew that panic only breeds more panic, and if the troops heard their ground commander crying and puking, it could render them all worse than useless.

"Lieutenant, get a hold of yourself and do your job," Parker hissed over the airways, prompting a few seconds of silence.

"Yes, Sir," came the quieter response, as he kept his finger on the transmit button and issued orders to his troops to fan out and search the area, but to stay in pairs.

That didn't do the unlucky bastards at your feet any good, thought Parker to himself.

"Sir?" came a voice from behind him. He turned to see a man approaching with a clipboard and sheets of paper attached to it, reading as he walked.

"The attack was on one of our drone re-broadcasters," he said, offering no introduction, "They must have used some kind of electronic device to knock it out," he finished with a shrug that made it obvious he had no idea what had actually happened.

"Can it be put back online?" Parker asked the man.

"Yes, probably, just not from here," he said. Parker nodded and turned back to the command desk.

"QRF two, Command," he said, then cursed himself for broadcasting on the wrong frequency.

He turned to the woman, who was holding up one finger to him, asking silently for a second to finish what she was doing. The index finger folded away and was replaced by an upturned thumb; she had patched in the secondary reactionary force.

"QRF two, Command," Parker said again.

"Command, QRF two, go ahead," came a cool response.

"QRF two, report to Citadel to escort engineering team to incident location," he said.

"Roger."

Parker looked at the board. The reactionary force was in place, with two thirds of them fanned out to provide a loose cordon as the remainder searched the area. He had no doubt that they would find no trace of the villains responsible for the attack, and he was mindful that the downing of a drone section control module was a prerequisite of whatever crime they planned next.

Parker ordered his final reactionary force to stand by at

the most central location in the city, ready to deploy anywhere they were required at a moment's notice.

"Someone inform the Chairman," Parker said.

"We've been trying, Sir," said a boy still in his teens, sitting on the same long bench as the woman controlling the radios, "can't raise him in his office or at his residence."

Parker hesitated for a long moment, then ordered, "Track him."

"Can't do that, Sir," replied the boy awkwardly, "nobody has the access to do that."

Parker's lips tightened to a thin line but he said nothing. He would be called to account for what had transpired, and for what would transpire in the immediate future, so he turned back to his job and concentrated on doing the best he could until ordered to stand down by the duty major, who was likely already struggling into a uniform to bustle into the command centre and take over.

———

"Sir," said the soldier as loudly as he dared from an arm's length away as he shook the sleeping man's shoulder.

"Sir," he said again, more insistently and shaking the shoulder more forcefully, before stepping smartly back to avoid any retaliation. The sleeping man jolted awake, momentarily unaware of his surroundings before the fog of his alcohol-induced sleep cleared.

"What?" snapped the Chairman, rising from the chair where he slept and knocking the empty glass from his lap to the carpeted floor.

"Some commotion outside," said the non-uniformed guard retreating to look out of the window.

Nathaniel stretched, slightly uncertain on his feet as the alcohol had not had sufficient time to purge itself from his body in his sleep. He pulled back the curtain in time to witness a troop-carrying van streak past the residence.

"That's the third one, Sir," said the guard, "has to be the QRF."

Nathaniel said nothing, just nodded. Without another word, he picked up his fitted leather jacket and strode to the door and pulled the handle, cursing silently that the door was locked, not realising the irony that he had threatened others for leaving it unlocked.

He left the residence, leaving the door open behind him, and walked quickly with uneven, long strides back to The Citadel to find out what was happening.

———

The pure-born regained the safety of the chambers below the citizens' residence blocks to the south. They were filthy from the tunnels, and all but the two black-clad members of the mission force were out of breath from the exertion of their escape.

Jenna was the first to snap.

"What the fuck was that all about?" she asked to nobody in particular.

Adam kept his mouth closed, waiting to see the outcome and unsure if the others knew what had happened.

"We had to create a diversion," Mouse said by way of explanation, "we had to make it look like we were going after a different target, otherwise they would have realised we were hitting that storeroom and done an inventory. If they found out what we've taken, then the plan is screwed."

"So what was the thing you threw?" asked Jonah.

"It's called a *Crunch*. A small electromagnetic bomb," Mouse said, "I don't understand it fully, but it goes off like a bomb without the explosion and knocks out anything electronic nearby. Those towers control the drones in their areas, they've got them dotted around all over the city. Right now, they'll hopefully be thinking that we are after something somewhere else and that was a diversion, like last time."

"So what did we get?" asked Adam in his oddly quiet voice.

In answer, Mouse delved into his battered bag and produced two items with wires dangling from them. Nobody knew what they were, except Mouse and Fly, given the looks on their faces.

"A retinal scanner and biometric fingerprint reader," Mouse declared, as though saying what the devices were would explain them. Before anyone could connect those dots, Jenna turned to Adam.

"How did those two guards spot you?" she asked, accusation heavy in her voice.

"They didn't," Adam said, turning to look at Eve.

The girl had jumped up silently on top of a large pipe and was swinging her dangling foot casually.

"What?" she asked, her cat-like eyes shining brightly in the gloom.

"Why did you kill those guards?" asked Mouse.

Eve shrugged, as though the events of earlier no longer held any interest. The atmosphere in the room grew instantly colder towards her.

"Did they see us?" Mouse asked. Eve shook her head and resumed the swinging of her foot, which had stopped when everyone had turned to look at her.

"Did they see *you*?" he asked her. She turned to Adam, something unspoken in her eyes. She wanted to know if he was going to throw her to the wolves. For some reason, completely unknown to him, he didn't.

"I think they noticed something," he said carefully, unaware if his attempt to cover the truth would be believed or not, "I was about to take them down when Eve killed them."

Silence hung in response to his untruthful statement. The eyes looking back at him were a mixture of under-standing, relief, and anger. He didn't dare glance in Eve's direction, not daring to risk her breaking the spell he had cast with the lie.

"Okay then,' Mouse said, turning for the door to leave, "let's get to work."

Adam loitered at the back of the group as they filed through the doorway. His right arm shot out to snatch at the thin, sinewy arm of Eve. She instinctively twisted around out of his grip and used the sheathed sword to brace his arm as she pinned it and looked directly in his eyes. Those eyes flicked down once and she followed the gaze, seeing the tip of a wickedly curved blade held close to her stomach.

The message was clear; *you can break my arm but I can gut you.* Eve smiled wickedly and released the pressure on his trapped arm.

"We need to talk,' Adam hissed at her. She smiled wider and nodded her agreement.

———

The Chairman burst into The Citadel twelve minutes after leaving the residence. The brisk walk in the chill night air had gone a long way towards clearing the effects of the fierce clear liquid on his mind and body. A young Captain he did not recognise gave a succinct report of the night's events, and detailed a response that the Chairman thought wholly appropriate to the situation. The failures to apprehend the terrorists were not down to the man's actions and orders, but the Chairman kept his mouth closed and nodded his replies to save the officers and soldiers present from detecting the smell of the spirits on his breath.

"Coffee," he snapped over his shoulder, not checking to see if anyone was there to receive the order. He heard hurried footsteps behind him and waited for a mug to be presented to him.

The coffee was different from what he was served in his office. It came in a thick, china mug and not a fine glass. It tasted bitter, earthy, stewed, and as he took a long pull on the dark liquid, he decided that he preferred the rank and file drink more than the refined version he was served.

He didn't like to feel separated from his troops like that; he had shared the front line with the men and women under his command and he decided that from now on he would drink the same coffee as they did.

This daydreaming confirmed for him that the alcohol was still coursing through his body, and would be vying for a democratic say in his decisions, so he focused his mind once more.

"Captain," he said as he looked at the young man, "assemble a brief report and bring it to my office when the duty officer arrives to relieve you."

With that, he turned away and walked to his office where he stripped off his coat and forced himself to void the contents of his stomach into the toilet, before washing his face and drinking the coffee down in one.

CHAPTER TWENTY-TWO

TWO SIDES OF THE COIN

The Chairman's head pounded, but his face remained stern in an effort not to betray the effect that the alcohol and the interrupted sleep had so graciously bestowed on him. The two Majors and a Colonel in the room eyed him warily but said nothing.

The young Captain again gave his report on the events, the management of which had now been taken over by more senior men. He was precise, to the point, and kept his opinions brief. In short, he wasn't trying to show off or cover his actions, which told the Chairman that he believed he had done the right things. As he spoke, the door opened after a single knock and in strode a Major not much older than him. His heels snapped together and a salute was offered up, which Major Stanley mirrored, albeit with much less enthusiasm and youthful alacrity. Waving for the man to continue, Stanley nodded a greeting to the Chairman, who tilted his head slightly in return, then sat to listen.

"As I was saying, Sirs," Parker said, "I detailed the

initial reactionary force to establish a cordon before investigating the location of the incident."

"Where was the patrol?" Stanley interjected.

To his credit, Parker didn't hesitate or check the paperwork under his arm.

"Industrial sector," he said, 'warehouses and stores mostly, with some factory units currently not in use."

Stanley nodded to himself, deep in thought, "And how were they killed, have we established that yet?" he asked, eyes up and glancing between the two men.

The chairman said nothing, so Parker gave the information he possessed.

"Sir," he said, the first hint of hesitation creeping into his voice, "the first units on scene were very distressed. Both soldiers had been…" he paused briefly, searching for the most appropriate word without seeming emotional, "cut up, Sir. Dismembered."

"One was decapitated, the other was stabbed cleanly straight through the throat after having his hands and rifle sliced straight through," growled the Chairman in a low voice. He closed his eyes for a fraction of a second longer than a blink before opening them again and looking at his audience, "similar to the recent attack, the terrorists appear to have used very sharp knives or similar weapons."

Stanley nodded, absorbing the troubling news with outward calm, "What were they after?" he asked, voicing the question the Chairman wanted answered, because in his hungover and sleep-deprived state, he couldn't see it himself.

———

"What happened?" James demanded, making Mouse feel

infinitely more uncomfortable than he normally did when forced to speak to people.

It was amplified by the fact that James had summoned him and other members of Command to a room where the lights were brighter than the murky gloom he was accustomed to, and felt most comfortable occupying.

"After we were discovered..." began Mouse, eyes cast downward and slightly closed as he replayed the events to give commentary.

"*Before* that," James snapped.

Mouse made a show of sighing heavily, letting everyone in the room know he was unhappy at being treated in that manner.

Squinting again and moving his hands in slow gestures as he ran through the memories again, he spoke.

"We followed the tunnels without any problems," he began, his body weight shifting as though he was re-enacting the events physically in fast forward, just muted through the medium of recital, "we got above ground, found the storeroom we needed, and we went inside with the others standing guard..."

"Who is we?" James demanded again.

"Me, Fly, Jenna and Jonah went inside," he said with a patience he did not feel, "and the *stalkers* stayed on the roof to watch."

Eyes flickered around the room, looking for any reaction to the new moniker he had gifted to their pair of black-clad, trained killers.

"A patrol approached from the direction we came in from," he said as he squinted his eyes tighter, "two-man foot patrol, standard equipment with rifles and sidearms. They were talking as they approached, so they weren't targeted to the area because of anything we did; we got in cleanly," he turned his head slightly, as though craning his neck to see through his closed eyelids, "As they approached, Eve dropped from the roof and took them out. It was quick, but one of the soldiers turned his light on so he might have seen her. I took their helmet memory units and we ran."

He opened his eyes and straightened fully, then shrank again to his normal, hunched stance as though he permanently expected to be berated.

"Why?" asked another man, younger than James but seemingly just as unfriendly.

"Why what?" Mouse asked, not out of belligerence, but because there could be lots of 'whys' about what he had just said. The man sighed in exasperation, letting everyone know that he thought Mouse was an idiot.

"Why," he said slowly and drawing out the word, "did you take their equipment?"

"Because I suspect that they can record what the soldiers see," Mouse said silencing the offensive man who talked to him like *he* was the stupid one, "and if they'd seen Eve before she cut one's he…" he stopped himself, "I didn't want to take the risk that they had recorded her."

"And before you ask," he said, turning to face the man who had offended him, "they probably won't figure out what we were after at the place where they died, because of the diversion."

———

"What did they do then" Stanley asked as he paced the office, "if the drone station attack was the diversion?"

"I don't know," said Nathaniel, his voice barely above a whisper but his head beginning to feel less like it was in an industrial press. His stomach was still sour and a glance at his watch told him that his new regular adjutant should be in place now. He was torn between not wanting to see her in his current state and needing breakfast ordering from The Citadel's kitchens.

He leaned over his desk, scarred forearm exposed as his sleeves were rolled up to his elbows, and hit the intercom button.

"Sir?" came the velvety-smooth voice from fifteen feet and a wall away.

"Nadeem," he said, his voice stronger and somehow projecting a kind of smile, "please have breakfast sent in for myself and Major Stanley," he requested. Nathaniel looked up to see Stanley smiling at him.

"You were saying, Major?" he asked, thinking that he had missed something.

"Nothing, Sir," Stanley said, dropping the smile with some difficulty, "I've had some already, but I'd never turn down another meal."

Nathaniel nodded, then remembered his thoughts from a few hours previously, "and Corporal?" he said as he hit the intercom button once more, "get our coffee from the same place as the command centre."

Stanley's eyebrows went up again, then dropped as though he thought the eccentricity were an irrelevant distraction.

Parker had been dismissed, as he was hours overdue finishing his night duty, and the more senior minds were taking responsibility for scouring footage and reports from The Citadel and surrounding areas, searching for any hint of what the terrorists were after.

"We are assuming they followed the same pattern as previously," Nathaniel said as he rose from his chair and stretched the stiffness from his back, "and that the drone tower was brought down to have our eyes turned there whilst they did something somewhere else." Stanley sat and watched as he paced and verbalised his logic, "but what if the drone tower *was* the target?" he asked.

"Then what was the outcome, and how did it benefit them?" Stanley posed back at the Chairman.

"Good question," he said as he arrived back at his chair and slumped into it heavily, "no fucking idea."

At that moment, there was one knock on the door and it swung open for Nadeem to allow a tray-bearer to enter. Nathaniel pulled down the sleeves of his shirt unthinkingly. The tray was placed gently on the desk and the bearer removed themselves from sight quickly.

They were one of the subservient members of the ruling class; not intelligent enough to become an engineer or scientist, nor physically capable enough to be diverted to a military career, but some jobs still needed doing in The Citadel, where a normal citizen would not be permitted access.

Nadeem watched the woman scurry away and covered the distance from door to desk in four long-legged and gracefully confident strides to pour two mugs of steaming coffee from the pot. She turned and left the room with the same actions and shut the door.

Both men's eyes lingered on the now closed door where the perfectly fitted uniform skirt had disappeared from view. As one, they both snapped out of the spell they had found themselves under.

"Sir," Stanley said inquisitively as they both began to eat from the plates loaded with meat and bread, "can I ask you a personal question?" he asked, almost embarrassed.

"Major," Nathaniel replied through a mouthful of bacon, "it was a pyrotechnic device which was rigged to blow when we entered one of their tunnels. It was a very long time ago and it didn't kill me because I was the third in line," he said, giving the official account of how he came to bear the ugly scars.

"I, er," Stanley said awkwardly, "I knew that Sir, I read the report."

Nathaniel frowned at him, making him guess which bit he was annoyed about.

"It's about Nadeem, Sir," he said, leaning to his satchel and pulling out the personnel file which the Chairman had temporarily forgotten all about, "she's clean. Completely. I was going to ask if you had any, er, any…"

Nathaniel swallowed and took a gulp of coffee as he leaned back to watch the younger man squirm.

"You want to know if I have any personal intentions with a non-commissioned officer under my direct supervision?" he asked dangerously.

"Well, Sir," Stanley said in a small voice, "now that you say it like that…"

"Yes, I have, unless your review uncovers something I don't like," Nathaniel said, looking Stanley directly in the eye with undisguised challenge. "Shall we return to the reason you are in my office to begin with, *Major*?" he finished, adding emphasis to the new rank in case Stanley had forgotten who had elevated him to the position he now enjoyed.

———

Mouse had explained. He had answered every question asked of him, despite those answers appearing to frustrate the members of Command.

"I fail to understand why you wasted an irreplaceable device on attacking a drone tower which offered us no tactical advantage," stated an older woman who had remained silent for most of the debriefing.

Mouse huffed a big sigh again, unable to disguise his contempt for the small-mindedness of the people he was forced to answer to and rely on.

"I've explained that," he said with an edge of hostility in his voice, "if I hadn't, then the soldiers would look around where the two were killed. They would check the storeroom, and would eventually discover that we had taken a retinal and a biometric scanner, even though they are older units, being stored because they weren't working efficiently." His answer had become a blatantly condescending explanation, but he no longer cared. He wanted to go back to his bed, or his screens to continue exploring the digital hallways of The Citadel's computerised memories and systems.

"If they figured out what we took, then they would re-write all of their security protocols and identification algorithms, which would shut me out and I'd have to start again, which would probably let them figure out that we are in their systems. I took out the drone tower so they would think that was a diversion like the last time."

He was slightly short of breath after he had finished his petulant rant. At no point had he made eye contact with any of his interrogators, so it appeared that he had argued with the rough patch of dusty concrete in front of his feet.

"Get it?" he added, "Now they don't know what we went there for and are probably searching everywhere else in the city to see what we did do—or what *they* think we did—when we didn't do it."

Blank faces looked back at him.

"Okay," said James finally, "so you're assuring us that it was actually a successful mission, and our plan isn't compromised?"

"Yes," Mouse said tiredly, "because I used the Crunch, and now they probably won't figure out what we are really up to," eyes cast once more between the members of Command.

"It's what the Nocturnals called the device," James offered, prompting Mouse to take his turn at not understanding. James waved a hand dismissively at his unspoken question

"Very well then," James said, "How long before you can carry out the next part of the plan?"

Mouse thought about it.

"Three days minimum," he said, "but I need a day to look through their reports and see what they've made of last night."

With that, he was dismissed to return to the shadows where he felt instantly more comfortable and less exposed. As he left the room he saw the two stalkers, trained to kill from the shadows, whereas his own skills lay in knowledge over action. Both were with their chaperones and neither spoke, merely kept their eyes cast down in resting wait.

Returning to the darkened tunnels and concrete corridors beneath the harsh world above, Mouse went via his room, where his small cot occupied a space in the wall. Fly was swinging gently in a hammock tied between two large pipes and didn't offer any greeting. He and Mouse had been in the same space for much of their childhood, and the small man with the uncanny ability to break locks had learned to ignore the other small man, with the similarly uncanny ability to manipulate anything computer related.

Mouse pulled across the curtain which separated his sleeping alcove from the rest of the underground world, but gave up on finding sleep almost instantly.

He knew there was no way he could rest now, so instead he got back out of bed and made his way to the computer terminals where he could wander through the abundance of information The Citadel's servers provided.

Sitting down and flexing the fingers of both hands to emanate a ripple of cracks from his knuckles, Mouse typed out the letters in amongst a series of symbols and numbers to find anything he could about the *Nocturnals* James had mentioned.

Back in the chamber Mouse had just occupied, Adam stood in the centre of the rough floor and tried to remain still as he explained what had happened. He hated having to explain to the older people why he had and hadn't done certain things they expected from him. He bit back a dozen retorts about their expertise being squandered in the dark; that if they knew so much better, why weren't they out there risking their lives?

His naivety showed through, with his failure to understand that the people in the room with him had risked their lives every single day. They risked their lives at that very moment. They risked their lives when they lived their duplicitous existence and smiled as they went along with the Party propaganda, which was far more difficult than swinging a blade in the dark.

Adam had justified his and Eve's actions and had been dismissed. He left the room in angry frustration and avoided eye contact with the girl on the way past.

Eve traipsed in, shoulders slumped and eyes cast downwards in preparation for being told off like a small child.

Her sullenness was evident, and the mood she had cast over herself affected not only her own actions, but the responses and attitudes of the people who needed information from her.

She saw it as an interrogation. As an affront. An insult to her abilities and intelligence. She let all of this hostility show when she answered the first question.

"Are you ok, Eve?" asked the man sitting in front of her as he leaned forward tiredly.

"I'm fine," she snapped, "why wouldn't I be?"

Behind her, Cohen let out an exasperated sigh of embarrassment.

"He's asking," she explained in an intentionally condescending tone, "because you were attacked by two soldiers and had to kill them." She let that hang.

"How do you feel after killing two people, Eve?" she asked slowly, unintentionally pushing too far and shaming the girl. Eve's eyes shot up to lock on to hers.

"I feel great," she said, feeling the collective gasp in the room as she had hoped for, "because all four of us got back safely without anyone getting captured or killed."

That silenced the inquisition, and the questioning took a more routine, sedate pace. Eve gave brief answers, still sullen but less hostile. Eventually she was dismissed from the room and the elders relaxed, exhausted by the girl's attitude and stubbornness.

Eve almost power-stomped her way back to her room, her cell as she called it, and said not one single word to Cohen, who scurried to keep up with the pace she set.

Eve heard the bolt slide across as soon as the door closed behind her, and she paced like a caged animal until finally the pent-up rage and frustration overcame her. She threw herself onto her cot and threw the blankets over her head to hide her tears from the room, in case that judged her too.

CHAPTER TWENTY-THREE

DUPLICITY

The insistent chirping from the alarm clock beside his bed dragged him out of a much-needed sleep after the events of the previous day. He had spent every shred of daylight in a windowless room poring over camera footage, city plans, reports from soldiers and their commanders. He had spent some time the previous afternoon dipping into the archives for reports on previous terrorist incidents to see if the past could influence his ability to predict the future.

That provided a distraction from the unsolvable problems, but still gave no answers.

He was eager to get back to his residence, which had previously been very humble and utilitarian. He now, however, enjoyed a residence more befitting not only his rank, but his privileged levels of access, which showed his true station. His new bedroom alone was the size of his previous residence, and this one had the added bonus of having quick access to The Citadel's kitchens. He had not needed to prepare a single meal since his elevation to a position of power, much to the disgust of his former peers who lived much further away from the comfort he now enjoyed.

He didn't know until he had glanced inside the Chairman's new adjutant's personnel file, but The Citadel administrative adjutant staff were actually housed only two floors above his new residence.

Through a serendipitous twist of fate, Samaira Nadeem lived almost vertically above him, something which he had mentioned to her a few days previously when he had first been given her file, and had opened the front page to be greeted with the basic information which included her residence.

He wasn't intrusive in the way that information was shared; he knew that she knew the Chairman had her file and was likely having her personally vetted for the position she had been allocated. As he left the Chairman's office days previously, he had nodded and acknowledged her smile of farewell by sketching a salute using the file in his hand.

"Investigating me, Major?" she asked with a playful smile of brilliantly white teeth in a voice like poured silk. Stanley was instantly under the spell that he suspected had been cast over the Chairman.

"Someone has to, Corporal," he said, equally as playfully as he decided to extend the conversation by spinning around and returning to her desk.

Flipping open the file to make a show of being open about it, he tried to convince himself that he was changing his planned schedule in the interests of a thorough investigation, which would obviously include his personal opinion on the young woman.

"Oh, I see your residence is by my own…" he said, trailing off as he became worried she would take offence at the inappropriateness of the comment.

"Oh, how delightful," she exclaimed with another dazzling smile. She leaned over her desk in a conspiratorial way and he found himself drawn in to mirror the gesture, "I've only just been moved there and I don't know anyone," she told him, as though imparting some kind of dangerous secret, "I haven't even found the residence gymnasium yet," she finished.

Stanley found himself fighting the physical effects of an elevated heart rate, and was rendered utterly powerless to stop his mouth opening and letting out the words.

"Two floors below mine," he said instantly, "I was planning on going there in a couple of hours."

"Thank you," she said, "maybe I'll see you there?"

Stanley did see her there. In fact, he could barely contain himself before arriving precisely one hundred and twenty minutes after he spoke to her. He tried to seem nonchalant, tried to not be obviously watching the arrival of every person through the double doors secured only by a biometric thumbprint reader.

When Adjutant Corporal Samaira Nadeem did eventually walk through the doors, a whole forty-six minutes after the estimated couple of hours, Stanley's heart leapt in his chest and his smile beamed like that of a young boy. He quickly ordered his facial expression back into cover and set the hard-working image of a fit, young Major with Special Operations access on it, waiting for her to notice him.

She didn't, and began running on a curved machine that used her body weight to propel the heavy belt along in response to the effort she put in.

She put in a lot, and ran hard for almost five minutes. Stanley knew this because he had positioned himself on a machine to lift heavy weights as he watched from her blind spot. When he saw her slowing, he began another set after adding an extra metal plate by moving the pin lower down the stack, and instantly regretted his decision as she climbed down from the running machine to half turn and stretch her long legs. As she turned, she saw him struggling to complete the movement and drop the weights back onto the stack with a loud noise.

Feeling instantly foolish, Stanley caught her eye as the smile broke out from the sweat-glistening skin of her face.

"Major," she said as she walked towards him.

"Ah, Corporal," he responded breathlessly, "how have you been?" it was the first thing he could think of to say, and made him feel awkward as he had seen her a short time before and they hardly had much to catch up on.

"I've been a good girl, thanks," she said, intentionally playfully as her eyes quickly and expertly scanned the cut of his shirt over his chest and shoulders. She seemed to like what she saw, at least Stanley hoped she did.

"I'm going to hit the squat rack," she told him, making him unsure if it were an invitation or a statement. His awkward delay in responding made her spell it out for him, "You coming?" she asked.

Now, on the fourth consecutive night they had spent together in his comparatively luxurious new residence, he felt the need to lay down some rules to prevent displeasing their personal, and overall, boss.

"We can't be seen together," he said again before she hushed him with a finger to his lips.

"I know, and we won't," she told him. The reason the alarm was set so early before their work days began was so that she could put on her gym clothing and sneak out of his door to the stairwell and down two floors for her morning run. "I still have to finish investigating you," he said with a boyish smirk as he whipped up the covers and dived underneath to make her giggle as he tickled her.

"Stop," she gasped, "I'll be late if you don't stop!"

"So be late then!" came the muffled reply from under the sheets, as the giggling became a gasping moan.

———

Adam had tried to speak to Eve after they had been summoned by Command as soon as they regained the safety of the tunnels beneath the Citizens' residences, but the small, older woman had spirited the girl away.

The miniature, at least in stature and not in deadliness or skill, female version of him twisted to look back over her shoulder as she was marched away. Just as she went out of sight, his eyes grew wider and stuck in an expression of utter bewilderment; the girl was sticking her tongue out at him.

He made to follow them but was intercepted by Mark.

"Where are you off to, boy?" he asked him, placing a hand on his shoulder.

Adam snatched at the hand as soon as it touched him and bent the thumb painfully inwards, making Mark bend at the waist instinctively to relieve the pain. Adam held the thumb there, bracing the wrist and the arm with it as his eyes followed the girl's exit. He released Mark, who stood and glared at him angrily.

"I'm not a boy," Adam told him dangerously, in that quiet voice which seemed to bypass a person's ears and arrive directly in their thoughts, "and why didn't you tell me there were others like me?" he asked with hostility.

Mark fought to control himself for a few heartbeats, chest rising and falling as he struggled to rebel against the chemical cocktail of adrenaline coursing through his veins.

"You know what you need to know," Mark answered

testily through gritted teeth, "and trust me, *Adam*, she is not like you."

The others all melted away and Adam was left in his own room where he paced to try and calm his brain. It was spinning and moving like a drone; erratic and fast. He trained in an attempt to focus his mind, then ate and tried to rest. He had stripped off his black suit and cleaned his weapons, having favoured a pair of small and wickedly curved knives this time; cleaned them even though he hadn't even drawn them since he had left his room the previous night, save to threaten to disembowel the girl when she tried to snap his arm.

This was the part he hated most of all. They kept him locked up in the dark, wound up like a compressed spring until they needed him. Then they shut him away again and never explained why or how things happened. He wrapped his lower body in a rough, threadbare towel and tried to read by candle light.

He was disturbed by the door opening, and leapt to his feet to challenge Mark about what had happened. He froze, because the figure who slipped through the door and closed it as silently as possible was not Mark.

The figure was small, and moved like a shadow, because she was still wearing the black suit, although she seemed to have left the sword behind. Eve stepped around the sparse furniture as she scanned the room, evidently comparing it to her own but showing neither disdain nor jealousy. She hopped lightly to land her backside on a wooden unit where she sat and looked down at him.

Her eyes searched his naked torso and made him feel that she was assessing where to put her blade to best effect. Adam snatched up a worn short-sleeved shirt and threw it over his head before pulling it down roughly. His eyes scanned the ground and he located a similar pair of loose trousers, which he bent to retrieve, and went behind a screen to swap for the towel he wore so as not to feel vulnerable.

When he reappeared, he found that Eve had not moved, and still wore the same mischievous and mocking smile.

"You wanted to talk?" she asked.

They spoke for hours. Each taking turns to fill the other in on the various stages of their lives and training after he had begged her to explain how she was walking around free. They had both met people who had trained the other, and they delighted in impersonating their trainers as though they alone on the planet shared a private joke.

Eventually Eve arrived at her point.

"Why did you lie to the others?" she asked him suddenly. He opened and closed his mouth as he searched for the answer; both for her and for himself.

"I don't know," he said eventually, and truthfully. "Why did you do it? Why did you kill them when you didn't need to?" he shot back.

As it was Eve's turn to search her soul for an answer to a question she didn't fully understand, her head cocked and her eyes looked up to the gloom of the ceiling.

"I liked it," she said eventually, and truthfully, "and I've been waiting to see if they are as dangerous as I've always been told. They aren't," she said, dropping her gaze and looking through him with an intensity which burned, "they are easy to kill. Too easy." She sounded disappointed.

Adam shared her disappointment, if not all of her feelings. He, like her, had been trained his entire life to believe that the evil party soldiers were superhumanly strong and fast, and would kill both of them with ease unless they trained harder and learned faster.

They lapsed into silence as each waded through their memories and feelings, having learned that neither was unique. After a period of time neither could accurately guess at, Eve spoke in her quiet echo of a voice.

"I hate it here," she stated simply, "there has to be a better life than what they let us see," Adam said nothing. He had some of the same feelings, but had never voiced them before and especially not so emotively as Eve had just done. He looked inside himself, finding that whilst he didn't enjoy many aspects of his life, he did like it there on the whole.

He had trained for his entire life, swallowed everything they had told him about his enemy and had been disappointed to find them nowhere near as fierce and dangerous as he had expected. Had hoped.

Eve hopped down from her perch as suddenly as she had sprung up to it, waved him a mischievous goodbye with the tips of her long fingers, and slipped from his room.

Minutes, later having avoided only one person in the tunnels easily by leaping upwards silently and holding her body weight suspended between two pipes, she walked back into her own room on silent feet. Stopping only to gently adjust the blanket over the sleeping form of Cohen, she lay down and closed her eyes.

CHAPTER TWENTY-FOUR

ESCALATION OF VIOLENCE

The Chairman entered the room carrying a rough, white mug in one hand and was followed by the new Major. Nobody in the room among the most senior officers in The Citadel really knew what he did, and that very fact alone made it obvious that it was something none of them was authorised to know. As such, the new Major was treated with a wary and fearful respect which he enjoyed without disguise.

The Chairman waved a hand over the assembled uniforms as he sat and clanged the mug onto the polished table top.

Major Stanley only wore rank insignia on his new uniform, and had evidently disregarded the need to wear his name badge. Even so, the rest of the men gathered there knew his name. The only other person in the room to do the same was the Chairman, and the similarities between the two were an insult to any man who felt that the chain of command was based on seniority, and not merit or favouritism. Some suspected that he would forgo the need to wear standard uniform entirely soon, and emulate the Chairman in his leather coat, cut to appear uniform in style.

"Let me recap, gentlemen," Nathaniel said in a tone which made it clear that he was unimpressed.

Not angry, not disappointed, but severely, obviously and dangerously unimpressed.

"After four days of investigation, we have absolutely no idea who killed two of our soldiers, although it is clear that the same terrorists are responsible for the last attack; no idea what they wanted or why they attacked the areas that they did." He paused to scan the room for any sign that someone had something useful to say, "We don't know what they were after last time, we don't know what they were after this time, and we have four dead soldiers cut to pieces on the streets of The Citadel, despite having extensive camera drone coverage. Tell me if I have any of this wrong?" he challenged them.

Nobody spoke, and nobody met his eye. He snorted his derision, which Stanley took as his cue to embarrass them further.

His fingers danced across the tablet in his hand and flicked towards the large wall opposite the Chairman. He and Nathaniel were the only two men who didn't have to turn to see. The footage played with no response from anyone. Stanley played it again more slowly, knowing that of everyone who had seen it, only he and the Chairman had noticed anything amiss. The film showed once more, slower this time and zoomed in on the street.

Still no response.

Stanley played it again, only this time he walked to the wall and pointed at the grate in the concrete, then pointed to a shadow hovering still nearby.

As the others watched on, that shadow disappeared unnaturally. Groans of understanding and gasps of shock rippled around the table as they finally saw what was being pointed out.

"Yes, gentlemen," Stanley said, "someone is tampering with our CCTV."

Nathaniel cleared his throat and swigged from his coffee cup. He pulled a ghost of a face which Stanley knew meant that the dark liquid had grown fractionally too cold for him. He swallowed it down and addressed the senior staff.

"We still have no idea how deep this rot goes," he told them, "but as of now every person working in or having access to the CCTV system is a suspected terrorist sympathiser. I fear further that our intelligence services are failing." He let that hang heavily, and saw at least four pairs of eyes swing to Colonel Edward Samson, who was the most senior man present and in overall charge of that department.

Samson glanced at the nearest man, the Major to his left who was the Chief of Drones, who resolutely ignored his pleading look. Samson said nothing and swallowed nervously to bob the lump in his throat below the fleshy jowls.

A soft man, thought Nathaniel, *unaccustomed to pressure.*

"Make no mistake," he growled at the congregation, "I will replace each and every one of you here with officers who show more ambition and results, should I not find out answers soon. Now," he said as he straightened and changed the subject, "the issue of how we respond is a delicate one. I feel that we need to make more of a point. The masses do not know about the incident, and more public punishments would only serve to ignite the fires burning in secret." He paused to adjust where his cup was, turning the handle so that it matched the nearest edge of the large table at a perfectly perpendicular angle, "I feel that we need a change in the security arrangements at the residence blocks," he finished simply.

He glanced up to look at the eyes glued to him, each of the assembled officers wary and fearful of both him and the terrorists.

"Major Stanley will give you your orders," he said before standing to leave the room. The others hurried to stand up to show their respect as the Chairman left.

Stanley sat and leaned back to survey the officers. The cautious respect metamorphosed into a myriad different responses, each one Stanley enjoyed exquisitely.

He saw anger, fear, jealousy, even outright loathing between two men who showed their disgust at being tasked by a mere upstart Major, who was probably younger than their own sons, who in turn were likely still Captains in perpetuity.

"Each residence block is to be granted a master-at-arms responsible for their safety. The role is to be part of the citizens' community, and to address their fears," he said with a smile, knowing that his words and his intentions were polar opposites, "It's something that used to be called *hearts and minds*," he smiled at their confusion, so he made plain his—the Chairman's—expectations.

"Guard commanders, I expect the files on your toughest, most overbearing and cruel soldiers by morning," he fought down the smile he could feel building in anticipation of his next instruction.

"Dismissed," he said before sitting back in his chair and watching as a room filled with more senior men than he filed out to follow his orders.

All but one of those men accepted their place in the world, and Colonel Samson strode angrily to the Chairman's office. Corporal Nadeem was on duty at the adjutant's desk and rose smoothly as the angry old man bustled with as much importance and alacrity as his portly frame could muster.

"Good morning, Colonel," Nadeem said as she delicately intercepted his path, forcing him to either push her aside or stop. He stopped, and not even her dazzling smile and charm could dissuade the man from making the mistake he was about to insist upon.

"Out of my way, *girl*," he snarled as he walked through the door uninvited and unannounced.

Nathaniel was standing leaning against the front of his desk as he read a small sheaf of reports and messages taken in his brief absence. Nathaniel calmly returned the papers to his desk and smiled at the intrusion as though Phillips' demeanour wasn't an overt hostility filled with disrespect.

"Colonel," he said equably, "what a pleasant surprise. I trust you have had your orders?"

"Yes, Sir, I have," he said, the colour of his slack jowls rising crimson from the neck of his tight uniform, "and I must protest."

"Protest, Sir?" Nathaniel said, "Protest against what? My orders?"

Samson seemed to notice for the first time the dangerous predicament he had barrelled into and now sought desperately for an escape. His bluster threatened to abandon him entirely.

"No, Sir, not your orders…" he tried.

"So what could be so wrong, Colonel, so offensive to you that you feel the need to enter my office in such a manner?" his voice was calm, measured, and infinitely more frightening than if he had shouted.

"Sir, please," he stammered, "I must protest that I am being given orders by a mere Major," he blurted out, "a major who only days ago was a young *Captain*..." his mouth flapped open and closed like a landed fish. Nathaniel dropped his shoulders, tilted his head a fraction and looked at the old man kindly.

"Colonel," he said almost in shock, "I must apologise," he let the words hang as he watched the fat man before him straining at the seams of his uniform relax in triumph, "I apologise because I now realise how much it must offend you to have a Major doing such senior work based on merit and ability, when an overpaid, overstuffed sack of lard like you claims superiority through seniority." His voice had still not risen, but the temperature had dropped suddenly in the room.

Nathaniel pushed himself away from the desk and now stood towering over the old man.

"I trust that none of the officers under your command feel similarly aggrieved at receiving their orders from your senior Major, who I know has been effectively running your entire department whilst you do nothing. So again, Colonel, I am very sorry that you feel that way. Corporal?" he said looking over Samson's head.

"Yes, Sir?" came the smooth response, making Samson spin to see that the attractive young woman had not scurried away when he had entered the office.

"Inform human resources that the Colonel here has decided to retire, effective immediately, and that Major Louise Barclay is to replace the Colonel in both position and rank." He nodded and cast his eyes back to the speechless man.

"There you are, Colonel. Oh sorry," he smiled as he

reached up a hand to unclip the stars from his collar, "*Mister* Samson, now you never have to follow orders from a mere Major ever again. Good day to you, Citizen."

Samson stumbled from the office, his head awash with fear and regret, wishing that he had swallowed his pride and kept his mouth shut.

CHAPTER TWENTY-FIVE

THE OVERSEERS

Colonel Barclay was escorted into the Chairman's office, where she shook hands with Stanley after saluting Nathaniel. He had kept the stars he had removed from her predecessor's uniform as he had stood powerless to say anything, and planned to give them to his replacement. Seeing that she had already located a set of rank badges befitting her new station did not dissuade Nathaniel, and when he explained where the offered stars came from, he saw her face crease in a slight smile of evil glee as she accepted them happily.

A stack of personnel files rested on the edge of the large desk, each one with a brief recommendation from their supervising officer. The role of the master-at-arms for each residence block was an ingenious idea initially dreamed up by Stanley and polished into their current plan by Nathaniel. They settled into chairs and each read through the dossiers in silence, speaking only to offer thanks for the passing of documents between them as they drank filtered coffee from the pot which had found a permanent home in the Chairman's office. When one had finished they waited in silence for the others to catch up.

Nathaniel stood and stretched, still feeling robbed of sleep after his interrupted night and active hangover, and sorted the files into a single stack.

"So," he said, "take twenty-three and pick six," as though declaring the task would make it any easier. It was not as simple as that, and they all knew it.

Picking a soldier too prone to violence would cause a risk of disorder, one too lenient would be totally counter-productive. One with proclivities towards mistreatment wouldn't necessarily be a negative point, but those proclivities could also be causes to ignite social disorder. He picked up the first file and opened it.

"Sergeant Davidson," he announced, "disciplined twice for excessive force used in training and disobeying an order. The former isn't a problem but I don't like the latter."

Barclay cleared her throat, "Sir, the order he refused was given by a Lieutenant half his age…" she said, leaving the rest open to individual interpretation.

"So he refused to carry out an order that had no place to be issued to begin with?" Stanley mused. Barclay nodded.

Nathaniel dropped the file onto an empty spot on the desk and picked up another.

"Sergeant Du Bois," he read uncertainly, pronouncing it *doo-bwah*, "Du Bois? Really?" he asked as he looked up to the others to meet blank looks. He cast his eyes down to the brief assessment of his officer.

"Sergeant Du Bois has served on the frontier, having been posted there as a private evidently early on in his career, after he was discovered giving additional rations to farm workers," Nathaniel paused to shoot a confused glance at the other members of his think tank, "Why has he been recommended for this role? Has someone not read between the lines and actually sent us a caring soldier?"

"No, Sir," Barclay interrupted the rhetoric, "it seems that the frontier has, er, *changed* him." Nathaniel regarded her with an eyebrow raised in interest.

"He has survived three years on the frontier and is the only surviving member of the unit he was assigned to when he got there. He's actually being transported to The Citadel now for reassignment, having earned promotion through Corporal and to Sergeant based largely on ruthless fighting and a keen intellect; that and staying alive.

"The outgoing Captain reported on him before he was rotated away from the unit to say that the man was 'more capable than any Lieutenant' he has had under his command, which I take to mean that Du Bois actually commanded the company in a practical sense. He's clever, Sir, and by all accounts, violently cruel."

Nathaniel smiled wolfishly.

"I like him already."

———

It took them almost the entire day to pick the six best candidates, and for their orders to be dictated for later writing-up formally by Nadeem.

Their real orders would be given in person, by either Stanley or Barclay, and they would be left under no illusion as to what they were required to do.

Barclay took her leave as the sun was sinking behind the huge building of The Central Citadel, leaving the two men alone. Nathaniel found the coffee to be cold, and instead of walking back to the desk he cracked open the door and called for Nadeem. The young woman appeared and leaned her upper body through the gap, as she held onto the doorframe, and raised a leg behind her for counterbalance.

She was wearing the white shirt and had removed the uniformed jacket.

"Sir?" she enquired simply.

"More coffee, please," Nathaniel said.

"Yes, Sir," she answered equably, then added, "after that I am due off duty unless you need me to stay?" She risked firing a glance at Stanley, who intentionally kept his gaze on the paperwork in his hands, despite not seeing a word on the page, in case he betrayed himself and smiled at her.

Nathaniel thought before answering, "No, that's fine. Please put an order through for coffee and some food, and then you may enjoy your evening as soon as your replacement arrives."

He nodded to her graciously, seeing her return the gesture and straighten up to leave.

His eyes scanned her toned legs and back as she turned away, and Stanley swallowed hard to fight down his jealousy. Rising from his chair to change the subject, Stanley stepped closer to ask Nathaniel in a hushed tone, "Sir, what about Project Erebus? Can't we use them against this kind of insurgency?"

Nathaniel regarded him casually for the briefest of moments, making the younger man feel like he was being assessed. Speaking suddenly, Nathaniel answered him, "No."

He offered no further explanation, making Stanley suspect that he was being tested to see if he could figure out the reasons why for himself. He was tired, his eyes were dry from being inside the air-conditioned room for so long, and his head was foggy because his concentration was wandering to the long legs which had been sitting outside the room he was in for so long.

"Too strong a reaction?" he asked.

"Yes," Nathaniel replied, just as someone knocked on the door, and a woman entered bearing a tray of sandwiches and coffee. The two men waited, saying nothing until the woman left without a word, and Nadeem's replacement at his desk shut the door after her. "Yes, it's too strong, but?" Nathaniel enquired of Stanley, waiting for him to arrive at the conclusion.

"But they're a precision weapon, and we don't have a precise target?" Stanley tried.

"Precisely," Nathaniel said with a mouthful of sandwich, "Let our new overseers turn up the heat, but in the meantime, I want to put one of the projects on a quick reaction force."

Stanley nodded, taking on the responsibility for the task and its many inherent problems wordlessly.

They discussed plans as they ate, coming to agreements and surmounting the stumbling blocks their logic encountered. The two were, as far as possible, becoming something resembling friends. After they bade each other goodnight and left for their residences, Nathaniel recalled that he hadn't yet received the report he had requested on the adjutant Corporal, which occupied a lot of his unfocused thoughts.

Stanley had declared her 'clean' but he hadn't heard the specifics he wanted; he had wanted to know enough to figure out how she ticked.

In the mood for more company, he stopped in the bland rooms he occupied in The Citadel only to drop his leather coat over the back of a chair and pick up a bottle of something.

The short walk along the empty corridors and deserted

stairwells late at night calmed him. He found the door he was looking for and knocked formally. Authoritatively.

After no response came from inside he tried again, louder this time and mindful that he did not want to disturb the other occupants of the corridor and feel obliged to explain himself. Instead of trying a third time, he returned sullenly to his own quarters and drank alone, no longer feeling relaxed by the emptiness he experienced in the vastness of The Citadel.

———

Two floors below that door, knocked on with such an air of leadership, the occupant of that room rolled between sheets intertwined with a man just as tired and in need of company as the one who had rapped on her door out of loneliness.

CHAPTER TWENTY-SIX

WAITING FOR THE PUNCHLINE

Sergeant Du Bois found himself unsettled by his return to The Citadel. He had spent the uncomfortable journey in an armoured vehicle convoy, cramped in the windowless rear among the officers rotating back to what they evidently felt was safety.

He kept his mouth shut. As the only non-commissioned man on board, he knew the others were wary of him. A mixture of slightly older and much younger men sat around, clearly not wanting to openly discuss their relief at making it out in front of the wild-looking sergeant, with his bushy beard the colour of rust, and eyes which spoke of horrors they had not experienced. He hadn't even changed his uniform since his last duty and the dried blood flaked off occasionally to serve as a reminder that the frontier was not a place many got to leave.

He ignored them, openly showing the disdain he held for the privileged officers who spoke about the dangers they had faced as if they'd been face to face with the enemy, when they hid behind men like him and the men he had commanded. He knew these men had served their brief tour—mere months instead of the years he had endured—in order to make the next rank on their way up the chain of command.

When the brakes squealed to announce the beginning of the end of their journey at the gates to the city, Owen Du Bois rolled his shoulders and eased his cramped muscles in preparation for getting out.

His jaw and the muscles in his cheeks ached the most, as he had kept his jaw clenched tightly for many miles over bumpy ground to keep him from speaking out and shaming the loud boy of a lieutenant who regaled them all with stories of his exploits on the frontier.

You are so full of shit, little boy, he thought to himself, *that I'm surprised the others can't smell it.*

Du Bois knew with absolute certainty that he wouldn't have lasted a month in his company, where even the greenest boys had at least learned enough to keep their mouths shut and their eyes open.

As he stepped out of the troop transport and shuffled into the daylight amidst the twenty or so others returning, he felt totally alone as the only real soldier among them all. He dutifully traipsed into the building and waited in line until called forward to stand before a Major from the adjutant corps. A soldier held out a hand in silence for his weapon, which he reluctantly handed over. The hand took it, then reappeared to wait for his sidearm. With a snort of obvious disapproval, Du Bois unholstered it and slapped it into the outstretched hand hard.

The Major pointed a handheld scanner at him and waited a brief second for the beep to signify it had picked up his chip.

The Major looked down at the readout, back to the list on his desk, then back to the readout before looking up for the first time.

"Sergeant Du Bois?" he asked, looking at the paper-work, "Or is it Private?" he mused, looking at the readout.

"It's Sergeant," he said, "got promoted but never reprogrammed."

The Major noticed the lack of a 'Sir' but let it slide. He turned to the screen on the desk to input the information and find the corresponding tasking for the man, regardless of his previous or current rank. His eyebrows rose, and he glanced back at the man in front of him. The eyes which held unmasked malevolence, the tight mouth which he guessed would let fly a stream of profanity given the slightest provocation, the wild beard which should be removed immediately if he were to comply with regu-lations.

"Du Bois," he said, deciding to leave out the rank as though it were in question somehow, "The Citadel, block A, floor two, residence nine," he said. Du Bois' mind raced, but his face remained stony.

Why the fuck have I been allocated to The Citadel's officers' quarters? He thought to himself.

"There must be some mistake, Sir" he started, before the Major cut him off.

"Not on my part," he snapped indignantly, "the orders are signed by a Major... Stanley?" he said aloud, his voice indicating that he had never heard of any Major Stanley and held the irregularity of the orders in utter disdain. Normally, a non-commissioned solider returning from the frontier would be sent directly to troop barracks or onwards to a posting west or north. They would be effec-tively held at the guard post until their transports arrived, but never had he heard of a mere Sergeant—even if he had been made up rapidly from Private—be given quarters far more prestigious than the Major's own.

"It says that you are to report to Major Stanley at 0800

tomorrow," he nodded to Du Bois and turned his attention to a returning Captain in the line behind the Sergeant. He went next to the security station, where his biometric records were checked against the fingerprints on file, then his retina was scanned. The man operating the machines gave him a curt nod, then ignored him.

Du Bois shuffled onwards, stripping his functional uniform at the quartermaster's insistence and finding himself issued with a dress uniform along with workout clothes, footwear, and pyjamas. He took his small bag of new clothes and the folded stack of uniform into the locker room where he showered for a long time, creeping the temperature of the water higher and higher until it threatened to scald his skin.

He began to inch the handle on the shower back to the left, dropping the heat level as slowly as he had raised it until the icy water made the skin of his back shiver uncontrollably.

Stepping out of the shower and wiping his hand over the mirror to streak the condensation away, he regarded his reflection for the first time in months; true, he had seen his reflection on the frontier, but he had never fully relaxed, so that he felt as though he had never really seen himself until now. He ran the fingers of his right hand over the wiry ginger hair sprouting from his chin. He picked up the packet next to the sink, tearing open the wrapping and removing the single-use razor and shaving cream. He paused, knowing that there was no way the one razor could remove the months of growth, so he compromised by trimming the neck up higher beneath his chin.

Drying himself, he put on the stiff uniform and carried the rest to The Citadel. Scanning himself into the main doors of the building with the thumb of his right hand, he walked towards the residence blocks looking for A-Two-

Nine. Finding the door, and feeling more and more like an idiot, as he was certain that a mistake had been made; certain, too, that he would be yelled at by an officer at any point, before being sent back to the uncomfortable life he had grown accustomed to. He bent to press his eye to the scanner in the door.

A tiny light flashed from red to green in front of his eyeball, then the door clicked open for him to push it inwards the remainder of the way. He walked inside slowly, hoping that when they finally realised their mistake, he would at least get to enjoy the comforts for a short time. Dropping the bag of clothes on the wide bed, wider than any he had ever been permitted to sleep in, and stepping around the furniture in the room, he ran his fingers along the smooth edges. His bed. His desk. His large sofa and not one, but two armchairs arranged around a coffee table. He opened the wardrobes and found a robe as well as more loose clothing.

His reverie was burst when a knock sounded at the door.

Fuck it, he thought, *at least let me get comfortable before you kick me back out.*

He opened the door with a resigned huff after one last look around the suite; he hadn't even had a chance to look at the bathroom yet. He expected to find an officer of the militia, flanked by guards, to escort him to a shit-hole of a hovel and probably a demotion along with it; that fear had been growing since he had returned and found that his promotion to Sergeant appeared not to have been ratified.

Instead, he opened the door to find a smiling Major leaning casually on the doorframe.

The man wore nothing on the uniform but the badges of rank on his collar, he wore no headgear, and did not act like any officer Du Bois had ever met.

"I'm hoping you're Du Bois?" the Major asked.

He nodded. "I'm guessing you're Major Stanley?" he answered, connecting the dots between the man behind his residence allocation and the rank he wore.

"Yes," he said with a wider smile as he pushed himself off the frame and stood up, making him a couple of inches taller than the bearded and confused man. Stanley walked inside, and Du Bois stepped back so that he didn't have to crowd him to do so.

"Sir," Du Bois began, then stopped as another man walked in behind the Major. He put down a small bag and began to measure the length of the sergeant's legs and the circumference of his chest in between scribbling notes. Du Bois looked at Stanley, dumfounded, whereas the Major just looked amused. The two soldiers looked at each other in silence until the smaller man had finished. He nodded to the Major and left, closing the door behind him.

Stanley strolled to the bureau by the armchairs and opened it to reveal a bottle on a silver tray with glasses. He poured them both a drink and sat, inviting the still silent Du Bois to join him with a gesture of his hand.

"Sir," he began again as he sat, "I'd very much like to know what's going on."

Stanley sipped, still smiling.

"You are being awarded the rank of Sergeant Major, warrant officer class one," Stanley said.

The jump was huge, and turned Du Bois from a grunt into a 'Sir', at least to every other soldier not wearing officer's badges. The rank was not an officer's status, but it was something infinitely more powerful. It was the grey area between soldiers and officers. It made him truly something, and officers would refer to him as *'Mister'* Du Bois.

"You will be appointed as the Master-At-Arms for an entire residence block, and will be given a team of your choosing under your direct command. You will report directly to me," he finished.

Du Bois assimilated this information quickly before asking his next question.

"I assume this is a Special Operations thing?" he asked bluntly, making Stanley smile wider still.

"Whatever gave you that impression?" he said innocently. Du Bois said nothing in response, other than to wave a hand over Stanley's general appearance to encompass all of him. The Major gave a self-deprecating shrug to acknowledge that he did, indeed, look like someone in the Special Operations arena.

"Yes. Oh-eight-hundred tomorrow, I'll come and get you," he said as he rose from the chair and swigged the last of the measure he had poured for himself. "Call down for food whenever you like; perks of being in the Alpha block." He smiled again, leaving a shocked Owen Du Bois alone in the room.

———

At eight the following morning, someone knocked on the door of A-2-9, and after a brief pause, Du Bois opened it to find Stanley there, with the same small man who had run the tape measure over him the previous evening with skilled hands. He looked very tired, as though he had been awake all night, which Du Bois realised he must have been, because he produced a package. He opened it to reveal dress and working uniforms tailored to his frame and bearing the bold, wreathed insignia of his new rank. He left the uniforms laid out on the bed and left the room, taking his red eyes with him as he shuffled along. Du Bois was already wearing the uniform shirt and trousers issued to him from the quartermaster yesterday, and he was happy enough with the fit. He slipped his arms inside the new tailored uniform coat.

The experience was new and made him enjoy a sensation he had never felt before. He struggled for the right word to accurately describe his feeling, but could only smile at the way the jacket hugged his frame perfectly. He rummaged in the bag for an item of headgear, expecting to be back in the rigid discipline of military service.

"If you're looking for a hat, there isn't one" Stanley told him with a shrug, indicating that such trivial matters no longer concerned either of them.

Du Bois returned the shrug, straightening and flexing as he was unable to resist testing how well the custom-made uniform made him feel.

He buttoned the jacket and faced the Major, who had wandered around his residence nonchalantly looking over the décor.

He found it to be slightly lower in standard than his own, as well as being on a less convenient floor, and was happy that he still held an elevated position. Hierarchy was all.

Besides, he thought ruefully, *I'm unlikely to be packed off to a shitty detail when I've done my part.*

"What's on the agenda, Sir?" Du Bois asked the officer to interrupt his snooping.

"Breakfast," he replied with a smile before heading for the door and leaving the Sergeant Major guessing as to whether he should follow. He did. He was hardly hungry after an evening of reading the food menu and finally summoning the courage to make a call to the kitchens. He still suspected that the cruel joke being played on him would suddenly display the punchline and he would be cast back down to the level he understood and deserved.

When the order had arrived, he had thanked the

person bearing the tray and stared at the food, the quality and quantity of which he had never seen before. He ate until he felt sick, and even now he still felt full up.

Following Stanley through the corridors to The Citadel's canteen, seeing people nod their heads and offer salutes to them, Du Bois realised that the Major must have been part of something above the access levels of most people, and he suspected that he had just been selected to join the ranks of those who marched in the shadows.

The newly minted Sergeant Major knew better than to try and discuss his orders in an environment such as the canteen, even if it was in the heart of The Citadel.

He kept a staunch silence unless to answer a direct question, and even then, he kept the details of his experiences on the frontier very limited, unsure if his abilities and trustworthiness were being assessed. His abilities included knowing when to speak and when not to, in case he inadvertently provided someone unauthorised with information above their access level.

He ate a reserved breakfast, wary of making himself feel unwell again, and waited patiently for the Major to finish his own. The senior man must have woken with a ravenous hunger, either that or he had woken early to exercise. He wiped his mouth with a napkin and dropped it on the plate. Standing and abandoning the trays where they lay for others beneath their standing to clean up, the Major led the Sergeant Major into the depths of The Citadel for the orders which were written between the lines.

CHAPTER TWENTY-SEVEN

CREATING AN IDENTITY

Mouse had to dig deep down to the original specifications of the retinal and biometric scanners to fully understand how they worked, because the ones he had connected and tested were not functioning. Fly peered over his shoulder as he worked the keyboards, annoying him by refusing to sit down and let him work. Fly had no idea what the numbers and characters flashing over the screens meant, but that didn't seem to dull his need to watch what was happening. Mouse took a long, deep breath and let it out slowly, not intentionally to let Fly know he was annoying him, but more to focus his mind away from the distractions of people and back to the digital world he preferred to inhabit.

He had presented the idea, even led a mission to retrieve the two items and had almost faced catastrophic consequences when that mission went sideways, and now he realised he might have made a mistake. A very big mistake, based on an assumption.

The retinal scanner was easy enough; it just read and matched a recording of the scanned eye against the one saved to the database, and correlated the access level assigned to that recorded eye to the programming of the door it secured. That was simple; scan a new eye and save it in the database, along with a high-enough access level so as to be useful but not cause concerns to be raised.

The higher the access level, the fewer eyes were authorised to see what lay behind those doors.

The list of names with that level of access was obviously much shorter; and that meant an increased chance of discovery by adding a new name to it.

In the cases of the highly secured doors it was far better to hack the system and temporarily reduce the access level required for the door in question.

The biometric scanner was a different matter entirely. Most people believed that it was merely a device which scanned a person's finger or thumbprint but Mouse, lucky in that his obsessive nature made him unable to rest until he understood how a thing worked, had found that it actually connected to the chip embedded in the neck of the person using the scanner. That two-stage verification process actually prevented an authorised user from opening a door when they were dead, which is something he had planned to try in the near future. The anger he felt at his own lack of knowledge threatened to send him into a spiralling rage because he had been presented with important information he had not discovered.

Mouse hadn't found the reason for that two-stage security protocol change, which was suggested in a seemingly insignificant document buried in the archives, and there was no direct link between the current security measures and the recommendation for them.

Had he searched for the reason through a different route, he would eventually have read a short memo from a then newly promoted Major, a young and privileged one, who had just been assigned to special operations level access; this Major had recommended an overall change after an incident in Project Erebus.

The familiar name stung Mouse again, but he filed it away until he could dedicate the resources of his brain to the problem of understanding that too.

The document didn't explain what the incident was, but it detailed that the biometric scanners should be linked to an active chip to prevent a further security breach, then also listed an additional security measure in the Erebus-level elevators, whereby a secondary manual code had to be entered to power the exit. The decision-making process accepting these proposals and the subsequent work had been classified; hence it was moved to the archive servers, which Mouse did not realise he was disconnected from. These were intentionally stand-alone systems not connected to anything but power. The original memo had, however, somehow slipped the net and remained on the now open systems.

Not paying any attention to the hidden reasons for the change in security, Mouse racked his brain for a way to beat the troublesome obstruction to his plan.

His fingers stopped moving on the keyboards and he slowly leaned back. Fly recognised the change in his behaviour, knew better than to ask until Mouse was ready to speak, and waited patiently for him to come back into the world where everyone else lived.

He had to wait for a long time.

"We need to get into The Citadel's hospital stores," he said aloud as both hands flew back to the keyboards and new windows popped up to be filled with complex lines of code.

Fly remained patient, shifting slightly and feeling the

instant air of annoyance as the small movement dragged Mouse away from the digital rooms he walked through.

"There," Mouse said finally after what seemed like an eternity punctuated only by the furious tapping of keys.

Mouse didn't think to explain what or where *there* was, but he realised after the other man gave no answer. Shaking his head slightly, he glanced at the floor to explain.

"We need a working chip to use the biometric scanners," he said, "But we don't have chips and nobody we know *with* chips will have access to get through any doors, and they won't have matching retinal scans, and I can't change their access levels without making it obvious and putting them in danger," he rambled breathlessly.

Stopping to glance up at Fly, he saw that it hadn't dawned on him yet, or he hadn't explained it properly. Fly didn't know why he could change some things and not others, but a lowly factory worker suddenly having access levels to open weapons caches would seem strange to the Party.

"We need a new chip which hasn't been installed yet," he said, hoping that would explain what was on his mind.

"So," Fly asked with a furrowed brow, "you want to put *us* on the system that everyone has spent their lives trying to keep us out of?"

Silence.

"Yes," said Mouse eventually as he deflated slightly at the way his idea had been explained, "sort of…"

———

Mark startled Adam by bursting into his room without warning. The young man leapt from the cot he lay on, not asleep but daydreaming as he stared at the poorly lit ceiling.

He was thinking about the slim girl who could wield a blade with devastating brutality, a girl as dangerous as he was but with such an intoxicating air of mischievous energy that he had thought of nothing else since she'd left his room.

He rolled from the cot and landed in a ready crouch as his right hand found the worn handle of the wickedly sharp curved blade under the folded blanket he had been resting his head on. His right hand gripped the knife as his left whipped up in front of his face to complete the ready stance, only for his hands to sag and his legs to extend and bring him upright when he realised it was his mentor.

"You've got another job," he told the young man without greeting or preamble, "and you need to go as soon as it's dark."

"Is Eve coming?" he blurted out before he could master his own tongue, making Mark pause to glance at him as he was throwing open the cabinet which held his weapons.

"Yes," he answered uncertainly, fearing that the boy's focus was already failing because he had met a girl once, "it's a small job. In and out."

Adam said nothing more and slipped out of the loose clothing he wore, feeling no shame in his nakedness, before stepping into the black suit which masked the beacon of his body heat from the ever-present eyes in the skies.

Mark ran a thumb gently along the edge of a large, wide-bladed knife to test it for sharpness. Shaking his hand as the razor-keen edge parted the outer layers of his skin with frightening ease, he sheathed the big blade and tossed it to Adam who caught the twirling handle effortlessly and knelt to strap it to the outside of his right calf.

Standing after he had secured the first weapon, he added the pair of curved knives to the elasticated waistband, to sit just behind each hip. Mark shuddered internally at the sight of the two small blades; there was something so primeval and worrying about the look of them, as though they were the modern equivalent of the claws of some giant predator which had once preyed on human beings.

"I'm ready," Adam said, fixing the older man with a look of resolve.

Mark regarded the boy before him.

No, he corrected himself chidingly, *not a boy any more. He's a man now, he was the first time he took a life.*

———

Cohen was dozing on the sofa in the room with Eve, although like Adam the girl lay awake also. Their eyes suddenly widened and fixed on the doorway as the slight sounds of tortured hinges betrayed movement.

"Job," came a low voice from the shadows outside the door, prompting Cohen to groan as she struggled to her feet and rubbed her eyes. As she took her hands away from her face, she found herself looking directly into Eve's wide eyes, when she'd had no clue that the girl was even awake.

"Oh, shit-fucker!" she yelped, clasping one hand to her chest as she panted to regain her composure. The girl looked curiously offended and frowned gently, having taken a step back and adopted a subconsciously defensive pose as she moved.

"Don't bloody do that!" Cohen gasped at the girl.

Eve shrugged and relaxed, then pointedly glanced between Cohen and the wooden stand, where her black stick containing the deadly folded steel stood dormant. Cohen followed her gaze and looked back to meet her eyes.

She nodded once and the girl ghosted away to snatch up the weapon.

Maybe Cohen was groggy from waking suddenly and receiving a fright straight after, but she swore that she could feel the dormancy of the inanimate weapon come to life, like a machine powering up, as soon as the girl placed her hands on it.

Eve followed the older woman out of the door and through the subterranean maze to Command, where she laid eyes on Adam again.

———

"Mister Du Bois requires the new tactical package," Stanley said grandly to the woman wearing the white lab coat that everyone that far underground seemed to be sporting.

The woman nodded and turned away, wiping her thumb on her coat out of habit before holding it down on the reader and waiting for the door to click open in response.

The two men followed the woman inside, Du Bois marvelling at the surroundings as he had done ever since the Major had led him to an elevator which took them so far underground that the bewildered Sergeant Major felt suddenly claustrophobic.

The lab coat wearer showed them through to another section and motioned for them to continue. Both men found themselves at another secured doorway with scanners on both sides. Stanley waved Du Bois forward and watched as he placed his thumb on the scanner uncertainly. A bleep of warning sounded briefly and Stanley added his thumb to the equation via the scanner on his side of the door. The bleep sounded again, this time so mildly different in pitch that it went unmistakably from a negative to a positive sound.

The retinal scanners seated higher up on the walls above the biometric scanners flashed to life and a short tube extended from each side. Both men bent forward and waited for their eyes to be scanned.

A louder beep sounded, this one with almost a happy inflection, and the door clicked open. The two men stood straight in unison and walked through the door.

Du Bois seemed shocked that his lowly thumbprint and eyeball had opened up a door of such magnitude that he regarded his hand, thumb turned up, as though it didn't belong to him.

"You'll get used to it, Sergeant Major," Stanley said with amusement.

"I doubt that, Sir," he replied under his breath, marvelling as lights blinked into renewed existence to illuminate racks of weapons and other equipment the likes of which the man had never seen before.

"Well, fuck me sideways…" he said in quiet awe from behind his beard.

CHAPTER TWENTY-EIGHT

STING IN THE TAIL

Nathaniel took personal responsibility for overseeing the addition of one of the Erebus subjects to The Citadel's reactionary force. He had three scientists with the subject; the one that had been named Host.

Host was dressed in tight black armour, developed to be flexible and still offer protection, with each slab of muscle shrouded in a fitted plate of thin armour, which lent him the appearance of a human insect. Each of his hands could access no fewer than three weapons, and the high-tech headset was strapped carefully to his head.

The headset not only gave him vision in multiple spectrums, but provided a live feed back to the science team and ultimately to Nathaniel, to control him remotely through the earpiece by which he would give him commands. The scientists ran tests and spoke to each other, ignoring Host as he stared resolutely forward, not yet required to interact.

"Test sync," called the lead scientist, prompting action from the others.

"Sync active," said one, looking to the other, who was

making minute adjustments to a drone which had not been seen by most people until then. It's slightly smaller size and evidently different construction marked it out as more expensive and ultimately more secret than the standard drone which scoured the skies day and night.

The material this new drone was made of seemed almost liquid, as the dull black skin shimmered under the light.

The stealth coating had performed well, as had the shielded blades protecting its ability to stay airborne when under attack. In truth, the new drones were intended to mark a new era in the war on the frontier, where the success of obtaining a technological advantage over their invisible enemy was sorely overdue. The decision to link the behaviour and full attention of the new drones to the Erebus project subjects was an interesting proposal which seemed to divert very little in the way of resources, so Nathaniel had eagerly permitted it.

This drone, what the lab coats were calling a stealth-tethered-drone, was not attached to main grid. It could not be controlled or monitored by The Citadel control room, and was slaved solely to the transponder embedded in Host's equipment. Wherever he went, the drone would be watching in eerie, whining silence from above.

The method of deploying the asset to any trouble spot was also achieved by the use of drone technology. The party's engineers had toyed with personal transport drones for years, but they had always been deemed too low-powered and inefficient to deploy troops over any distance, because the drones had to be recovered and brought back by more conventional methods more times than was acceptable.

The use of these personal transport drones had been shelved, along with all their research, but Nathaniel's decision to use the assets as a QRF prompted the project to be unveiled once more, if only for two units to be readied for use. These two units were the best of the prototypes and were rapidly serviced to make them ready for deployment.

Host was equipped, strapped into the frame hanging under the big drone, with the slaved stealth-tethered-drone resting on the ground beside him, ready to reactivate and follow if needed. Nathaniel settled himself into the drone control seat, this time not deep in the bowels of the underground laboratories, but high up on the floor directly below the roof of The Citadel. The drone station had been retrofitted to act not as a control station for a flying toy, but to monitor the incoming feeds from the drone network, the stealth slave, the asset himself via the headset; to monitor also the CCTV network and direct line of communications running to the asset and The Citadel control room. He had shrugged out of his heavy leather coat and rolled up his sleeves to settle in for a long wait as he sipped the rough coffee from the cheaply made mug, which he enjoyed immensely as his most recent fad.

———

Many floors below him, having had his mind blown by the sudden turn in fortune he now enjoyed, and marvelling as he ran his hands over his new equipment and weapons, Sergeant Major Du Bois relaxed with a solitary drink before his first day as Master-At-Arms for residence block six.

The block where Command had based themselves.

———

Two floors below the Sergeant Major, similarly excited and

relaxed, a Corporal and a Major lay in each other's arms and neither of them considered the dangerous stupidity of what they were doing.

———

Elsewhere under the streets of The Citadel, hidden in the darkness as they wound their way through the dank tunnels, four people crept towards their target. Mouse had elected to travel fast and light, initially choosing just himself and Fly to go and get what they needed, hoping to remain undetected and hence not needing protection. He had been ordered to take others, and had chosen the twins to accompany them. But he had been overridden and forced to take the other two as well. He trusted the twins, he had worked with them many times over.

He trusted Adam, he supposed, having recognised a quiet and stoical nature about him, which belied the danger he posed to the enemy.

He didn't trust the girl.

He had been the one keeping watch during their last mission through the small window and had seen the movement as she sailed to the ground to kill the two soldiers. He'd seen no evidence that they had been spooked, even less to indicate that they had detected anything amiss or that they posed any risk of discovering them. Still, Adam had backed her up and sworn that the kills were necessary. His quick thinking to remove their helmet-mounted recording devices was a sensible one, not that he had shared the contents of that footage yet, after spending hours decrypting the security protocols.

Even he had shuddered at the screen, having to replay it and crank up the contrast to show a slightly darker shape in the inky blackness emerge flashing a brilliant and deadly strip of steel in the sudden harsh light.

It was punctuated only by a curious flash of bright red as the girl's fingernails swept through the shot. That footage then tumbled end over end, casting insane shadows as it went, before coming to rest and rocking slightly. At the very edge of the screen, he saw the girl cut the hands and rifle of the second soldier into pieces; like a cat playing with its food. It was clear to Mouse that she could've killed them both quickly and cleanly, yet she chose the manner of their deaths to be more gruesome than he thought was efficient.

That footage ended as his own concerned face filled the corner of the screen and snatched away the camera, shutting down the recording.

Now, forced into a mission sooner than he would have liked, pressed into taking a protection detail that he didn't feel he needed, nor did he fully trust, he stopped at a junction as he mentally checked the map in his brain.

"Here," he said, indicating an access port to the world topside up a short ladder, nodding to Fly to take the lead and to check the cover for signs of alarms. He repeated his trademark pose of pushing up gently with his upper back as his head was turned sideways, inch by inch as he shifted position to see every gap and be sure that the hatch didn't house a nasty surprise for them. He slipped through, expecting the others to follow instantly, and Eve sprang up the ladder and rolled out into the darkness above with a disturbing lack of noise. Mouse was last out after Adam had joined the first two, and the cover was replaced undisturbed.

Mouse led the way, sticking to the shadows as he scurried towards their target in genuine mimicry of his namesake. Finding the building they wanted, Eve let out an undisciplined gasp as she marvelled at the height of it.

The medical centre wasn't the tallest building in the city by far, but Eve hadn't been anywhere near The Citadel as the others had been, so the sight was a marvel to her.

Fly hissed at her to keep quiet, receiving a sullen and murderous look from the girl.

With only her eyes visible, Fly thought as he fought to control an involuntary shudder, *that girl can really convey a strong dose of malice.*

The majority of the intelligence on their target building had come from Cohen, providing detailed information from memory and describing the turns of the corridors to Mouse, who listened with his eyes closed in still silence as he committed the descriptions to memory. In the dark they approached the hospital, which was operating only a night time skeleton crew for emergencies and to monitor the citizens and Party members admitted for treatment. They waited in the shadows, watching the lone soldier standing sentry on the rear doors where the equipment and supplies went in and the refuse went out. They waited close to forty minutes, none of them uttering a sound or being so undisciplined in concealment as to make any noise adjusting their position for comfort.

Three times Adam's ears detected the slight scream and whine of the tiny turbine motors indicating that a drone was overhead in the blackness.

Eve's ears pricked up all three times, the tiniest cocking of her small head searching for the direction of the sound, indicating that she had also detected the near silent betrayal at the highest end of the noise spectrum.

Fly and Mouse had pulled thin sheets from their pouches to disguise their body heat, just as the suits of the other two did, and sat still and silent beneath the thin cloth.

The guard, shuffling his or her feet—none of them could tell, given the covered face—eventually moved off on some form of predetermined patrol route to be conducted at set times.

Male, Adam thought, watching the way the faceless and generic enemy moved, *my height but bigger,* unable to switch off his hunter's assessment of a potential target.

Without a word, Mouse led them towards the doors. Adam followed, keeping to the rear of their small group with his right hand curled around the hilt of one wickedly curved blade. He cast his eyes back to the door and recognised the scanner as one which needed the eyeball of a Party soldier to activate, and thought that Fly would have some way of getting around the locking mechanisms without activating any alarms. He did, but that was not what Adam saw happen.

As Mouse bent to press his face to the device, Adam almost cried out to stop him. As he drew in breath to hiss a warning, he saw the tiny red light on the door blink to green and slide open. He closed his mouth, scanned the area behind them again, then slid inside after the others.

Following the maps in his head again, Mouse led them through the corridors illuminated only by emergency lighting, as most places were during the night.

Finding the storeroom he wanted from the legends stencilled above the doors, Fly set to work and undid the lock using two small pieces of bent metal.

As the slightest of metallic clicks sounded, they stepped inside and Mouse immediately began scanning the room for the data access port. Finding it, he unrolled a flexible keyboard and flipped up the lid of a small folding tablet, battered and held together with strips of tape.

Green symbols sprang to life and shot across the tiny screen, filling up the horizontal lines from left to right. He tapped at the keys as fast as Adam could wield the blades he carried, before ending with a flourish and a final heavy keystroke.

"Done," he said, "now the cameras which saw us come in have been wiped and are just looping the empty corridors they've been watching before. Let's get to work."

———

"Sir, Sir!" came the panicked voice of the intelligence analyst sitting in the small control room behind the Chairman. He didn't take his eyes away from the displays ranked before him, merely spoke out of the side of his mouth.

"What is it, soldier?" he enquired equably, suspecting that he knew the answer.

"The anomaly we've been looking for, Sir? In the CCTV system?" he panted, half terrified of the man he was speaking directly to and half excited that something was finally happening in his dull existence of staring at screens.

"Yes…?" Nathaniel said, his patience threatening to snap if the excitable boy didn't arrive at a meaningful point soon.

"The Citadel medical centre," he announced almost breathlessly, "it just did the same thing."

CHAPTER TWENTY-NINE

ONE STEP AHEAD

Mouse had organised them to work fast and quietly, posting Fly as a lookout simply because he had known him the longest and trusted him the most. Adam was reliable, he was certain of it, but the girl was both reckless and unpredictable. He wanted the sword-happy pair where he could see them, having elected not to bring them in the first place but finding himself overridden.

"How did you get us inside?" Adam asked him in his soft voice which seemed to appear magically inside his skull and bypass his hearing entirely, "Through the eye scanner?"

"Easy," Mouse answered as he lifted a sealed box and passed it carefully out to Adam, who passed it on to Eve, who placed it gently in order with the others. "I added my eye scan to their security system. And Fly's."

Adam opened his mouth to ask more, but a hiss of warning from the door made them all freeze. The faint sounds of voices and the giggle of a woman penetrated the door to reach their ears. None of them moved, and the sounds from outside their storeroom grew louder as the bass notes of a man's voice gave the tone more depth.

The slightest of Doppler effects echoed as the voices passed their door, punctuated now by the rapid clicking of the woman's shoes on the hard floor and the sounds of keys scraping into a lock, before a door closed on the opposite side of the corridor and muffled the talking and laughing.

None of the four infiltrators moved a muscle until the talking stopped, and other sounds took over which suggested that the detection of resistance fighters was not their main priority in exploring the depths of the medical centre during the night. As one, the four began to work again in the silent dark. As Mouse stretched out to reach the last box on the bottom shelf, he pulled it closely to him and flicked an extending blade from his pocket.

Adam marvelled that the loud *snick* sound of the blade shooting out of the handle on its pivot point was so quiet, but then knowing what little he did about Mouse and his frighteningly precise attention to detail, he thought he had probably worked for hours to make the action as silent as possible.

Mouse ran the very tip of the knife, honed to a razor's edge, along the tape sealing the box and gently peeled back the lid. Lifting out the white polystyrene packaging a millimetre at a time to prevent the high-pitched squealing noise it made as it rubbed against the ridged cardboard, he uncovered a dark, plastic box. Popping the clasp on it, he lifted the inner compartment to reveal three straight rows of tiny metal rectangles with two thin wires protruding from the short sides.

Mouse closed the lid, removed the inner case, then painstakingly replaced the package and pressed the flap of the box back down. Sliding it carefully back to the place it had come from, his hands indicated frustration to Adam as the next box he needed to replace the initial jigsaw puzzle wasn't already available to him. Adam snatched up the box from Eve, who was way ahead of him, and turned back for the next one.

Mouse replaced everything exactly as it had been when he had removed them initially, his photographic memory making it easy to ensure that nothing looked out of place.

Mouse muttered to himself after he had restored the final box, standing to look at the shelves from different angles to see that what was before him now matched precisely what had been there before. Adam caught the words he muttered.

"Twenty chips per case. Two cases per box. Seventeen boxes. Six hundred and eighty. Six hundred and forty to be safe…" he trailed off, working through the mathematical timeframe until the missing box they had come for would be noticed.

Another hiss from the door made them all go still once more, as though some genetic coding dictated that a predator was in their immediate proximity, and that movement equalled discovery. The giggling grew louder again, backed by the low rumble of the man's voice as he spoke quietly to the woman, who giggled again.

The clicking of her heels was slower now, all urgency in their movement gone after they had clearly achieved what they could not wait to do in the unused part of the hospital at night.

The four, who had melted into the shadows, reanimated as the reckless couple's voices receded from their vicinity. Mouse forced the case into his small pack and prepared to lead the way back outside.

———

"You can go now, soldier," Nathaniel said, investing his words with some of the edge he felt at the nervous presence making the hairs on the back of his neck tingle.

The soldier's attendance faded away and he returned the entirety of his attention to the screens before him. He had launched the heavy drone carrying the secret payload as soon as he had confirmed that the CCTV system had been tampered with, and had sent word down for the location of the intercepting signal to be traced. The drone carrying Host moved ponderously slowly, and reacted with as much poise and responsiveness as the heavy cows which occupied the stalls in the far-off farming districts. The shadowing stealth drone moved crisply, matching its every move to the geo-anchor of the asset called Host.

As the Mule, a name which Nathaniel had literally stumbled upon at that moment, came into view of The Citadel's hospital, he dropped the altitude with a sickeningly unsympathetic motion to the passenger it carried. An involuntary grunt sounded in the Chairman's earpiece, elicited from Host by the sudden drop in height and the momentary weightlessness, but no protest came.

He knew there wouldn't be one. Even a professional and well-trained solider could've kept their opinions on the driving to themselves, but they would harbour a resentment for the pilot, and that resentment could manifest itself as opinions or even actions in the future. Project Erebus had created precision tools without opinions or emotions, who wouldn't bear grudges and harbour resentment.

As soon as the Mule touched down near the rear entrance—an educated guess as he saw no logic in the possibility that whoever was tampering inside the medical centre would have walked through the front door—he hit a small icon on the screen to his right to remotely disconnect the restraints.

He flicked his eyes to the main display in front of him, seeing what Host saw through the headset he wore, and watched as the subject was pitched forwards onto the rough ground, where he fell to one knee before snapping his head up to scan a full circle of his battleground.

All Nathaniel had to do now was wait, but waiting was difficult.

He had a constant stream of outside information on the smaller screen to his left. The screen to his right had now switched from the control and telemetry of the Mule to the stealth-tethered-drone.

Need a codename for that thing, he mused, unhelpfully distracting himself, *the STD won't do, obviously.*

The screen to his left lit up red, indicating a priority flash message, just as voices behind him rose in volume and intensity.

"Attack on the south gate," came a shout.

"Host," Nathaniel growled into the mouthpiece on his headset as he hit the transmit button on the control panel under his right hand, "return to the transport."

He saw the central screen respond with movement as Host climbed back on to the airframe. Nathaniel glanced to the drone display and swiped his finger halfway across the screen to split the view between Mule and tethered stealth prototype drone tethered… thing.

Dammit, he thought, *the STD.*

Host's view flicked downwards as the buckles were reattached, and he launched the Mule into the air as harshly as it could move. The power readout read sixty-three per cent, annoyingly low given that the Mule was probably still within a long rifle shot of the rooftop it had launched from.

It took almost a full minute for the heavy drone to

climb, and all the time the smaller, more highly powered agile unit flitted around it as though the inanimate object were herding the more cumbersome craft. When Nathaniel settled out the climb and left the subject suspended above the potential battlefield at around eight hundred feet, the shouts behind him returned to more sensible sounds. An officer scurried forward, the sounds of his small shoes squeaking rapidly in Nathaniel's ears, and he cleared his throat for the Chairman's attention.

"A little busy," he answered as his hands ran over the controls and his eyes flicked between the screens. The small drone cycled through visual spectrums with far higher-powered optics than the standard fleet employed. It went from standard, to infra-red showing heat sources, to ultra-violet, to a radiation-detecting spectrum, to a movement tracking mode, to another screen which showed sound as a radiating shimmer of lines, and back again.

"Sonar!" he said aloud with glee. "It's a bat!"

"Sir," queried the small man standing somewhere behind his head.

"Nothing," Nathaniel snapped, "what is it?"

"Sir, terrorists have attacked the southern gate," he started, "there…"

"I know that bit," Nathaniel snarled, "I'm not deaf. Tell me what I don't know."

"Sir," began the officer again, unable to hide his wounded pride at having been scolded, "there is a fire there and soldiers have shot at the attackers."

"Any prisoners?" the Chairman interrupted.

"Two have been shot, Sir. One is still alive."

"Send QRF one and medical evacuation immediately," he ordered, never taking his eyes away from the displays to his front, "highest priority is the survival of the prisoner."

The officer hesitated, making small noises as though he

wanted to speak but wasn't certain that his chosen words were the right ones.

"Why are you still here?" Nathaniel enquired quietly, his voice full of threatening implied disappointment.

"Sir," he tried before clearing his throat again and speaking more loudly, "we thought that the asset you are commanding might be useful there…"

"Then you're an idiot," Nathaniel said almost to himself as he was dedicating only a small portion of his attention to the unimportant question, "the attack on the gate is a feint, obviously, and *my* asset is none of your concern."

The officer fled, defeated, to relay the orders and explain that his team weren't allowed to play with the secret project they were supporting. Nathaniel heard his orders being passed on but paid close attention to the display of his newly-named Bat.

He had taken over direct control of the craft, dropping it to about two hundred feet and holding it steady. Unlike the Mule, the Bat stayed rock steady, in as the far superior internal gyroscopes corrected every minor buffet of wind and thermal disruption. The over-powered turbine engines with their protected quad blades were instantly responsive to the most minor of adjustments he made, and the sensor suite on board scored a direct hit within seconds.

A smile of evil intent spread slowly across his face as he switched controls and began to home the Mule in on an intercept course.

———

The four of them stopped and huddled by the door they had entered through, pausing for Adam to scan the rear yard. He dropped from the window, pulled the hood of his suit up over his head and motioned for the others to stay where they were. Eve shifted, misinterpreting the gesture to mean that she was not part of the group told to stay put. Adam repeated the signal for her benefit alone, saw the eyes narrow at him, and turned away.

Placing a hand gently on the release handle, a one-way fire door, as safety played a higher card than security in many places, he willed the shiny black helmet of the returned guard to turn away.

As soon as the head swung right in a lazy scanning pattern, he struck. Pushing open the door with a muted click he stepped out and rose up to throw his right hand in a vicious, arcing hook and snag the neck of the soldier. He squeezed tight, knowing that physical reactions would override conscious thought and both hands would involuntarily reach up to protect the precious passage of air into the body. This action kept the soldier's hands clear of his weapons, for vital seconds anyway, and gave him enough time to resolve the situation quietly.

He knew that bloodshed would lead to death, and he didn't need a small army descending on them. He bunched the fingers of his left hand and struck one, two, three savage and deep blows with the extended knuckles into the armpit of the soldier until his left hand dropped lifelessly to his side as the nerves were in spasm and disarray.

With that single obstruction dealt with, Adam switched the weapon that was his left hand and morphed it into a single, solid protrusion which culminated in the first knuckle of his index finger. His right hand released the neck and spread flat on the side of the shiny helmet providing more purchase than it was probably designed for. He pulled the helmet in tight with his right hand, extending the left side of the neck and making the small join of neck and skull just visible where the jawbone met them.

Driving his left index knuckle into the exposed weakness, he heard a soft popping sound and the fight left the soldier immediately. He lowered the unconscious body to the ground in the shadows and turned back to catch the door before it slammed shut and made a noise.

He didn't reach it in time, and instinctively snatched his fingers back before the heavy door pinched them. The door stopped an inch from closing, and Adam glanced down to see the dull black tip of Eve's sheathed sword stuck in the frame where it met the ground. He snatched the door back open, glanced once behind him, and indicated for them to follow him outside.

———

The curious way that the sonar or echo-location vision spectrum was represented on the screen amused and mesmerised Nathaniel, and even though his hands moved over the controls and his eyes scanned between the three displays wildly, he couldn't help but marvel at how pretty the display was.

The sounds bounced back to his Bat, and radiated outwards from the source of the sound to show the ghostly interpretations of people shrouded inside those shimmering lines.

What he saw was undoubtedly a kind of scuffle, one which he had zero faith in being won by one of the Party soldiers unless they had seen significant combat. If they had, he reasoned, then it was highly unlikely that they would be picking up night sentry duty at the service entrance of a hospital. He switched the direct control from Bat to Mule and leaned forward in concentration.

The Bat shot back up vertically, racing on auto-pilot to return to its synchronised link to the asset, just as the asset raced downwards at an angle for the Mule to disgorge its lethal cargo in the path of the shimmering lines which were making their way fast out of the small yard.

CHAPTER THIRTY

ONE STEP BEHIND

Eve heard it first. She hissed a warning to the others but was ignored as they ran. She paused at the sound, registering it as nothing she had experienced before, and cocked her head to listen to it as she stopped. Adam glanced back and saw that she wasn't running. He stopped to call her to catch up but the words froze in his mouth.

He heard it too.

The high pitch of the whine indicated a drone, but the stronger note of its engines sounded wrong. It moved faster, changed direction quicker, and was gone over their heads in a flash, heading upwards as the engine notes faded.

Adam turned back to call the others to stop, but when he faced the way he had come from, the noise of another drone filled the air and could've been detected by a sleeping child. This new drone literally droned, as though it struggled to carry its own weight, and sounded more like four drones linked together.

The Mule was, in fact, constructed of four standard drones linked as one single propulsion unit. Four times the power, four times the torque and four times the carrying weight it was rated for. It also emitted four times the noise. Mouse skidded to a stop a few paces before Fly, as the noise came in louder from directly ahead, making the shorter man bump into his back hard and stagger past him.

As the shadows in front of him took the form of a large drone with a hanging frame which banged into the ground. Empty.

As soon as that sound met their ears, another sound pierced the air from behind them. This one was also unmistakable, although very ominous, and was the sound of a human landing on the concrete. Only the landing was controlled, and the human that had landed rose from one knee and turned back to face them, having disengaged the restraints, and leapt from the drone as it dropped before his targets. He, unmistakably he, had a shaved head, a murderous facial expression and was swathed in black armour, which seemed custom-made to fit his muscular frame. He looked directly at them coldly. The eyes regarded Mouse and Fly from through its eyebrows; intent clear and not boding well for them.

———

Nathaniel looked at the large screen directly in front of him with awe and exhilaration. Pressing a finger to the transmit button he spoke a single line into the microphone, "Capture or kill."

———

The *thing* in front of Mouse and Fly twitched its eyes momentarily to the left, then smiled. It looked human, it moved like a human moved, but it did not *feel* human.

What it did do was draw two vicious short batons from either side of its waist and flick both wrists savagely to extend them. As the metal extended in three parts, the ends took on a slightly blue glow and the air seemed to crackle almost imperceptibly.

Adam's mouth dropped open inside the hood protecting his face, and every single muscle he moved in response to the threat seemed so utterly and terribly slow. His fear of the ambush, and his impending sense of doom rendered him unaware that they faced no ordinary Party soldier, but Eve moved similarly only half a pace behind him, taking a wider route to approach the threat from the side.

———

Host stepped forward two strong paces and bladed his stance sideways to attack two-handed the first person in front of him as he whirled the batons. Mouse instinctively threw up his left forearm to ward off the overhead blow.

It was a combination of Fly shoving him forwards and to the side, and the fact that his arms were sheathed in relatively thick leather that saved him, initially, from the force of the blow and secondly from the sixty thousand volts running free in the tips of the batons, searching for a conductive target. He suffered a minor shock which threw his body into rigid tautness as he hit the ground hard, but the locked muscles kept his head and neck impossibly stiff and prevented his skull from crashing into the hard surface. Already their ambusher was twirling and swinging the batons individually and together as he attacked with each exaggerated pace forwards. Fly backtracked desperately with each progressive attack, evading with such a frantic urgency that nobody would believe he could triumph.

Host switched effortlessly from high attacks with the weapons to low attacks with his feet, the second consecutive sweep successfully taking the small foe's legs cleanly from under him and tipping his upper body painfully backwards.

The angle of his fall was steep enough to pitch the back of his head into the concrete where he went down hard, and stayed there.

Host stood, turned back to the one who had stopped spasming and now lay panting as blood ran from his mouth, just as another target erupted from the dark and made straight for him.

———

Adam had drawn his weapons as he ran without thinking. Now he burst into the fight without cognitive thought that the two small, hooked blades were little use against the far superior reach of the electrified batons his enemy wielded. Instinctively, he adapted his fighting style and tried his hardest to close the distance between them. He ducked the initial attempts to render him useless, rising up inside the reach of the soldier who fought with a skill Adam had never seen outside of his own training.

He punched and slashed and swung as desperately in attack as he had seen Fly dodge in retreat. He rose, punching for the neck of the attacker with his left hand, intending to open the vein beneath the black material and end the fight. His eyes widened as the blade found its target but failed to slice through. Ducking the responding blow, he rose and swung as the tip of the knife in his right hand caught in the midriff of the attacker, and Adam tried to rip it hard to tear the soft skin beneath. The material of the armour caught the blade and held it tight, seeming to bind around the edge as he forced it.

Taught never to reinforce a failed manoeuvre, Adam spun his hand over and shoved the razor-sharp tip of the blade hard in the opposite direction and was rewarded with a change in pressure as the point punctured skin and muscle.

The body he had just perforated gave no indication that it had been cut.

There was no sudden change, no reaction to the pain, which must have been incredible, and no natural response to the risk of death. Instead, the body reacted by slamming the hilt of the baton down hard just above Adam's right ear.

Adam dropped to the ground and, not bothering to release his two index fingers from the metal loops of the knife hilts, drew the single broad, long blade from his right calf.

The attacker leapt through the air, higher than any person had the right to jump from a standing start, and bore down on him as his muscles again responded far more slowly than his mind. Rolling forwards, counter-intuitively towards the threat, he reached up to slice the blade wickedly through the material and flesh of the lower leg that flew past him.

Landing heavily and turning as Adam rolled to his feet, the savage killer who had dropped from the sky to upend their underground world staggered slightly, glancing down to regard the growing puddle of darkness just visible in the gloom by its right boot. Tossing down the batons, Adam's daunting attacker steadied its footing and it drew a pistol from the holster on its thigh.

Just then, a sudden whistling sound ended in a sickening *thwack*, and a sliver of shining metal appeared out of the side of the attacker's skull, rocking it sideways.

In shock, it reached up to tentatively touch the object, but Adam rolled forward towards it and rose from the ground with the wide blade an extension of his right arm to chop down hard and sever the hand holding the gun. A single gunshot rang out as the dead hand hit the rough concrete, still holding the weapon, the flash from the muzzle lighting up their battle-field like a lightning bolt to provide a freeze-frame of horror.

Another whistling sound touched Adam's ears as he leapt back from the homicidal look in the eyes of the man he had dismembered. Eve emerged from the shadows and swept the long sword in three glittering, arcs.

The left arm, severed just above the elbow, dropped first to the attacker's boot before rolling to the ground to rest opposite the right hand still holding the gun.

The face turned back to Eve in shock, at either her sudden appearance or at the catastrophic damage she had just dealt him, and the second and third twirls of the straight blade opened up the neck to make the head tilt sideways before the final thrust penetrated the armour front and back to skewer the body through the heart.

Eve remained still in the killing pose for a heartbeat, then withdrew forcefully and spun the blade back into the sheath held in her left hand before the body had toppled forward to slam into the ground with a crunch as the bones in its face first broke the fall.

Eve dragged Mouse to his feet and steadied him as she glanced at Adam to indicate that he should already have Fly. He sheathed his own blades and picked up the smaller man with ease.

Mouse had regained enough composure to pick up one of the batons, seeing and feeling the shimmering electricity fade out in response to his touch. He muttered something but was ignored, eventually regaining sufficient consciousness to tell them which way their exit was through a mouthful of blood.

———

Nathaniel said nothing as the image on the main screen showed only darkness with the vague light displaying the dark blood creeping outwards from the dead body which carried his camera.

He carefully set down the headset and rose from the seat, removing the plug-in device which both recorded everything and gave him authority to access the controls.

As he stood, his anger erupted from him like a pressurised explosion. Like steam escaping a container, his anger attacked the weakest point in the structure and forced him to lash out savagely, knocking the small officer to the ground as a roar of impotent rage escaped his lungs and forced the skin over his knuckles white under the pressure of his balled fists.

The small gathering of lab coats huddled nearby, terrified of the rage and consequences of their inaugural test failing in the worst possible way.

"Recover everything to the Erebus lab," he snarled at them through gritted teeth, "and have the area searched thoroughly by a forensics team."

The officer struggled to his feet, wiping the blood from his eyebrow with horror. He had only thought to offer the secondary quick reaction force be deployed to aid the asset, but the Chairman had attacked him instead, and now slammed the door harshly as he stalked from the room.

CHAPTER THIRTY-ONE

NOTHING WORTH HAVING COMES EASY

Adam burst through the doors into the collection of rooms occupied by Command, still carrying the unconscious Fly. Eve helped Mouse, who could mostly walk by himself, but the result of the electricity he had conducted had left him desperately uncoordinated and disorientated. He had found their route back underground, but each choice to turn left or right seemed to cause him agonising pain to recall.

Eventually, after many distressing wrong turns, they wound their way back to safety. Adam sucked in a large lungful of air as his chest heaved, and was sheened with sweat from the exertion of carrying Fly. He was far bigger and stronger than any of the others, but dead weight was called that for a reason. Eve seemed no worse physically for having helped half carry, half drag Mouse back.

Half shouts of alarm and hissed questions filled the air and were ignored until the two injured men were set down. Questions were fired at Mouse, who simply shook his head, "Not here," he said weakly as he tried to stand and blink away the disorientation, "Command."

People came and went, Cohen and Mark appeared and both took their wards aside to speak to them privately.

They were debriefed, then left where they sat. Fly was taken away and Cohen followed to offer her medical knowledge, no doubt. Mark left the room, probably to check the accounts against others and whatever other information the secretive older generation had access to. He came back minutes later and asked for Adam's knife.

His left hand went to his left hip, the closest weapon to pass to him, but Mark held up a hand.

"No, the one that caught the other guy," he said irritably. Adam dropped his left hand and raised his right, flicking his index finger inside the ring on the base of the hilt and drawing the curved blade. Dried blood was still visible on the tip.

Mark took it carefully, avoiding the bloody end, then bent and drew the wide-bladed knife from the sheath on Adam's right calf without asking.

The older man stalked away towards Eve without another word. Adam watched on, unable to hear the words on the other side of the room but seeing the evident unhappiness on the girl's face as she was asked to hand over her sword. She did, eventually. Reluctantly. Holding on to it until the very last second when Mark's grip became strong enough to force a confrontation, then she released it suddenly, making him stagger a fraction of a step backwards.

Left alone now, the two black-clad killers gravitated towards one another.

"What was that thing?" asked Eve, just as Adam spoke with, "Thank you."

The two regarded each other awkwardly for a few heartbeats.

"You're welcome," Eve answered humbly, "Do you think you would've taken him if I hadn't been there?"

Adam felt instantly affronted by the implied challenge in her words, but before he reacted emotionally he saw that her face bore genuine concern. He asked himself the same question, running her words through his brain again to search for the truth of the answer.

"No," he said finally, "He was going to shoot me and I was too far away to stop him," and an unnoticed fact tickled his brain, making his eyebrows knit together. "Where did the throwing knife come from?" he asked her.

Eve smiled, turned her body sideways towards him and cocked her right leg onto her toes. Folding down a strip of black cloth identical to the material of the suits they wore she exposed a pair of dull, silver coloured hilts with cut-out loops; like halves of a pair of scissors. Plain, simple, effective slithers of sharpened metal weighted perfectly to the throw of a small hand. As quickly as she had revealed them she let the fabric fold back over her slim thigh, just when the door opened and Mark waved them towards him.

He led them in silence along the corridors as both of them lapsed into silence when he repeatedly ignored their questions.

———

"What the hell happened?" snapped James.

Mouse was still groggy. His tongue burned fiercely, even though the bleeding had finally stopped, thanks to Cohen thrusting valuable sugar sachets into his hand and telling him to pour them in his mouth. The blood stopped flowing within seconds of the precious sweetness hitting his taste buds, but the metallic tang still made him feel nauseous.

"We were attacked," he explained again, his voice sounding thick and syllabic, "by a soldier."

"Be specific," instructed another member of Command, more softly than James had spoken to him.

"It wasn't a normal soldier," he explained, earning a snort of derision from James as he stated the obvious, "it—he—came in on us via a drone I've never seen before. It was a kind of personal transport drone." He paused, seeing the eyes meeting each other in the room.

They knew about them then, he thought, *thanks for telling me, you bastards.*

"He had weapons I've also never come across," he went on, "I brought back the electrified baton that he hit me with, but it's like the guns; it doesn't work without a chip."

"Did you get the chips?" James asked, betraying the fact that he had forgotten about the original mission objectives in light of the surprise appearance.

"Yes," he said, "a whole case."

He anticipated the next question and turned to Cohen, who he knew worked in the medical centre they had just broken into, "How many births a week?" he asked her.

"One or two," she answered, "never more than eight in any month."

Mouse's eyes rolled up slightly as he calculated the timeframe.

"Six-point-six years," he muttered, then louder, "six years to be safe until the missing case is noticed, within the parameters we know, obviously," he finished.

"So, what happened?" James snapped again, having allowed himself to be distracted by the facts of a largely successful mission.

———

The door to Stanley's residence was hammered on, startling them both from a blissful sleep and inducing panic.

They scrambled from the bed, her to snatch up her clothes and run on tiptoes for the safety of the bathroom, and he to throw on trousers and wait until she went wordlessly out of sight before opening the door.

"I'm coming," he called out croakily. Opening the door, he found the Chairman standing in the doorway, chest rising and falling and the face bearing a vicious look of frustrated rage.

"Sir," Stanley said, his face falling and his mouth opening to begin a lame explanation of how it had started, but he was cut off before the apology could start.

"Command suite," Nathaniel snapped officially, "as soon as you can, Major." Then he turned away and fast-paced along the corridor.

Stanley shut the door and leaned heavily against it, the adrenaline in his body making his breathing ragged and deep. The bathroom door creaked open an inch and the half-dressed Samaira Nadeem peeked a single, terrified, almond-shaped eye around the doorframe. Her clothes had been thrown on as desperately as Stanley's own, and she seemed shocked at the sudden disturbance.

Stanley shook his head, meaning to convey that they had not been discovered, even more that the Chairman's middle of the night visit was for some crisis in the Party and not a personal matter.

Neither of them spoke. Stanley continued to dress, pulling on a plain tactical uniform with no badges of rank other than the Major's stars on the collar, and he nodded to her once as he left the door.

Samaira Nadeem's nerve broke then, the fear of

discovery and the consequences of their illicit attraction overwhelming her with the potential consequences. She knew from experience that adjutants who denied the Chairman or displeased him found themselves relocated to dangerous or dead-end postings.

For that to happen to her would render all the hard work at engineering herself close to the Chairman utterly pointless.

———

Stanley strode into the large briefing room to find Nathaniel sitting at the head of the large table, a device plugged in to the port on the side of the large tablet he held. He had thought to grab two cups of coffee on the way into the room, and was sure to make eye contact with a junior officer he passed and order that more be brought immediately. Sitting and placing one cup next to Nathaniel, he sipped in silence as the man worked the tablet with a furious anger. Finally, he swiped a finger from the tablet to the wall with evident wrath and picked up the coffee.

Stanley half turned to see the large screen, which showed three different views. The view on the right nearest him was drone telemetry, on the left side was an information feed, but the majority of the screen was taken up by a first-person view. Nathaniel sipped the coffee and pulled a face at the heat. Swallowing it down, he sat back and spoke in an angry monotone.

"I activated Host from Erebus," he began without emotion, "he was carried by a prototype transport drone, called a Mule, with another prototype shadowing him. I call that the Bat, for reasons you'll see shortly."

He sipped again, accustomed to the heat now, and

went on. "The camera footage anomaly you found after the attack last month?" Stanley nodded his understanding, "We had identified the signal which preceded the hack, and it was detected a few hours ago at The Citadel medical centre. The QRF were deployed to an attack on the south gate, the obvious distraction, so I kept Host in a holding position at the hospital."

He leaned forward and put the coffee down, then tapped with one finger at the tablet to skip the replayed footage forward ten seconds at a time. The screen on the right cycled through different visual spectrums until a curious grey screen began to pulse with shimmering lines.

Stanley stood and walked towards the large screen, tilting his head as the shimmering lines took the ghostly form of people running. Nathaniel paused the playback.

"Sonar?" Stanley asked as he regarded the freeze-frame image.

"Echo-location," Nathaniel replied quietly, "hence the name…"

"…The Bat," Stanley affirmed in interruption.

The footage sprang into life again.

"Now check the main screen," Nathaniel told him as he returned to his seat. The tablet was tapped and the screen filled with the moving imagery on the central display. The first-person view was curious, and the sound of whistling wind came through the hidden speakers in the room.

The way the camera moved made Stanley belatedly realise that the camera was attached to Host's head. The view was descending fast, a grunt emanating from the speakers. The gloom took shape to display a top-down view of two people running towards the sinking drone, then it glanced down and a rough hand was clearly displayed flicking the release catch on a restrain harness.

The clasp came free, and another grunt of effort sounded as the dark screen spun. Stanley was shocked to realise that Host had jumped from the moving drone at about twenty feet in the air.

The concrete rushed up and the camera shuddered violently before rising up and panning to regard two shocked, terrified looking men.

The sounds and movement of the camera lent him the feeling of being there, of being the person behind the camera, yet somehow detached,

The Chairman's voice boomed out after a click. The view showing and the angle on the men put Stanley in mind of the way a predator discerns which prey to single out.

"Capture or kill," came the command, and the camera view jerked as Host drew the weapons.

———

It was daybreak by the time all four had been questioned and released to sleep. All four had told the story from their own perspective, each one differing slightly due to the intricacies of angles and perceptions, but each told fundamentally the same tale.

"Do they have any idea who or what you are?" was the final query thrown at Mouse by James.

"I don't think so," he answered. Full of false confidence.

———

The screens froze, showing just a dark-angle anonymous city street as the left side of the screen grew gradually darker where the blood seeped outwards to soak the concrete. The two men sat in silence, staring at the empty wall before them until finally one of them spoke.

"Who," he asked slowly, "the bloody hell were they?"

"I have no idea, Major," Nathaniel spoke softly, "but I would very much like to find out."

CHAPTER THIRTY-TWO

OTHER AVENUES

Sergeant Major Owen Du Bois, Master-At-Arms in overall charge of the safety and security of Residence block six, strode almost brazenly through The Citadel streets. He didn't believe in travelling the two miles by convoy, and the men assigned to his new unit walked with him in loose patrol fashion, marking them out instantly as different from any other squad of Party soldiers, as much as their newer model submachine guns and uniforms did.

His men, assigned to him doubtless because they frightened their officers and had been as flirtatious with insanity as he himself had been, proceeded in a ragged formation as though patrolling an urban war zone. They did not march in a tight, regimented formation, and the few citizens making their way to their allocated early work assignments scattered in the path of the approaching squad.

Du Bois alone was bare-headed, shocking the scruffy workers with uncommon eye contact and the wild ginger beard, which he saw as something of a company standard. He was telling the world that he was there, he was not afraid, and he did not need to hide who he was. So shocked were the regular people to see a uniformed and armoured soldier not wearing the trademark reflective black full-face visor that he rapidly became a spectacle.

Which is precisely what he wanted; he wanted to represent a symbol of fear to them until they gave up their secrets.

He had willingly become their personal devil.

He carried only a sidearm on his right thigh, and a short, extendable baton on his left hip in a cross-draw position. He strode purposefully, menacingly, and he enjoyed every fearful look that shot his way.

His morning briefing had been fast and strained, as Major Stanley gave him a shortened, sanitised version of the night's events. Of the two terrorists shot in the feint attack on the southern gate, one still lived, although in critical condition and unlikely to remain alive for long. Du Bois willed that he would live, as he was hopeful for an opportunity to try his hand at interrogation. The man would have to get his strength back before that. The dead man and the survivor had both been positively identified as residents of block six, that fact already bridling Du Bois' sense of professional pride, as though he felt simultaneously let down and angry.

Major Stanley had advised him that he had a relatively free reign in terms of tactics, but that whilst he and the other members of Special Projects were analysing the evidence from the attacks, Du Bois should explore any other avenues he saw fit to arrive at the truth.

Already having been given a free-reign to bring terror to the masses until they fell in line, the additional permission to do whatever he felt was necessary electrified him as much as the baton he carried would do to anyone he used it on.

Du Bois absorbed that information with relish, and

decided that he should introduce himself to his wards in the most effective format he knew: an inspection. Treating the residence block like a barracks full of trainees, he would storm in early and search everywhere for cleanliness and compliance.

'Contraband' was a loose term which could be interpreted to mean anything that the soldiers found in context to their feelings about the citizen concerned. With permission granted hurriedly by Major Stanley, Du Bois had ordered that all work allocations deemed to be non-essential would be shut down for a day, allowing his team to search and question each resident.

For their safety and security, he mused to himself with a cruel smile.

Arriving at the high-rise, he posted a pair of guards armed with assault rifles at the two entrances and exits, and tapped at the small touchscreen fitted into the sleeve of his uniform on the left forearm.

It was pre-programmed to allow control over the block, and as soon as his team were inside he locked the exits and announced his presence by accessing and activating the public-address system.

"Residents of block six," he began confidently, feeling the air change as the hundreds of people inside all jumped in fright at once, "Good Morning... I am Sergeant Major Du Bois of the Party's Residence Security Team," he declared grandly, investing the newly-formed unit with pride and importance.

"All work allocations are hereby cancelled, and all citizens must unlock their doors and prepare for their residences to be searched." He paused, a smile creeping across his face from under the beard. "Thank you in advance for your cooperation," he finished.

Clicking off the address system, he gave two quick

hand signals to the assembled thirty soldiers inside the entrance lobby, watching as all but two scattered to scour the ground floor.

Two helmeted men flanking him, chosen mostly for their equally large size and intimidating appearance, followed him to the elevator and stood resolutely in silence behind each shoulder as he carefully pressed the button for the third floor.

Fear and intimidation are tactics, he recited to himself. *Never allow your enemy to get comfortable, and never let them predict your next move.*

With that in mind, he strode directly to the door of the residence where the man injured in the failed attack lived, drew himself up, and knocked politely on the door with a jaunty rapping. He stepped back, gestured for his enforcers to step aside, and put on his best smile with his hands clasped behind his back.

A woman answered the door timidly. She peered through the crack with red eyes, knowing that her husband had not come home and connecting the block search to that fact instantly. Du Bois' smile grew wider.

"Good morning," he said genially, "may I please come in?"

His manner and bare-headed appearance totally threw the woman, who was expecting the door to be kicked inwards and her small apartment torn apart. She expected to be thrown to the ground, hooded and cuffed, then dragged away for questioning, never to be seen again. She realised that she hadn't responded, and her manners took over.

"Yes, please do," she said meekly, opening the door and gesturing the soldiers inside. Only the man with the red beard walked in, the other two stayed outside and turned their backs to guard the door against any interruptions.

"Thank you," Du Bois said as he fixed his smile on her. Stepping inside, he made a show of wiping his feet on the threadbare mat before being invited to sit.

"Please, sit. Can I offer you anything?" the woman asked, nervous and confused about the turn of events.

"Just water, please," Du Bois said as he gently perched himself on the edge of an old chair. The woman wiped clean a glass and ran the tap, testing the water with her finger until she judged it appropriately cold enough to drink. Returning to the table, she sat and offered the glass to the soldier. He took it gratefully and pulled a long sip from the glass before regarding the drink.

"You know," he said conversationally, "when I was on the frontier, the water never tasted the same," he told her softly. She just stared, too nervous to move or speak.

"Rumour said it was because the enemy poisoned the water supply," he carried on, "but I think it's just that water tastes different when you go to new places." He took another long drink and set the empty glass down with precise care. Still the woman said nothing. He turned to regard her. She was about his age, but the constant fear and worry seemed to have aged her. She wasn't unattractive, just very plain and fearful.

"Do you know why I'm here," he asked quietly.

"To search the block?" she asked timidly, echoing his statement of intent via the announcement.

Du Bois smiled sympathetically. "Do you know why I am *here*, in your home?" he asked specifically.

The woman's eyes glazed wetly and she looked down as her lower lip began to quiver.

"My husband," she said so quietly that he had to lean closer to hear her words.

"Yes," he said, his voice barely above whisper, "your husband. Do you know where he is?" he asked.

The woman cried now, although silently, and shook her head forcing a single tear to drop to her drab trousers. She wiped it away absent-mindedly.

"He's in The Citadel," Du Bois told her, seeing her elation at the news that he lived suddenly overcome in the same breath as she formulated the chances of his remaining alive. "He's being cared for," he said, shifting in his chair to place one gloveless hand on hers. She didn't recoil from his touch, but he felt her stiffen involuntarily.

"What is your name?" he asked her, genuine emotion filling his words with kindness.

"Georgina," she answered with a sniff.

"Well, Georgina," Du Bois said sweetly, "it's a pleasure to meet you." She glanced up and met his eyes briefly, smiling her thanks. In that instant, she saw that whilst his smile and his words conveyed kindness, his eyes betrayed him. For a flash, she saw through the orbs into a soul so foul that she shuddered and pulled away her hand.

Du Bois stood fast and put one hand on the edge of the table, flipping it backwards through the air as he took one long stride towards her and loomed high over the shorter woman.

His right hand grabbed a painful fistful of her hair, whilst his left squeezed tightly around her chin and forced her eyes to meet his. She was paralysed with fear, only her eyes showing an ability to communicate.

"You," he snarled in her ear, "will tell me everything you know about your husband. Who he spoke to, what he did yesterday, and who organised it."

He told her, not as a question but assuming with absolute certainty that she would share that knowledge as an inevitability.

"Take off your clothes," he ordered her, releasing her

as suddenly as he had attacked. She stood still, shocked and immobile.

"Now!" Du bois said with a genial smile, clapping his hands to hurry her along, "we don't have all day!"

She straightened herself and shot him a look of loathing.

"Or I could go back to The Citadel and beat your husband until he tells me what I want to know," he paused, rubbing his beard with thumb and forefinger, "although with him being unconscious and everything, I'd probably just kill him by accident…"

She said nothing, but hesitantly began to unbutton the collar of her shirt. She shyly tried to cover her naked upper body with her hands as she fumbled with the waistband of her trousers, making Du Bois grow impatient.

He said nothing, just fidgeted until she stepped out of her clothes and stood undressed before him, wearing nothing but a defiant look of hatred. He walked slowly forwards, circling around her and tracing a finger along her stomach, over her hip and settling at the base of her spine.

"Put your arms down," he told her.

She didn't move, so he grabbed her hair roughly again and tightened his grip, dragging the small woman into the rear bedroom.

The two faceless guards outside the door heard the crash, heard the sounds of panicked movement inside, then nothing but the rhythmical sobs from the woman, muffled by the door between them.

The two helmets glanced at each other, then turned back to face forwards with their arms folded.

———

A little over six minutes later, Du Bois opened the door and stepped outside before closing it carefully.

"One down, gentlemen," he said, "where next?"

One of the two soldiers gave him a location only two floors above, and Du Bois led them up the stairwell.

"A change of pace, perhaps?" he enquired of the two guards. Neither of them responded, as he expected neither of them to. Bracing himself, he drew up one boot and kicked hard. He didn't aim at the lock, but instead at the lower hinge. The weak door exploded inwards, shredded from the anchor points in the wall and hanging pathetically from the weak chain used to secure it from the inside.

Du Bois stepped over the threshold and fragments of wood, seeing a man struggling out of a chair to stand. In two fast paces, he was in front of the man, hitting him hard in the solar plexus and smiling in satisfaction at the sounds indicating that the man could not breathe. A woman's scream cut the air in fright, and he leapt over furniture to block her exit as she huddled small and continued to scream. Du Bois leaned down and made soothing noises to shush her. Putting a hand on each arm he gently lifted her up, all the while making the noises intended to quieten her. She stopped screaming and looked up at him, just as he let her go and reached across his waist to draw the baton. Flicking it behind him casually, he raised the tip to the soft flesh beneath her chin and forced it against her with a grimace of bared teeth.

She went rigid and made a gargling noise, then fell backwards to crash heavily into the table, which splintered under her weight.

Du Bois let out a whoop of elation and excitement.

"Bag'em and tag'em, boys," he shouted, climbing over the wrecked room to leave the apartment, as his goons picked up the immobile victims and forced black hoods over their heads, before forcing their hands behind their backs to apply the plastic locking strips around their wrists.

"Call in the transport and get them locked up at The Citadel," he told them, prompting the two helmets to glance towards each other again.

"You're not coming, Mister Du Bois?" one of them asked. Du Bois turned and regarded them, the rictus of insane glee evident on his face reflected back at him from the visor.

"And miss all this fun?" he asked, "No. I'll see them when I've finished playing."

CHAPTER THIRTY-THREE

INCIDENT DEBRIEF

The door to the briefing room clicked shut and was locked by Nathaniel. Twenty people were inside, talking animatedly between themselves and ignorant of his entrance. It was about to become clear to them that they were now part of something important, whether they wanted to be or not.

"Ladies and gentlemen," Nathaniel announced loudly, calling for instant quiet. Everyone obediently sat round the table, leaving Nathaniel and Stanley on their feet.

"Ladies and gentlemen," Nathaniel said again, more quietly this time, "you are here because you are either already involved or are required to be involved in understanding the events of last night."

He looked tired and drawn, more so than Stanley did, and he suspected that his own reflection was sufficient to frighten children by that point. Nathaniel looked at him to take over.

"There is a two-level security protocol in place as of now," he explained, "those of you who have Special Operations clearance will meet underground following this briefing. Everyone else will remain in this room to work. Understood?" his eyes scanned the room for nods of assent before carrying on.

"Okay, as we know, elements of a terrorist faction are active inside the walls of the city. A diversionary attack was conducted on the south gate, which was unsuccessful..." he glanced to the Chairman to see if he wanted certain facts made public about that attack, mainly that they had captured one surviving terrorist, but the slight shake of his head made the Major leave that part out, "...but at the same time there was activity around The Citadel's hospital."

"The CCTV system is compromised, we still don't know how, but we *are* able to identify the signal used when they hack our system. The hack showed the cameras inside the medical hospital on a loop, so we can't see what they are doing in there, but we are working on that." He paused to consult his tablet.

"Captain Williams?" he asked the group.

"Sir," came the reply from a short haired brunette towards the far end of the table. The way she sat high in her chair made it obvious that she was a tall woman.

"Captain, you will be collating data around the access doors in and around the hospital. Cross reference these with the expected patterns of staff and soldiers on duty." Williams nodded her understanding and compliance, "We need that as a priority," he finished.

"Colonel Barclay will task the remainder of you. Now, if everyone with S.O. clearance could please come with us?"

At that, eight people rose to leave the room with the two senior men, leaving the head of intelligence services to coordinate the investigation.

Everyone that followed Nathaniel and Stanley to the elevator leading to the sub-basement levels was a scientist, indicating a marked difference in the required skill set for that part of the investigation.

It took tedious minutes for them all to scan their thumbs and eyes. If even one of them did not have the clearance, then the elevator would not move. Eventually, crammed into the metal box as they hurtled downwards, they spilled out into the Erebus lab complex. Nathaniel led the way, stopping and turning abruptly after half a dozen paces.

"I want the post-mortem examination of the asset done immediately, and the footage is to be reviewed first for any trace of contact with the terrorists. That is your priority —*identify them!*"

With that, he turned away again, making a beeline for the nearest source of caffeine, with Stanley flanking him. The scientists scurried away to their tasks. Nathaniel poured two mugs and took a seat in the closest office, not caring one iota for who it belonged to or whether they would be displaced by the presence of the two exhausted officers. Leaning back in the chair and putting his feet up, he sipped at the coffee, finding it just the right temperature to be gulped.

He hated waiting for his coffee to cool down, as he invariably left it too long and found himself swallowing down the cold dregs before he finished the cup.

"Sir? They should have the knife out of the asset's head soon," came an announcement from the doorway shortly afterwards, making both men jump, as neither realised they had drifted off to a state close to sleep. Nathaniel looked up and nodded, watching the man in the lab coat retreat.

"Are you a betting man, Major?" he enquired curiously.

"Not usually," Stanley answered honestly.

"What odds would you give on that knife not having any fingerprints on it?"

"Two to one at best," Stanley answered, hesitating before posing his own question, "What odds would *you* give on the knife having prints, but none that match our database?" he asked.

Nathaniel looked up, lowered his feet from the desk, and stared at the man.

"I knew I promoted you for a reason," he said with a grim smile of empty success, "I'd bet nothing on that, as I have suspected for a while that we don't control everything we claim to."

"Outsiders?" Stanley probed.

"Outsiders. Insiders. It doesn't matter," Nathaniel said ambiguously, "it means that we aren't in control as much as we thought, and if the masses realise that then we, Sir, are fucked." He sighed heavily, leaning back and rubbing his face as he roughly calculated the desperately uneven balance of citizens to Party members, and that was just in the city surrounding The Citadel and not the outlying zones.

"You've accessed the archives that *aren't* networked, right?" the Chairman asked him from behind his hands, meaning the stand-alone database of information requiring the highest clearance.

"Yes," he replied, "some of it."

"Did you figure out why we have to use drones now, and don't use the aircraft to bomb our enemies?"

Stanley hadn't seen it in black and white, but he had read enough of the lines to figure out the message between them. "No fuel," he stated simply, not enough of an inflection on the word to warrant it being a question.

"No fuel left," Nathaniel confirmed, "Hence the hydrogen-electric propulsion we have used for years. It's not that there isn't oil," he explained, "It's just that we lack the ability to refine it. Did you get to the part about the wastelands? The Frontier?"

Stanley hesitated, "No. What about it?" he said, still reeling from the openness of the conversation.

"Where to begin?" Nathaniel said tiredly, "the lands outside of the cities under Party control are habitable," he said, unravelling the years of education and the basis of belief. Belief in the power of the Party being required to keep the population safe and prospering.

Stanley said nothing. He swallowed, waiting for more truth than he was sure he wanted.

Nathaniel also said nothing, hoping that the irascible Major would have discovered these facts for himself by now, and that he would not be forced to explain.

"Only three people have access to that information," he said, "myself, obviously, now you, and the Chairman," he said, leaving the invitation open as he knew Stanley would be unable to resist prying. He didn't disappoint him.

"Where is the Chairman, Sir?" he asked carefully. Respectfully.

"Hidden in a residence nearby," he replied, "completely devoid of his wits. His mind has abandoned him, and now he rants about the *others* coming to tear down our walls."

Stanley swallowed.

"Which *others?*" he asked quietly.

He made eye contact as he took his hands away from his face, "the ones who aren't us, I imagine."

Further discussion was interrupted by the same lab coat peering into the office. "Sirs? We have fingerprints from the knife…" he said, trailing away into silence.

"And?" Nathaniel asked.

"And, um, and they aren't on our database, Sir."

Nathaniel and Stanley looked directly at each other.

"Good job you didn't make that bet," Stanley said to Nathaniel.

CHAPTER THIRTY-FOUR

FEAR OF THE DARK

The most dangerous time of any person's life serving on the frontier is the switch between day and night on the front line.

The Party had learned from past mistakes. Each overlapping team of incoming and outgoing soldiers was staggered, so as not to leave any single stretch unguarded, as eager soldiers retreated to thank their luck at surviving. Although past mistakes had been made, analysed, and countered, mistakes were still made. Had Captain Smith and his perpetually nervous Lieutenant taken more personal control of their troops instead of cowering behind a weakened line, weakened by their own demand for additional personal sentries, then they might have been able to prevent disaster.

That disaster could have been prevented, if only the incoming commanders—Smith and Shaw—had shown bravery and leadership. If they had not run to their bunker and hidden. If they had taken the time to walk the front lines, to inspect the men and their positions, they might have noticed the subtle changes which denoted danger.

That disaster could, however, still have been prevented as those outgoing troops were relieved. If, when the troops had taken position to dig in for the first rotation of night duty, Smith and Shaw had been leaders and been brave, the slight operational changes might have gone unnoticed. As it was, they simply gave their orders to the company's Sergeant, then made straight for the command bunker with their personal escort of four soldiers.

The Sergeant was no replacement for the one they had just lost with no notice as he was rotated back to The Citadel, something which the bearded man with the piercing eyes had evidently kept to himself. But neither of the officers paid enough attention to notice the ramifications of that.

Instead, three hours into their night duty in the pitch black, illuminated only by weak starlight and the night vision modes of their visors, disaster struck them hard.

As one, every soldier panicked as his visor's electronics shut down. Each man's head spun wildly as their eerie view of the world outside of their helmets went black, plunging them into a terrifying darkness which spelled death to all of them. Men hit at the helmets in that vague human belief that mild violence will render electronic equipment viable once more. As the first shouts rang out, the lack of noise discipline betraying the abject fear that they felt, the first screams erupted from the entrenched positions.

———

The shrouded creatures had inched forwards from the concealed entrance of the tunnel leading deep into their labyrinth network, as the sun disappeared from the horizon behind them.

The slight movements of the shapes which were indiscernible from the rough, undulating landscape, made it impossible to tell how many there were. Undetected by any sight mode the soldiers facing them possessed, they crept as one slow-moving wave; like a thick liquid oozing slowly across a surface with the slightest of assistance from gravity.

As one, the skulking wave of creatures stopped. No signal came, no sign that they communicated vocally or by any conventional method. A muted click sounded, followed by an almost imperceptible pressure wave emanating outwards explosively. Only the smallest of changes could be detected somewhere deep in the inner ear, and only if the owner of that ear were calm and concentrating.

Seconds later, the darkness ahead seemed to come alive with frantic rustling, then shouts of fear and alarm as the men and women with the shiny black faces realised they were blind.

The shapeless ooze of creatures moved forward, low and animalistic, and the sounds coming from the trenches ahead changed in pitch and intensity. Shouts of panic and hissed orders morphed into wet, gargling sounds and then screams of agonising pain and terror.

––––––

Smith and Shaw's faces swung together to meet and lock eyes in frozen fear.

Their own visors had remained active, as had those of the four guards posted outside their haven, but they were not to know of the equipment failure of the men to their front.

"Two of you go and find out what's happening," Smith snarled at the guards outside, after trying and failing to raise anyone on their small squad-net radio. Smith continued to try to raise someone, anyone, via the radio set after the guards had gone. The way he spoke betrayed his cowardice, as he must have believed he could threaten and bully the radio into working if he spoke into it harshly.

A scuffling sound outside the door made both officers freeze in panic. Before either spoke or tore his eyes away from the door, it burst inwards and a handful of small shadows flowed through the entrance, illuminated by the softest glow from the single, red-lensed light in the bunker.

Smith almost shrieked in terror. His body was reacting in such a primeval way that it felt as though animals had hunted him down, instead of a human enemy making an attack. The utter, bowel-loosening terror he felt did not prevent a flash of logic hitting his consciousness. *They never make large-scale attacks on our positions,* he thought to himself, annoyed that the enemy were not following the rules in his head. *Do they? This isn't fair!*

His internal whining was cut short as one of the shadows flowed over the ground and emerged upwards to crack him hard on the flesh between shoulder and neck. The agony of the collarbone breaking made his legs turn to liquid, just as his bladder lost all semblance of control and he hit the floor sobbing, the acrid smell of ammonia creeping outwards. The agony did not last long. He watched in silence as one of the creatures unclasped the protective vest with small, human hands, and tore open the uniform.

They are human, he mused, as though discovering that truth behind the rumours made his imminent death something less than a total failure.

His fear rose again as he saw the flash of a blade reflected by the dull red glow, but before his scream could erupt, it was cut short.

Shaw had stood and tried to draw the sidearm from his

right hip. A wicked crack had sounded and his right index finger exploded in pain.

Shaking his hand away from the gun involuntarily, a second and third blow rocked his head first left, then right to drop him to the hard floor where he remained motionless. Just as his consciousness slipped away, he heard butcher's noises, and saw the bloodied heart of his superior officer pulled from his chest as a knife slashed at the sinewy tubes trying desperately to hold it in place.

He felt footsteps stop next to his face and rolled slightly to look up at two shapeless shadows.

"Lahda dre dyowl?" one shadow hissed at the other, the inflection making it obvious that a question had been asked about Shaw's fate.

"Negedhek," hissed the other shadow in response, *"drei an taklen."*

With that, the speaker melted away as it hissed, *"Skapya,"* and the other knelt down to him. Just before the short stick hit his head again to tip him fully into the blackness, he caught the slightest reflection from two large, cat-like eyes in the weak, red glow.

CHAPTER THIRTY-FIVE

INTERRUPTED INTERROGATION

"Ian Anderson," said Colonel Barclay after consulting the clipboard in the hand of her aide, before returning her attention to the glass in front of them.

"Factory worker," she continued for the benefit of her superior, "worked in units which made plastics and chemicals."

"So he had access to accelerants?" Nathaniel enquired with an unreadable expression. He was not angry at Barclay, and he felt she was too useful and senior to intimidate for mere amusement. He regarded the unconscious man on the other side of the glass, swathed in white bandages in the hospital bed and attended by two nurses. The operation to save his life had been touch and go, but after two successful revival attempts, the man's bleeding was staunched and his heart restarted. Nathaniel was fighting the balancing scales between wanting the information in the man's head and being unable to interrogate him properly for fear of killing him too easily.

"We can assume so, Sir," Barclay said carefully, "I'll review security protocols there and rotate the soldiers." She had not raised herself to the position she now held by making such simple assumptions, and her tone of voice implied as much.

The Chairman huffed as he turned away suddenly, somehow conveying to Barclay that he wouldn't be guilty of making that assumption either until the full facts were known.

"What else do we know?" he asked as he set a brisk pace that the female Colonel matched with long strides.

"Captain Williams has spoken to all hospital staff," she said, not needing to consult any notes this time, "and patients for that matter. The only anomalies are a pair of nurses who couldn't account for their whereabouts accurately."

"Meaning?" Nathaniel said brusquely without slowing his pace.

"Meaning that they said they were somewhere else when their security logs showed one entering the basement level and then one of them exiting a short time later."

Nathaniel stopped and turned to her with a mild look of hilarity on his face. "And Captain Williams thinks that could be linked to the terrorists' activities?"

Barclay blushed slightly, having also figured out the mental arithmetic of the facts and come to the same conclusion. "She is adamant that it requires investigation, Sir."

The Chairman snorted a bark of a laugh out loud, startling Barclay's aide and seeing him visibly jump in fright.

"Let me know the outcome of that investigation," he said with evident amusement as he resumed his direction, albeit at a slower pace than before.

"And the residence blocks?" he asked, changing the

subject quickly as he liked to, if only to see if the person he was speaking to could keep up.

"Focus was obviously on block six," she told him, "as Anderson lived there with his wife." She spoke about the man as though he were already dead. *Which, in many ways, he is,* Nathaniel thought.

"Du Bois brought his wife in, as he did the parents of the dead man," she paused to crane her head over the clipboard once more, "a Michael Simms."

"Ah," Nathaniel answered, deep in thought, "who has the lead on the interrogations?" he enquired.

Barclay had no need of the clipboard that time, and a look of such distaste took control of her face as to be undisguisable.

"Professor Winslow," she said, the name almost sticking in her throat. Her evident revulsion amused Nathaniel again, making him surprised that he could find so much entertainment in the aftermath of a catastrophic personal failure and a series of terrorist attacks.

"You are aware of the Professor's methods?" he asked her, surprising her that he evidently knew what she did. Or at least what she suspected.

"I, er," she began, fearful that she had stumbled onto something that she didn't fully understand and may have shown her cards early, "I understand that the Professor is an expert in cognitive reprogramming," she said formally.

"Yes," replied Nathaniel, "he is. And he's also a disgusting little man who abuses his subjects."

It was the Chairman's turn to see shock on Barclay's face, and that amused him also. She stood there with her mouth open, struggling to assimilate the facts that not only did the Chairman know about the abuse, but that he seemed to be allowing it to continue. He held up a hand to prevent any comment in front of the aide, who appeared to be trying extremely hard to appear like he wasn't listening.

"I have plans for him," he explained with a dismissive wave of his hand, "another time. For now, let Du Bois have the first shot at her."

With that, they resumed walking in thoughtful silence for a few seconds until Nathaniel dismissed her. He carried on walking alone, never followed by the pack of aides which other senior officers led around The Citadel. He liked that Barclay had a bag-carrier, and that she didn't delegate all of her responsibilities to junior officers, much as her predecessor had done this to her.

"Now, as for the…" he began before Barclay's aide cut him off with a squeak.

"Sir," he stammered as his shaking hands tapped at the screen of his tablet, "there's been an attack on the frontier," he said breathlessly.

"There are attacks on the frontier every month," he said in an almost contemptuous voice for the young man's excitement, before he found himself cut off once more.

"Not like this, Sir," he said, wordlessly turning the tablet around and showing him the screen."

Nathaniel stared for a long moment, tapped the screen once to get more information, then turned on his heel and powered his large frame down the corridor out of sight.

———

Mouse felt as though he hadn't slept for days. Sleeping wasn't one of his strong points, nor was it something he did much as his brain never seemed to slow down enough for slumber to find him unless he was exhausted. His neck was stiff and his head throbbed. He could barely speak as the swelling of his damaged tongue prevented him from doing so without significant pain.

That suited him fine, as talking to people was one his least favourite activities anyway.

Cohen had tried to insist that he be forced to rest alongside Fly, who had regained consciousness but was in a poor state. He couldn't turn his neck to one side, and even the side he could look towards was so painful as to threaten to rob him of his senses.

The concussion made him dizzy and confused, so much so that he accepted his forced bed rest happily, but Mouse could simply not stay still. He was beginning to suspect that there were great vaults of information which he could not access, even given his covert and parasitical infiltration into The Citadel's computer systems. He began swimming in the deep lake of letters, numbers and symbols which made great sense to him and baffled so many others. In truth, he had set up the system to be inaccessible to almost everyone, even though a far more user-friendly operating system could easily be employed, which anyone having the slightest knowledge of computers could navigate.

That wasn't intentional, he simply didn't think to set up the system for anyone else to use. He sat and walked with his fingertips, first taking a casual stroll through the daily messages and alerts for anything of note. His eyes grew wider as he saw more important information in any daily briefing note than ever before.

He threw himself into each subject, burrowing deeper via different access routes and individual department databases until he knew the full facts regarding each part, before standing up and running to Command in desperate need to share the information and plan a response.

There was nobody there. None of them had come

down in the morning, navigating the access tunnels through the basement of the block above.

Mouse paced in his frustration at the prospect of having to wait until they returned that evening. His pacing led him to where Fly slept, unable to bring himself to wake him. He bumped, literally, into Jonah as he fast-walked through the dark tunnels and explained part of what he had learned. Jonah urged him to keep explaining as he stopped at a door and knocked softly. His sister answered the door in silence, just a whisper of wavy hair half covering an eye in the crack of the door as it opened. Her eye switched between her brother and the nervous-looking Mouse, and she opened the door the remainder of the way, having communicated almost tele-pathically with her twin as she recognised the look on his face.

She was wearing loose trousers and a dull coloured vest top which Mouse thought must have been white at some distant point in the past. Mouse, inappropriately and distractingly, noticed for the first time how her slim body seemed rock-hard under the thin layers of loose clothing, and realised that he had only ever seen her dressed for battle before. Shaking away those thoughts, he asked the twins a question.

"Should we get the others?" he asked, seeing their eyes dart to each other's briefly and come back to shake their heads in unison.

Just as the three of them turned for Mouse to lead the way back to the room where he felt most comfortable, a petite shape dropped from the ceiling ahead of them.

As it emerged from the gloom, it took the shape of the murderous and reckless girl they had just unanimously agreed to leave out of the conversation they were about to have.

"What should you get us for?" she asked sweetly, in her echoing voice, which chilled Mouse to the very core.

The three of them glanced again at each other, then relented.

"One of you can go and get Adam then," she said, threat heavily evident in her words as she made it clear that she didn't trust any of them not to ditch her if she went. Separating one of the twins was the tactical choice for so many reasons and she made it almost instinctively; divide and dominate.

CHAPTER THIRTY-SIX

THE AUTHORITY OF NECESSITY

"Wait, wait," Adam said as he stopped pacing and held up his hands with eyes screwed shut. "You're saying that there was another attack last night, a distraction for our mission, and that they have one of them?"

"Yes," Mouse replied, eyes cast down and growing ever angrier at the unwavering look Eve aimed at him, "the prisoner is in The Citadel and we have no chance of getting to him," he explained, "but that isn't the real problem."

All eyes were on him, making him even more uncomfortable, so he shut his eyes and continued, "what's important is what is happening up there. Now." He held a single finger aloft, pointing directly upwards and confusing them all.

"We are under block six, which is where most of Command live, except they are all trapped in there and the soldiers are searching everyone's residences. It's locked down tight; nobody in or out. They've taken the man's wife."

"Whose wife?" Jenna snapped, annoyed and confused by the circuitous explanation.

"The man they captured. The one being held inside The Citadel. But they have her in a building *near* The Citadel and not *inside*."

Eyes found other eyes in the gloom as they searched the chaotic account of what Mouse had learned for meaning.

Mouse sighed loudly and opened his eyes to focus them on an unseen spot on the far wall.

"We can't rescue the others today, and Command are all trapped in their homes, but we can get to her. Georgina."

Silence.

"Shouldn't we wait for orders?" asked Jonah.

"No time," Eve said, just as Mouse opened his mouth to say the same.

"So, what?" Adam asked incredulously. "We just go out in daylight and wander around?"

"No," Mouse said as he rummaged around in his pack, "we go and get her." He finished as he produced a handful of tiny, silver objects and a roll of tools.

"What are they?" Jenna asked, the only person present not to have seen one yet.

"Chips," Adam said, "like the ones everyone else has inside them."

"Oh no," Jenna said as she stood and walked towards the door. Her brother flanked her. "No way are you plugging me into their system," he said in support of his twin.

"I'll do it," Eve said, hopping down to the ground from her perch with a ghostly lack of associated sound.

"Me too," Adam said as he started towards Mouse.

"You'll have to do me too," the smaller man said, "I'll talk you both through it as we go."

———

The lack of parental supervision for the naïve human weapons of the Resistance did not hinder their abilities one bit. Eve volunteered to go first, and lay face down on a table they had cleared.

Mouse used a clear liquid to sanitise the chip he had pilfered from the supply, amending his calculations to cover the fact that he had falsely reported how many chips they had taken.

He used the same liquid to wipe over her thin neck before glancing once at Adam. "Hold her," he whispered.

To the girl's credit, she only stiffened and gasped as the knife made a small incision just below her hair line. Her body remained stiff as the chip was placed carefully using tweezers into the small wound which welled with blood. The chip seemed to come alive, the two tiny wire tendrils burrowing into the bulging blood and pulling itself in to connect to the flesh below the skin. Mouse wiped away the blood and pinched the two halves of the cut together before squeezing a small tube of glue over the incision.

Almost instantly, the cut closed and stayed that way. Adam relaxed his grip and let the girl up from the table, seemingly no worse for the experience.

"Your turn," she whispered to him as her fingers delicately explored the bump on her neck. Adam lay down and gripped the edges of the table.

He didn't utter a sound as the knife cut him, but squirmed as the tiniest sensations tickled his spine. He imagined the wire tentacles of the chip plugging themselves into his spinal column. He felt as though his bellybutton was being pulled inwards with the smallest of threads and the feeling made him whimper an involuntary sound that prompted a snigger from Eve. He felt the skin pinched tight and then a curiously warm feeling as the glue fused the two sides of the skin together.

"Now, you two do me," Mouse said breathlessly, clearly fearful. He gave them clear instructions which they followed to the letter. Cut, insert chip, close wound. The task was simple, but the transition was terrifying.

As Mouse stood, he explained the modifications he had made.

"I've disabled the anti-tamper setting," he said, "so the chips won't kill us if we remove them."

Adam and Eve shot each other a desperate, terrified look in answer, their faces making it clear that they had agreed to something without knowing the full facts. Mouse ignored their looks and began tapping away at his terminals.

"I've pre-loaded your profiles onto The Citadel network," he said as he typed, "and I've activated your security access protocols to the most common high level—that way you should be able to access most things, but I can override certain doors if they are too secure. Thumb." He said, gesturing to the biometric scanner they had stolen.

Adam went first, putting each digit in turn into the reader until his full set was synched to his profile. Eve followed suit, then both took turns to scan each of their eyes. He went through all three profiles, adding their access levels, before he cursed out loud.

"Shit," he said, more to himself than them, "I don't have the write-access to add you to that."

"What?" Adam asked.

"Nothing. Now, the target building is about a mile from here…"

Nathaniel sat in his office, waiting for Major Stanley to arrive to discuss the most recent of the catastrophic problems he was facing.

His screen blinked to life at an incoming message. He glanced at the small box which popped up, ready to ignore and dismiss it as he did almost every message which crossed his desk, but something made him stop.

The message read simply, *'Authority to access S.O.'*

He had to personally accept any request for Special Operation access, something which he had insisted on many years before, and clicked on the box to expand it. The applicant details were blank, merely linked to a file which held no information. Snatching up the phone he called human resources and demanded the details of the personnel file identified only by the number on the application.

"I'm sorry, Sir," came the nervous response from the other end of the phone, "that file isn't on our database."

Nathaniel put the phone down and remained still as he thought. Stanley knocked on the door once and entered without waiting, just as Nathaniel threw himself up out of the chair and stalked towards the door.

"With me," he snapped, forcing the exhausted looking Major to spin on his heel and catch up. The Chairman said nothing as he strode at a pace close to running towards the elevator leading down to the labs. His impatience broke and he began to jog, Stanley matching speed and desperate to know the need for such uncommon urgency. Both men scanned their hands and eyes and waited in tense impatience as the metal cage sped downwards.

As the doors opened into the lab, Nathaniel burst through them and bawled for a scientist by name. The small man appeared and enquired diffidently as to how he could help the Chairman.

"Run the prints again," he demanded, offering no explanation.

"But Sir—" the scientist began but stopped as the tall man whirled on him with a fury. He gave no reply, merely turned on his heel and ran to his office. Nathaniel paced, emitting a nervous tension like an electrostatic field as he waited. The small man reappeared, seeming more terrified than before.

"Still no record?" Nathaniel demanded of him.

"No, Sir," the scientist stuttered, seeing the big man relax, "I mean, yes." The Chairman stopped still, and regarded the man. He felt as though trapped in the jaws of a beast slowly closing its mouth to consume him, unless he explained quickly.

"There is a record, Sir," he said hurriedly, "but it's an empty file. Just a number."

"Show me," Nathaniel growled. A small crowd had gathered now, and he scanned them all with his cold eyes, prompting them to flee back to their original tasks.

"Here, Sir," said the scientist, gesturing at his computer screen.

The Chairman glanced once, matched all five digits up with the number he had memorised from the message on his own terminal, and for the first time in years, felt scared.

———

Adam pulled on his black suit, adding the two long knives he had used on his inaugural visit to the world above. He added the other wide-bladed knife to his right calf again, in place of the one which had been taken from him by Mark when his hooked blades were also removed.

Eve was less happy. She heavily favoured the long sword which she wielded effortlessly, ever seeming as if she and the blade moved independently yet linked in a deadly form of symbiosis, despite its length and weight. Instead, she was forced to beg access to Adam's personal arsenal, finally selecting two matte-black, heavy, curved machetes.

"They're kukris," he told her, receiving no answer as she twirled the two blades around. She chose them as having the longest blades, but found that she loved the sheer weight towards the point of each edge, and marvelled at the impetus each weapon carried as she swung them in lazy practice arcs. Deciding that each could easily decapitate an enemy, she smiled and slid the wide knives into the sheaths behind her back.

She still carried the two remaining throwing daggers on her right thigh. When both were armed and ready, they locked eyes and the girl nodded to Adam. He responded, returning the curt nod, attempting to convey a sense of mutual understanding. A camaraderie. A meaningful gesture which told her that they were in this together.

She ignored his response entirely, and walked out of the room, leading the way back to Mouse in his computer workshop.

They found him with his head bent low over something, wires snaking between the item and his gadgets. He didn't look up when they entered, but both had the sense that he was fully aware of their presence.

"Done," he said, sitting up and unplugging the wires and lifting the thing he had been working on from the desk.

Adam went cold with the hint of memory as he recognised it. The electrified baton which had buzzed through the air when he had tangled with the thing that Eve had killed seemed somehow less malevolent in Mouse's hand.

And yet, when he stood to give himself space and flicked his wrist to extend the metal sections, the familiar crackle of electricity made him shudder.

Eve looked confused for a moment, then asked him, "Your chip?"

"Yes," he replied as he pressed a button and collapsed the weapon to stop the current running through it. "I can also use their guns now, too," he mused, tucking the baton into his belt, "as long as I can figure out if they are tracked or not."

That last comment made them all think a little deeper about the truths they had grown up believing; did Command just feed them lies to keep them safe and infinitely more careful, or was the mighty Party so powerful and omnipresent that they really could track anyone and anything?

"How will you know?" Eve asked.

"Take one of their guns and plug it into this," he said, patting the small tablet and folding keyboard they had seen him use to hack the system in the hospital. Mouse snapped out of his theoretical world and looked at them both.

"Shall we?"

CHAPTER THIRTY-SEVEN

ADAPT AND OVERCOME

As Nathaniel was already inside the Erebus labs, his snap decision was made easier by sheer proximity. Grabbing the nearest lab coat roughly, he gave his orders using as economically few words as he could to save precious time and not waste more by explaining everything in detail. Stanley marked his senior, flanking him in readiness, even though he doubted whether he knew what the man was planning.

The fact that he had ordered not one, but both remaining Erebus subjects readied for deployment—in broad daylight—worried the young Major slightly. He watched as every lab coat on the level ran around preparing everything for the deployment with such alacrity, knowing that it could only be fuelled by the anger in the Chairman's voice.

The two assets, Shadow and Reaper, were armoured and equipped before being declared ready. Both stood stock still, emotionless expressions on their faces, as their bodies bristled with weapons and exuded a transparent lethality. Nathaniel stood in front of both of them and returned their eye contact.

"Escort me," he said as he looked at them both in turn, "bodyguard detail."

Stanley didn't realise they could be put into close protection mode, but then he recalled that much of the assets' lives had been under the direct control of Nathaniel and his team of pet scientists.

Stanley was well aware, as was just about everyone in The Citadel, of the Chairman's personal aversion to a protection detail, so this recent development gave him pause.

What did he just learn? He thought, *What could have been so unnerving that he activated these two to protect him?*

Nathaniel's next move made his intentions clearer, as he threw off his heavy leather coat whilst halfway through the doorway into the armoury. He unbuttoned his shirt and dropped it on the ground before selecting a black, long-sleeved top and forcing it over his head. The fit was intentionally very tight, and despite the speed with which he moved, Stanley saw half a dozen faces react to the scarring up his left arm. Nathaniel pulled on an armoured vest and began strapping it tight, pausing only to make eye contact with his junior officer and raise an eyebrow.

That eyebrow spoke volumes.

It asked why he wasn't already doing the same.

Stanley's only response was to strip off his own uniform and follow suit. The Chairman added only an electrified baton to his equipment, relying on his brutally heavy handgun which never left his side, but Stanley elected to add a baton and a submachine gun of a design not seen worn by regular troops.

He added three elongated spare magazines for the gun

and clipped them onto the vest before selecting a heavy black greave which he slipped over his left forearm.

So, Nathaniel thought wryly, *you* have *been studying.*

Stepping back, Stanley checked he had sufficient room in his immediate surroundings and clenched his left fist to activate the device protecting his forearm. Instantly, the thick covering whirred and exploded outwards, fanning out to form a shield of overlapping composite plates. He regarded the shield for a brief moment, then released the clenched fist and watched as the shield retracted as fast as it had deployed. He glanced up to see Nathaniel looking at him.

"I don't like knives," Stanley said simply in answer to the implied question. Nathaniel nodded his response.

Turning to snatch up two headsets and tossing one to Stanley, the Chairman announced loudly to the lab, "I want a control room up and running in the next thirty minutes," he said, "Colonel Barclay will be in charge." With that, he strode out of the armoury alongside Stanley, who fell in step, the two of them tracked robotically by the two assets who seemed to pay no heed to one another.

"Get us transport topside," he snapped, "and I want Bats tethered to all of us." Stanley glanced at a female scientist as he walked past, seeing a desperation on her face mixed with a worried misunderstanding at the orders she had been given.

"The prototype drones," he said as he leaned towards the woman, "and a response van will do us nicely," he finished as he stood tall and resumed his pace.

"But, Sirs!" came an exasperated shout from behind them. Nathaniel stopped and turned slowly.

"Sir," came the pleading voice again, quieter this time, "the lab exit protocols?"

Nathaniel had considered this, the very protocols he

had demanded be upgraded years ago at great cost in time and materials to the Party. He paused, looked at each of the surviving assets in turn, trying to gauge their understanding.

"That's my decision," he said, turning back without another word and leading his procession of four to the elevator. He used his thumb and right eye to access the doors before stepping inside, then turned to the assets.

"Reaper, Shadow," he said commandingly, "turn around." They did, without any other response.

Reaper's eyes flickered to her side, catching the slightest glimpse of Shadow doing the same to her. As their gaze locked briefly, the unmistakable sound of six keys being hit on a number pad reached their ears. The eye contact broke, and Reaper's face twitched as she fought to control a sneer of a smile.

To their credit, the lab coats had managed to order up a van by the time the four heavily armed people exited the elevator. They scattered the uniformed minions of The Citadel as they strode powerfully towards the wide, stone steps leading down from the main doors. They blasted through the security station unchallenged as people scrambled to get clear of their path. They were parting the human waves, moving forward with a relentless impetus which radiated something almost deadly.

Those who made way for them stared at the spectacle, fearful at seeing their Chairman so hell-bent on violence, but more worried about the two killers flanking him.

None of the four returned the frightened looks of those people; two through sheer concentration and two through a simple inability to recognise them as important. To Shadow and Reaper, these people were an irrelevance until such time as they received an instruction to treat them otherwise.

They piled into the dull, grey van, its electric engine running silently and ready to propel them forwards. A driver was provided, helpfully, as Stanley was prepared to climb behind the wheel to save the Chairman from having yet another strain on his temper.

"Where to, Sir?" the driver asked. Straight to the point, luckily for him.

"Stick centrally," Nathaniel answered impulsively, then added, "no, south. Run laps on the residence district. Are you fully charged?" he asked, meaning to enquire about the battery power of the troop carrier.

"Ninety-six percent, Sir," came the answer from the front. Nathaniel nodded to himself, the small gesture reflexive and not designed to communicate anything to anyone. Leaning back in his seat he held the button over the right earpiece on his headset.

"Barclay, are you there?" he said in a muted, professional tone that he reserved solely for radio use.

"Here, Sir," came the reply, moments later.

He saw the eyes flicker in response to the voices in the ears of both assets and his Major. The driver gave no indication that he was tuned into their net, which suited Nathaniel just fine. He was there to drive.

"Are we up and running?" he asked the microphone.

Barclay came back instantly, listing off the resources at her immediate disposal, "Yes Sir, I have feeds from four, er, *Bats*, launching now. They are tethered and inbound. I have city-wide footage and three operators, I have QRF one on immediate deployment readiness, I ha…"

Nathaniel cut her off.

"Tech support," he said irritably, "I need active monitoring of the last security personnel file to request access to Sierra Oscar," he said, reverting automatically to the use of the phonetic alphabet to describe Special Operations, removing the chances of a misunderstanding. "And have them look at the most recent files uploaded to be sure they are real people."

A pause on the other end as Barclay assimilated the information and quickly concluded the meaning of it.

"We have ghosts in the machine, Sir?" she enquired in a quieter voice, as though she didn't want the nearest personnel hearing her words.

"I believe so, Colonel," he replied grimly, "and I want immediate notification of any of those access codes being used."

"Roger, understood," Barclay responded, "callsigns?" she asked, meaning to set up their small net formally as the sounds of frantic business rattled around her.

Nathaniel regarded his team and smiled.

"Marauder," he said.

A pause sounded after the choice of callsign set the tone for the operation.

"Marauder Actual, reading you five by five. Stand by for updates. Control out."

———

Making a journey to the perilous world above was a relatively new thing for all three of the pure-born, heading along tunnels to the holding facility nestled in the shade of The Citadel. The ponderous twists and turns of the tunnels led them in a long path of necessity until they reached the building they wanted, again trusting Mouse's uncanny ability to read the map in his mind after staring at the screen for a second to memorise it.

Despite their call for immediate action, the delays caused by inserting and programming the chips meant that the sun was already starting to sink and the time when Command would reappear was fast approaching.

Fly remained in and out of consciousness, and would be of little help even if he had elected to come with them, but the twins resolutely refused. Both wanted to wait until Command returned and gave them orders which could be followed without the need for independent thought.

"When was the last time you remember there never being anyone coming down from upstairs? The whole block is still on lockdown and I think we are on our own." Mouse reasoned with them desperately, "Something really bad is going on, and we don't even know if anyone from Command will ever be back."

Despite this logical approach, Jenna and Jonah outright refused to join them.

The others decided that they would not, and could not, wait.

———

By the time they had made even a third of their underground journey, high up in the residence block above their starting point, a man with a wild-looking red beard whooped once more in elation.

Du Bois had spent the day overseeing and supervising the various searches conducted systematically on each floor of the block until he found something which piqued his interest. Sometimes it was an object which had not been issued by the Party, and he either questioned the owners on the spot or simply had them detained and transported. Other times it was a look he and his soldiers received, or some attempt by the citizens to communicate without being heard or seen that would send him flying into a sudden, violent rage or merely pointing a lazy finger at the target of his choice.

He hardly noticed the passage of time but when he realised that his team had finished with the block, it was almost the close of the working day. He had thirty-one prisoners to have what he called 'discussions' with; primarily the young woman who would doubtless be less than happy to see him again, or the older couple who would remember their beatings at his hand for the rest of their lives.

Satisfied with a solid day's work, he removed the lock-down from the block and dismissed his team to stand down, with the exception of his two personal guards. He set off with a jaunty spring in his step as he walked away from the high-rise, deciding to head straight for the detention centre and eat before he could torture some weak people for information and sheer enjoyment.

——

As Jenna and Jonah sat in silence either side of Fly's makeshift hospital cot, coaxing him into drinking some water and gently speaking to him when he had regained his senses, the door creaked open and James spilled into the room with his eyes scanning wildly and carrying an obvious sense of desperation with him, as though he rode it like a wave.

"Did they get down here?" he demanded with more than a hint of desperation in his voice. Two other people joined him, indicating the slow trickle of Command returning, just as Mouse had assured them that they never would.

James looked at the faces, not finding the one he was looking for.

"Where's Cohen?" he snapped, "has anyone seen Cohen?"

Silence.

If she was alive and free to move, she would have been the first one there. Fearing that they had taken her, James' heart sank; not out of any love for the woman, but mostly because he needed her ideas to rationalise his own. Just as his fear and panic threatened to overcome him, an obvious fact found his brain like a pin finding a balloon.

"Where are the others?" he asked in a hoarse voice, fearing the answer but not realising how bad it could be.

"Gone," Jonah said, seeing him almost collapse, "gone to free the prisoners taken from upstairs."

CHAPTER THIRTY-EIGHT

CHILDHOOD MONSTERS

Shaw's collarbone burned with an intensity he didn't think possible to bear. The pain of being roughly carried when he regained consciousness was so extreme, so unprecedented in his experience, that it had caused him to pass out again.

He sat with his back leant against a rough wall now, the agony of having dragged himself upright still a very raw memory, and he tried to assess the damage.

No crunching when it moves, he told himself in a vain attempt to offer reassurance, *so I think it's just fractured.*

His meagre medical training had granted him just about enough knowledge to tell the difference, even though the pain told him that a thousand hot lances must be spearing the flesh of his shoulder and arm every time he moved.

Hell, every time I breathe too fast.

The room he occupied was so dark, so utterly devoid of light with which to give depth and clarity to his surroundings, that he was forced to rely on his other senses to try and gather information about his captivity. When he had first gasped back into alertness, crying out in sobbing yelps of pain as the fire burned in his cracked bone and as he grew aware of the insidious thumping in his head, he had lain where he was for minutes, just breathing.

It could have been hours, but without sight he found that he suddenly had little idea about anything.

So reliant were people on their eyes, that he wondered how anyone could live in such an inhospitable place, existing without light.

He had been stripped of his helmet and visor, rendering the technology he trusted to give him sight in the dark as useless as his tears, and he found that he had lost almost all of his uniform and equipment along with it. Using his hands, or at least his left hand as his right was only comfortable if he held it tight across his chest and made no attempt to engage those muscles, he discovered that he was sitting on rough ground which seemed like packed earth. The walls appeared to be made of the same material, like half-wet mud had been hit hard with something dull and heavy, and he could make out no change in light to indicate if there was even a door in the prison he was in.

His first hour spent awake, apart from the tears and the confusion, was wasted on trying to figure out if he was alive or dead. When he finally knew with any certainty that he did, in fact, still live, he wasted yet more time trying to comprehend why.

Why hadn't they killed him, he thought. Why hadn't they eaten his flesh or cut out his heart like they had done to Captain Smith?

The recollection of seeing that barbaric act returned to him fully then, along with the hollow crunching sounds as his Captain's ribs were pulled back from the flayed chest to expose the organ.

Shaw expelled what was left in his stomach then, and with no reference point to aim for he succeeded only in covering his right side in the foul bile. He felt no sense of loss for the man whose fate had been intertwined with his own; a brotherhood of responsibility through mutual failure.

Now, using the coldness of the ageing vomit as his only available point of reference, he carefully felt his way around the inky blackness.

He surmised that the room was circular, with smoothed edges at all points, and no ceiling that he could discern. Pacing lengthways, at least he assumed it was lengthways, he reckoned that he was in a chamber around four metres in diameter. He had thrown up somewhere around the centre of the room, slightly towards what he was calling the left face, even though the roughly circular shape allowed no such bearings.

It could have been a day, or an hour, or just minutes since he had woken—enough time for the vomit to cool and send a shiver up his spine as it wormed its gelatinous way between his toes when he stood in the puddle—but he had no concept of anything outside his personal hole, when a noise above him gave him a sudden point of focus.

Craning his head painfully backwards and letting out a weak cry of pain, he adjusted his posture and looked sideways with his head cocked over.

A feeble light showed the height of two men above his head, bathing the hole with the smallest washes of illumination.

An oubliette.

That was the first word that his mind conjured up from his history lessons.

He was in an oubliette, and he was not going to escape from it. In the grey gloom merging with the black, he saw the hint of shapes of two hooded humans, and he swore he could see the luminescent glow of four large eyeballs high above him. He opened his mouth to speak, but his throat was so dry that he only croaked and coughed.

Before he could regain his composure, what little he possessed, he heard sibilant hissing noises from above.

"Pan mednas an dyowl?" hissed one of the hooded half shapes. Shaw stopped and swallowed. The voices were half-whisper, half-echo, and all frightening.

"Praga nyns ladha a'n?" answered a deeper voice, still in a whisper, but again with an inflection which made him aware that a question had been posed.

Shaw, not comprehending the words, was suddenly aware of a feeling more than any fact. He was aware that they were discussing him, and likely his fate and future, as though he were a *thing*.

An *it*.

An *amusement*.

A possession taken on the battlefield. A thing without rights or feelings or any tangible worth. Something to be hurt, experimented on, used, discarded without remorse or forethought. The realisation gave him pause, and a sob escaped his trembling lower lip. The irony of feeling like a lowly citizen of the Republic under the dubious protection of the Party was lost entirely on him. The oppressor had become the oppressed.

The sounds from above sounded raspy and amused. Shaw heard what sounded like a rapid panting noise, with a hesitant edge as though the voice had been recorded and was now being replayed, only in reverse.

He steeled his resolve and stared hard at the barely-visible shapes above him, his jaw set hard and his eyes blazing with anger.

The laughing noise stopped as suddenly as it had

started, startling Shaw with the knowledge that the shapes he could barely see could obviously see him clearly enough to make out facial expressions; then it started again, only far louder.

Shaw bit his tongue for as long as possible under the onslaught of mockery, before his impotent anger exploded from him volcanically.

"Fuck you," he blurted out in a voice somewhere in between a sob and a snarl, "you fucking animals. You…" he struggled for the right word, "you *monsters*."

The laughing stopped again as suddenly as it had started. Although he could make out nothing more visually than he initially could, he shivered with a sudden chill as the hooded figure above shifted unnaturally.

"Hebask diskwitha," it said, the voice echoing with heavy sarcasm and sincere threat, *"Keth,"* it added with utter contempt.

Shaw slumped back to the rough wall and sank painfully to the hard-packed earth.

"Keth," he said aloud to himself. That was a word aimed solely at him. About him.

It was a label, and it did not fill him with confidence.

————

Adam's mind raced as they made their winding way through the black, subterranean walkways. The paths formed part of a long-forgotten network; as often dead-ended as they were successful in linking with the other rat runs. The infrastructure that had originally built these tunnels favoured materials which were never seen—or felt —on the surface anywhere where any of them had ever been before.

The curved edges of the walls were comprised of many

smooth segments, as though each piece had been fitted individually by hand, and where the years and layers of grime fell away under his fingertips, the cool textures made him feel a connection to the time before.

The time before their enemy ruled over everything. Before people had to live in fear of their rulers. Before the world became fenced enclaves of industrial concrete, and the skies above them buzzed with the whine of the drones that watched everything they did.

The three of them did not speak, not even when a partially collapsed tunnel blocked their progress and Mouse hovered in silence, eyes tightly shut, as he analysed the map tucked deep inside his brain for an alternative route to their target. Like water finding gaps in a structure, like a soft, green shoot punching its way out to sunlight and freedom through the irregularities in a roadway, their inexorable flow towards their objective seemed unstoppable.

They had been raised to fear the mighty Party and their army of soldiers. Had been educated to cower in dread at the thought of the Chairman leading his troops of faceless robots to terrorise the good citizens, who wanted only freedom from tyranny.

They had been cultivated and pruned like puppets to believe that silence and hibernation in the shadows underground would keep them safe, if only they followed the instructions of their elders without question.

They had, all of them, been lied to.

Their truth, they now knew, was one of pure manufactured convenience. They were capable of so much more and learned that they had little to fear from the soldier-drones they had believed to be terrifying. Even the actual fear they felt when facing something far more dangerous, something infinitely more lethal than they had expected to

DEVON C FORD

encounter, they had fought and killed it together in mere seconds.

They would not be so poorly prepared the next time. They would not hesitate.

They were going to war, going rogue, and going to bring terror to the *enemy* for the first time.

———

Owen Du Bois had seen evil. He had experienced terror; pure, unadulterated, bowel-loosening, gut-wrenching, bladder-voiding fear. He had seen the shifting shadows, like a cloud half seen at night, and he had heard the screams of the men under his command. When he had first experienced the way the enemy attacked, he had pissed himself like a child fearing discovery by an abusive parent.

He had cowered in his trench, heard the guttural and sickening butcher's sounds of the soldier to his right dying, and he had found his courage.

He felt that it was a simple exchange. He had died that night, died of fear, and was reborn in the violence which gave the darkness light. Swallowing his childish panic, he had taken a single, deep breath, let it out, then depressed the trigger of his rifle to unleash a long burst of fully automatic fire directly towards the sound of the fight.

He did not know if he had hit or killed any of the enemy, even if he was certain that he had killed the soldier who was being cut open only metres away, but he had stood tall and brave in his trench and he had never felt fear since that night.

He had met the demons of his childhood, and although he had never stared one down face to face, they no longer held the power of fear over him.

In The Citadel, the soft city of safety and security,

where nothing came at him from the silent dark like an animal hunting him, he doubted he would ever feel fear again. Having lived through the horror of the frontier for the long months he had spent there, only to find himself reunited with society and a bigger hierarchy than before— only this time with an unthinkable boost in power and status—he had to find the thrill which fuelled him in places other than combat.

He found his ecstasy in making others feel the fear that he was now immune to, and having spent an entire day drinking in the palpable anxiety that his mere presence brought on in the citizens, his thirst was still not yet satisfied.

He finished playing with the bowl of porridge he had taken from the small canteen in the holding facility; he liked the thick and dry consistency of it when it had been made so many hours before, but food seemed to hold no joy for him. Pushing away the bowl and ignoring the signs ordering that he tidy up his own tray—that was for people who felt fear, he believed—he made his lazy way towards the exit.

The two gargantuan guards he had ordered to flank him, if only for the amusement it gave him to see people's reactions to them, stood tiredly and shuffled towards him.

Both had removed their helmets to eat and still carried them under their arms. Neither looked intimidating without the reflective black face plate, and he now found their appearances disappointing.

"Stand down, both of you," he told them, "back to barracks and wait for more orders."

Both men straightened and nodded their dismissal.

"Sir," they chorused, and left.

Du Bois smirked to himself. His new rank was a curiosity. A military grey area. An ancient remnant of an old system long outdated, but still very much relevant.

To the troops he was a *Sir,* even if they weren't to salute him. To the officers, who he still had to salute, he was a *Mister,* and enjoyed more benefits and privilege than most junior officers ever would. His status and position, he assured himself, were hard-earned rewards for passing through hell and reaching the other side, just to look back over his shoulder and ask, *Was that it?*

Now, sucking the last of the gooey oats from his teeth, he rolled his neck on his thick shoulders as he limbered up to question the woman.

Again.

CHAPTER THIRTY-NINE

WHAT GOES AROUND

The three underground killers reached their destination. Mouse used his tiny, red-lensed torch to show the way up, and went to climb the short ladder offering access to the world above, but crashed back down to ring a stony echo through the long tunnel as the first rusted rung gave way under his weight.

Rubbing at his shin rapidly to try and scrub away the pain, he waved the others away and began again, placing his boot on the next rung up and testing it more carefully this time. It too gave way, and Mouse shone the weak light up the six rusted steps to the grate above as his brain tried to work out a solution. The light found a trickle of moisture coming from high up in the tunnel wall, showing the source of the corrosion, but unhelpful to any suggestion of solution.

Eve's small fingers snapped gently, making the light swing to bathe her in a soft glow as she pointed first to herself, then to Adam, then upwards to the grate above. Adam nodded his understanding, crossed over his hands and clasped Eve's. She moved towards him as he turned his upper body, pulling her in and pushing his hands upwards. She leapt as the threshold of inertia took her, jumping easily to place her right foot on his right shoulder and her left knee steadying her balance on the opposite side.

Adam stepped forwards twice, placing them both directly under the grate, and planted his feet wide. Mouse took a step back and kept the low light on them as Eve effortlessly stood and lifted her left foot to stand on his shoulders.

Her head almost reached the grate, but try as she might there was no movement in the metal plate at all. After the fourth attempt, she whispered that it wouldn't budge, and Adam lowered his body in a squat to allow her to hop vertically downwards from his shoulders to drop only a short distance to the ground.

"We have to go back one access point," Mouse said softly, his eyes open, having taken the opportunity to consult his mental map as the human tower separated to become two people again, "but it's by a factory unit," he said, leaving the rest unfinished.

They were not active during the night, where the only things moving were soldiers and drones. They were still in daylight hours, and even if the factory shifts had finished, the Party soldiers might still be around. Three pairs of eyes flickered amongst themselves, looking for alternatives or objections, and when nobody spoke, they split and began to move back the way they had come from.

Minutes later, they were climbing the rungs of the access ladder and watching as Mouse inched the grate upwards to peer carefully around the full circumference on display.

He didn't declare that he could see no dangers, didn't waste time telling them an irrelevant fact, merely pushed harder and slid the grate aside as noiselessly as possible before slipping upwards into the fading daylight. Eve followed, eerily making no sound as she moved, and Adam was the last to pull himself though the portal as he spun in his crouch to replace the grate and disguise their presence.

All of them blinked. All had been under lights before, but none had really seen daylight, even if it was at the lowest ebb of its daily cycle of intensity.

Skulking away into the shadowy alleys between the big factory buildings, they crept towards their target.

"Wait," Mouse hissed, fumbling in his bag and bringing out his tiny tablet and folding keyboard, "data point," he said in simple explanation. The others kept watch front and back as Mouse slid his flick knife into the gap in the housing of the metal box and popped the lock open. He pushed aside the mess of wires and selected a bunch, separating the different colours and attaching clips which spiked into the wires inside the plastic. Those spikes and their clips were attached to other wires, which ran back to Mouse's tablet. Agonising seconds ticked past whilst all of them were left wide open to the slim chance of discovery in daylight, as Mouse ran his fingers over the keys with all the expertise of a professional working in life-threatening conditions.

"In," he muttered to himself, before continuing to tap away. He wasted no time glancing up to either side fearing discovery; he trusted that the others knew their business well enough to leave the computers to him, and to deal with any guards themselves.

"Fire alarm… activated," he commentated, "doors locked…" he muttered before pulling the wires from the wires and shoving the battered equipment away in his pack.

"Let's go," he said to them, "before they realise that The Citadel isn't burning down."

———

"Marauder, Control," came the crisp communication through their earpieces.

"Go," snapped Nathaniel.

"Fire alarms activated at The Citadel," she said, the sirens blaring behind her cool tones, "and exits are all on electronic lockdown, over."

"All received, wait one" Nathaniel answered as he closed his eyes and his lips fluttered almost imperceptibly. He was thinking, theorising, playing a lightning-fast war game in his head before making a snap decision.

"Control, remain on station unless you physically see a threat. Confirm," he said.

"Marauder, confirmed. We are in lockdown and will remain active," Barclay answered, "working on activation source, wait out."

Nathaniel didn't bother responding. If there was something to find, some trace of the signal which had caused his headquarters to act so bizarrely as to simultaneously declare evacuation and lock the soldiers and workers inside, then Barclay and her technical support team would find it. Until such time he would have to wait for the breadcrumbs to drop, and he preferred to remain mobile on the ground as he waited for that to happen. Moving, even if it was in circles, felt better than waiting.

Stealing a glance at Stanley, he guessed that the younger man was less patient or at least let his impatience show through more. As for the other two passengers, he doubted they had an opinion either way, as both stared resolutely forward, wearing blank expressions.

The Chairman did not have to wait for long.

"Marauder, Control," came the voice again, this time with more intensity and, he suspected, a hint of excitement.

"Go," he growled, shifting to lean forward in his seat.

"Stand by to copy grid reference for hack, over."

Nathaniel snatched up the mobile terminal from the seat beside Stanley, who had logged in and kept the screen active to prevent it from locking and requiring the passwords to be inputted again.

"Send," Nathaniel said curtly, barely keeping his finger on the transmit button long enough for the word to be heard at the other end in his anticipation of being able to input the coordinates of the first scent of the hunt.

"Citadel grid reference: eight-eight, three-four, over."

"Received," Stanley said as he leaned over the Chairman's shoulder and watched as he typed in the correct grid coordinates that he had heard, "Confirm: eight-eight, three-four, over."

"Confirmed," Barclay answered, "grid co-ords for confirmed hack. Factory district, east of The Citadel. Bringing up manifests, stand by."

Nathaniel had listened to the exchange, but his mind was already past the conversation, past the location of the hack, and diving headlong into the purpose of the cyber-attack.

He scrolled out on the reinforced mobile terminal, some hybrid cross between a chunky laptop and a small suitcase, and stared at the screen for a second.

"Disregard," he said, taking his finger away from the keys and hitting the transmit button on his headset, "the factories aren't the target. Send QRF one to grid, eight-eight, three-one. Confirm eight-eight, three-one. Send them from the north, repeat, the north. Read back."

"Marauder, Control. Reading back QRF one via northerly approach to grid eight-eight, three-one," Barclay confirmed. Nathaniel didn't respond, he knew she understood, and raised his voice to the driver.

"Back to The Citadel, then east to the holding facility," he said in simple instruction. The driver said nothing. Merely nodded and took the next right turn to press the accelerator harder as soon as the road straightened.

"Holding facility?" Stanley asked Nathaniel.

"An educated guess," Nathaniel said as he tapped at more keys before spinning the case to show Stanley the list of citizens, ranked neatly beside their photographs, taken for questioning that day.

"Du Bois' team detained three with suspected terrorist markers, six suspected sympathisers including the families of last night's prisoners."

One prisoner, one dead body, Stanley thought to himself, deciding that the pedantic interruption wouldn't help anyone at that moment.

"As well as plenty of others which I'm sure were for either sport or a demonstration of power," he paused to lock eyes with his Major, "that's where I think they're going" he finished almost triumphantly.

"I didn't think you were a gambling man, Sir." Stanley offered with an evil half-smile.

"I'm not," he answered, "but when have you known me to be wrong about something?"

———

Professor Winslow had dismissed the attending guards, sealed the observation area and upgraded the security status temporarily so that nobody could access the room and watch him through the one-way glass. Now, feeling as alone as he could with the struggling and gagged girl writhing on the bed, he anticipated the enjoyment of a fresh subject.

Georgina, her left eye half-closed as a kindly memento from a faceless soldier, fought against the restraints as soon as she had seen the chinless, bespectacled scientist. Her sense of self-preservation fired deep within her, prompting an adrenaline-fuelled frenzy as the foreboding feeling threatened to paralyse her if she did not fight. The sycophantic smile on the pointy face could not disguise his malevolent intent, and the urban myths of citizens being tortured by Party scientists was suddenly so believable.

He made shushing noises as he walked to the bed she was propped up in and restrained to by her ankles and wrists. He continued to sooth her ineffectually as he unclasped the thick, wide belt which held her torso down, and her thrashing increased as she gained more control over the impetus of her small body weight, but she still could not force the gag from her mouth to scream out in rage and hope of rescue. Winslow was bucked backwards by the impact of one hip, forcing the false smile to drop and unveil the cruelty hidden just below the surface. He stepped closer and raised his right hand to strike her, but she froze and stopped her struggling to lock eyes with him.

I dare you, her eyes said dangerously, *I fucking dare you.*

Winslow stopped, frozen to the spot by the malevolent force of the look she gave him. His face cracked into a smile again, a genuine smile of wicked amusement this time, and he lowered his hand to turn on his heel and leave the room.

Georgina's chest heaved as she fought to regain her breath through her nose, blowing snot down her cheeks to mix with her tears of fear and hatred.

Winslow reappeared and only at the exact moment she

recognised the item in his hand did her thrashing struggles begin again, only harder and faster in intensity.

As the ugly scientist approached her cautiously, mindful of the pointed end of the hypodermic syringe needle, he tried to secure her sufficiently to stick her with the needle to chemically pacify her; not too much, because he wanted her awake.

He liked seeing their fear.

Just as he was about to thrust forward to inject her thigh, the intercom crackled loudly in the room. Winslow froze, listening to the obvious sounds of a man clearing his throat.

"What do you think you are doing?" enquired the speakers, diffidently and full of polite request.

Winslow turned to face the reflective glass and the observation room hidden behind it.

Who the hell..? Winslow thought impotently, *that room is locked...*

He opened his mouth to demand that the anonymous voice explain itself, to insist that the interruption was uncalled for and that he had full authority over the entire facility. Before he could utter the words, the speakers crackled once more.

"I asked," they said, "what you think you are doing…"

"How dare you?" Winslow blurted out, "I am…"

"I don't give a shit who you are," declared the voice again calmly, as the sound of a switch being flicked transmitted from the next room, "I asked what you think you are doing with my prisoner."

The glass went hazy, then cleared from reflective to opaque. Winslow, frozen to the spot still with a syringe in his hand, stared at the glass in shock.

Soldiers and guards were so much a part of the furniture in his world that he never gave them a second glance;

not even on the occasions when they weren't wearing the creepy reflective visors and he saw that they had human faces underneath. But the sight of this man made him feel fear.

The shimmery, blue haze of the toughened glass did not obscure the malevolence on the face of the bearded man standing tall and proud and immovable in the observation room. Winslow hesitated, swallowed twice, then tried to speak.

"How did you access that room?" he croaked, doubt evident in his tone. Georgina, similarly motionless at the interruption, smiled to herself at seeing the man without a chin and a sickening gleam in his eye so fearful of the newcomer. Her eyes stayed on Winslow and the syringe he still held.

"With my thumb," answered the bearded man equably, "the same way you did, I imagine."

Winslow hesitated and swallowed again, the pronounced movement of the lump in his throat more evident for his lack of a sturdy jawline, and tried to regain some power and composure.

"This is a Special Operations project, which you are not cleared for, so please leave the observation suite at once," he tried, attempting to sound as authoritative as possible.

The bearded man didn't move.

He didn't even shift his gaze which, much to Winslow's discomfort, seemed to be trying to bore a hole through his forehead. Winslow tried again.

"Who are you, soldier? Identify yourself," he demanded, squaring his small, thin shoulders.

The man behind the glass said nothing, and remained still, watching them. Wordlessly, suddenly, he turned away and flicked the switch to return the glass to a reflective surface. Winslow breathed out, more in exasperation at the interruption than anything else, and returned his attention to the girl.

Instantly, Georgina's struggling began again just as intensely as it had been before; almost as if the power supply had been temporarily interrupted and was now restored. Before Winslow could gauge his administering of the injection, the door behind him burst open.

Winslow recoiled from the girl in terror at the noise. Nobody should be able to access the doors, not without Special Operations clearance, and he doubted that any mere soldier below senior officer rank would have such access.

He also knew that the doors could not be kicked open, so in the flash of thought he was permitted before his space was invaded, he recognised that the intrusion must carry the weight of authority in some way. He had no chance to verbalise any of this, no opportunity to discuss the rights and wrongs of appropriate authority.

The bearded man entered the room, prompting a string of screamed obscenities from the restrained girl, and Winslow watched in horror as he crossed the room towards him in three, long strides. Instinctively, the scientist leaned back and raised his hands defensively, still holding the syringe.

Du Bois stopped short, looking down at the cowering man who could only match maybe half of his body mass, and contemptuously reached forward to slap him hard across the face with one gloved hand. Winslow's face registered pain, shock, and most of all disbelief.

Du Bois cuffed him again, harder this time, like a cat playing with a kill with its claws retracted so as to prolong the enjoyment.

Winslow yelped aloud at the second blow which skewed

his spectacles, and his attacker snatched the syringe from his grip, then shot his left hand forward to grip his thin neck roughly.

"What's this for?" Du Bois asked, no malice or threat in his words, only curiosity.

Winslow gasped for air as his feebly thin fingers grabbed at the restriction wrapped around his throat.

Only choking noises gargled from his throat, and Du Bois leaned his ear closer to the man's face.

"Sorry?" he asked, speaking intentionally loudly, "What is it for again?"

Winslow still couldn't manage to utter a word, and the clamping around his neck became stronger as Du Bois' face contorted in a rictus of contempt. He released the scientist, who gasped extravagantly loudly and reeled away from his assailant. Du Bois followed him, and just as the man in the lab coat was preparing to speak, he back-handed him hard across the face with his left hand and spun the man. As he flapped against the wall, holding the left side of his face, Du Bois stepped close and neatly speared him in the upper arm with the syringe but held his thumb over the plunger. His left hand slammed hard against the wall just beside Winslow's head, and he bent his face forward to meet the smaller man's at an uncomfortable distance apart. Winslow squealed weakly, like a child having a tantrum.

"What," he asked quietly, "is this for?"

"It's a," Winslow coughed, spraying spittle and bad breath into Du Bois' face, "a sedative. To make her stop fighting,"

Du Bois leaned back, using his left hand to wipe his face, then glanced between the struggling girl and the impaled scientist, before squeezing his thumb down and pulsing the cool liquid into Winslow's flesh.

He gasped, staring at the needle still protruding from his shoulder, and watched as Du Bois stepped away to stroke the hair of the madly thrashing girl as he shushed her gently.

"Why would you want her to stop fighting?" he asked over the grunting and keening sounds emanating from the girl.

Winslow couldn't answer, as he was sliding down the wall as he melted into unconsciousness.

———

"There," Mouse hissed to the others, pointing towards a service door in the gathering gloom. They all felt happier now that the sun was setting, as though they felt like they were on an alien planet walking around in daylight. Eve slipped forward, placed one eye surreptitiously to the small, reinforced glass window, then held her thumb over the scanner as she glanced back to Mouse. He nodded once, reassuring her that it would—should—work.

Placing her thumb with the shiny, red nail onto the reader, she watched in awe as the small red light blinked green and the door opened a crack. She withdrew her thumb with a smile, pulled open the door, and slipped inside low to the ground as the others followed.

———

"Marauder, Control" came Barclay's crisp voice. Nathaniel thought he heard a hint of excitement, but it may just have been his own excitement transferred to the information receiving part of his brain.

"Go," he growled.

"That profile has activated a security door, next quadrant over, at the holding facility" she said. Definitely an air of excitement there, as though his hunches were now being understood by others. As though his genius and his superior tactics were now obvious.

"Understood," he answered, nodding to Stanley by raising his chin towards the driver up front. Stanley nodded back, turned in his seat and ordered the driver to make for the holding facility, only a little faster than he was currently going.

CHAPTER FORTY

SHOWDOWN

Had Nathaniel known about the Resistance's mirror efforts to his own Project Erebus, he would have anticipated the showdown between Genesis and Erebus with an evil, gleeful delight.

He suspected that the terrorists had superior skills to his usual rank and file, that much was evident in the discovery of the butchered bodies who hadn't even managed to discharge their weapons, and in the savage and stinging loss of Host. But to know that his own test subjects could be tested in equal combat with the best that the enemy could muster would have been a thought to give him great excitement.

He was not to know that such a test was imminent, but his excitement was still palpable to anyone who knew him well; to anyone who could read his body language and decipher his blank face, as he skipped up the steps to the main doors of the holding facility.

The attending guard at the door snapped to attention from his lazy leaning stance against the wall, but the procession of four heavily armed people led by the

Chairman himself was through the doors and gone before he could even salute. The guard looked around for any confirmation that what he had just seen had indeed happened, but he found nobody to corroborate that with.

Looking down the steps to the response personnel carrier that had opened its rear doors to disgorge the unexpected human cargo, he saw the driver get out and stretch his back after what seemed like hours behind the wheel.

He nodded affably to the surprised guard, who returned the gesture automatically, and wandered down the steps uncertainly to chat to his peer.

Nathaniel strode in, blasted through the security checkpoint unchallenged, and startled the ageing Major he assumed to be in charge of the facility.

"Report," he barked, as the man flew to his feet from behind a plain desk to show an unbuttoned uniform jacket.

The Major simultaneously tried to salute, button his coat, and stammer a response all at once, rewarding him with total failure at all three actions. Steadying himself in response to the cold look the Chairman gave him, he tried once more.

"Sir," he said, clearing his throat in an attempt to sound less surprised and incompetent, "all fine here."

"Really?" Nathaniel enquired with a wolfish smile, "so you don't have terrorists in your facility right now who have accessed the service levels?"

The Major's eyes goggled as though he had been squeezed in a man-sized vice. His mouth flapped open and closed as he searched for the words which could explain his lack of knowledge.

Nathaniel waved a hand as though to dismiss any attempt to make up for it, then continued.

"Mobilise your entire guard force," he said, adding, "*quietly.*"

The Major's hand stopped in mid-hover as it was reaching out towards the large, red button on the control panel near his desk. He seemed, luckily for him, to comprehend the necessity for subtlety quickly and retracted the movement as he switched his glance to fall upon a junior officer under his command.

"Matthews," he snapped, "mobilise whatever Cyclone forces we have on site, but do not use the alarms," he said, pointing a finger at the young man's face to emphasise his point. Matthews nodded his understanding. "Each wing is to be secured, in person," he added, meaning that the need for quiet was absolute.

Nathaniel nodded, then spoke again.

"Where are the detainees from this morning's block inspection?" he enquired.

"Ground level," he answered automatically, proving that he had at least some knowledge of what was happening in his own facility, "Charlie spur."

Nathaniel nodded his head as he thought. The facility had been constructed as a central, circular hub with three long wings that branched out behind it. They were predictably named Alpha, Bravo and Charlie.

The prisoners taken that day following the raid on residence block six must be, he told himself logically, the prize on offer to them.

Either they desperately want their people back, he thought, *or they are so frightened about what they will tell us that they have come to silence them.*

He turned away from the office and began walking out of the hub towards the gate on the far right. He heard the sounds of spoken orders, and the rustling sounds of men shrugging themselves into equipment. The Cyclone troops, he knew, were the branch of the military which specialised in the pacification of detainees. They had all undergone the same basic training as every Party soldier, but these men and women detailed to specialise as the party's jailers were given additional training.

Now, without calling in additional troops and making it obvious that they had discovered the intruders, Nathaniel glanced behind him to see almost twenty troops following him down the long, linking walkway. They were trained to use non-lethal methods to subdue a prisoner, as often the violence was an attempt to entice their death and prevent their information from being extracted forcibly. Suicide by soldier was a concept Nathaniel himself had experienced in the mining facilities to the north when he was a Lieutenant, and had made changes to the training processes as a result.

Adapt and dominate.

As he rode the head of the wave heading for impending conflict, he smiled in anticipation as the earpiece attached to his headset crackled to life once more.

"Marauder, Control."

"Marauder Actual, go ahead," he said confidently.

"Marauder, we are detecting an active hack from the facility," Barclay informed him.

"Details?" Nathaniel asked.

"Stand by… Charlie wing, ground level, guard station Echo."

"Received," Nathaniel said, then turned to the nearest soldier from the facility. It was Lieutenant Matthews.

"Guard station Echo?" he parroted to the young man.

"End of the spur, Sir" Matthews told him, "last station."

They followed the Chairman's lead and picked up the pace. "And bring a mobile control terminal," he fired over his shoulder, expecting that the order would be followed without question.

———

The three lazy guards sitting in the station were totally unprepared for an attack from their rear.

They were totally unprepared for an attack from anywhere, with all of their charges locked in small cells or under the direct supervision of other guards.

The three of them had the responsibility to monitor twelve screens, and those screens showed nothing of interest. If they'd had even a shred of awareness, if two of them hadn't been lounging with their feet on the table tops as though they were celebrating their laziness, they might have noticed the two black shapes creeping under the thick glass of their guard post.

Adam rolled silently under the door and drew a blade from behind his back to scrape at the doorframe. He glanced at Eve, who held one of the wicked and heavy curved black blades, although she had left it sheathed to try not to kill anyone. She nodded back to him and he scraped the blade again, knocking slightly as he did and hearing the reward of movement inside the locked room.

As the curious guard closest to the door stood and walked towards the exit to place one hand on the release handle, he peered out of the glass for any sign of the source of the small disturbance. As soon as he put sufficient pressure on the release handle to hear the click of the lock disengaging, the door was ripped outwards away from his grasp and the heavy hilt of a blade was jabbed hard into his throat. He reeled backwards instantly. Choking and unable to speak, he fell back against the workstation as a black, hooded figure unfolded from the doorway.

The other guards stood in simultaneous shock as their comrade fell back so violently.

As one, they saw the intruders and both sprang into immediate action, despite their previous state of rest.

One reached for his baton, only to find the sheathed, blunt, heavy edge of Eve's black kukri pinning his wrist to the desk with a sickening crack as the bone gave way under the impact. He drew his lips back from his teeth as he inhaled, ready to issue a scream of pure agony, before the slim girl struck him twice in the neck with her small, sharp hands. Choking, he pitched forward as she switched her gaze to see Adam, empty handed as he had sheathed the knife in case he used it and set off the alarms that a dead guard would cause, spinning as he avoided the items the soldier threw at him as he desperately tried to reach the panic alarm. Just as his hand reached out to press the button, Adam's right leg spun again and the foot connected heavily with the chest of his target, sending the man flying backwards as though pulled from behind by a huge force. He crashed into the wall and hit the ground, immobile.

Adam wordlessly returned to the first guard he had struck and wrapped his left arm around his neck to choke off the blood supply to the brain. After a few seconds of feeble struggling, the limp guard was laid down gently.

The one that Eve had taken was unconscious, the right hand flapping unnaturally on its shattered wrist as she dragged it towards the others. Mouse slipped inside and closed the door, plugging his small tablet into the data port as the others set about stripping wires to tie the guards up with.

By the time Mouse announced that he had killed the CCTV for the facility and began searching the guard post terminal for a prisoner manifest, the others had finished securing the broken, unconscious guards and returned to his side.

"Just down the hall," he said as much to himself as he thought out loud, looking at the facility schematics. The others waited in impatient silence as he worked, then locked eyes as Mouse exclaimed, "Shit!"

"What is it?" Adam asked.

Mouse glanced at Eve, swallowed, and told her, "They've got Cohen"

"Where?" Eve asked, her face unreadable and her body extraordinarily still. Mouse's fingers tracked across the keyboard for a few seconds before, "Next level above. Cell two-fourteen. Wait," he added as he hit the keys with the same intensity. "There. The cell door is now at your access level," he told her, seeing the girl wheel around and slip out of the room.

"Go with her," he told Adam, seeing the concern as the fighter's priorities were suddenly torn.

"I'll be fine," he told him, "The girl they took is just over there," he told him, pointing behind the young man at the corridor past the guard post.

Adam shot one final glance at the three slumbering guards tied together, then at Mouse who tried his hardest to make eye contact and convey a sense of calm, then he left.

Eve had to climb the stairs at the far end of the corridor, then double back on herself to reach the right cell. As she gained the threshold of the first wide landing, double doors ahead of her hissed as they opened mechanically. She froze, skidding to a stop as her eyes registered what she was seeing. A tall man stopped in front of a procession of armoured guards and his eyes shot wide as he saw her. She felt exposed, caught in the open, pinned by the light with no shadows to retreat to. Behind the man, who now smiled, filed so many soldiers that she could not count them. All of them had the insect-like shiny black faces of their helmet visors. They swooped fast to form a rough semi-circle around her.

She bladed her right foot forwards, sank her body weight onto her legs, and slowly drew the two wide-bladed, curved weapons from behind her back. The formation of guards stopped and waited, as though unable to attack her independently without an order.

One tried to sidle into position behind her, who she watched in her peripheral vision, until the body jerked and emitted a high-pitched whine before spasming and dropping limply to tumble down the metal staircase.

Rising in its place was Adam, one long knife blade wet and dripping with blood. He stepped forwards to mirror Eve's stance on her right side.

"I thought we weren't killing anyone?" she asked him out of the side of her mouth.

"I think they already know we're here," Adam answered with uncharacteristic comedy.

"True," Eve said as she cocked her head slightly, "what do we do now?" she muttered as she eyed the nervous heads of the arrayed soldiers reflecting the image of two killers dressed in black with weapons ready. The decision was made for them.

"Take them alive," came the clear, confident command from the man at the doors. Adam had a flash image of the man, flanked by an excited looking man. What caught his attention, however, was the expressions on the faces of the two soldiers standing behind them. The fact that any of them were showing their faces was an irregularity, but these two looked at Adam with a cold predatory nature which made his blood run cold for the briefest of moments.

He had seen that expression before on another face. The face of a man that he and Eve had killed.

He had no more time to assimilate this information, as the surrounding guards surged forward as one to attack. They were all armoured, all wore the eerily reflective black visors, and all carried only metal batons designed to incapacitate and not kill.

All of these facts both Adam and Eve were aware of, but their bodies responded with an instinctual automation which spoke of hours upon hours, their whole lives in fact, spent practising their craft. And their craft was killing.

Adam dropped low and rolled forward to rise effortlessly and bury the blade in his right hand into the brain of the soldier in front. It would have punctured cleanly out of the top of the head but for the protective helmet ironically keeping a killing blow inside and not out, he dropped again, dragging that blade free as he cut savagely across the front of the lower leg of another attacker.

He heard a muffled scream of pain and saw the leg go limp as the thigh bunch up to swell inside the reinforced trousers. He knew he had severed the ligaments and tendons keeping the knee cap in place, which had then obediently answered the call of the strong muscle above to rearrange the mechanics of the leg.

Turning away to his right, knowing that the spaces to his left and front were temporarily protected by a dead body and a screaming mess of thrashing limbs, he spun to bring both blades up to deflect the downward strike of a baton. As he moved, he caught sight of Eve and marvelled at the beauty and grace of her kills.

Eve had, when Adam attacked forwards, taken a step backwards and dropped into a vertical split, with one leg forward and one leg back. As she dropped and felt the swing of two batons pass high over her where her head had just been, she threw back her arms and buried the two evil blades into the midsections of her attackers. They were not parallel to each other, so whilst one blade bit terribly into the hip bone of the solider to her right, the one to her left suffered only a glancing blow which sliced the outer edge of the thigh deeply. Springing back to her feet without the use of her hands, Eve abandoned the blade buried in bone and spun to deliver a downwards kick to the back of the helmet belonging to the soldier with the leg wound. The scream which emanated from behind the visor sounded female but that didn't register with Eve. Just as Adam had found when he first went out, an enemy was an enemy and the Party made no such changes for gender.

She followed the kick with a swing of the blade still in her left hand, and felt the satisfaction of the heavy edge bite through material and sever the spine just below the skull.

Using her downward momentum, she rolled away and her right hand found the handle of her other weapon, which she wrenched free using her body weight as she spun back to her feet. The next soldier fell like a slaughtered animal as she struck downwards at an inward angle on both shoulders, pulling the blades free to turn and seek out a new victim. Her glance told her of the threat from her left, and she ducked to avoid the swing before raising her right hand in a sweeping arc and severing the weapon hand of the soldier. She dispatched another attacker almost absent-mindedly as her gaze was drawing her inexorably closer to the man who had given the orders. A helpful shout of rage sounded behind her and she turned to bury a knife into the helmet and split open the visor. As the body fell, she let go of the weapon and reached down for one of her two remaining throwing daggers. Spinning to aim from visual memory, she flicked her hand hard to send the knife spinning towards its intended target, only to see the knife spark as it clanged off a round disc on the forearm of the other man.

Stanley had seen it coming. He had sensed the ranged attack on a cellular level, and reacted without a single shred of cognitive thought. He thrust his left forearm across the face of the Chairman and clamped his fist down hard to activate the shield. He couldn't say how he knew that he wasn't the target, and why he had exposed himself to greater risk by protecting Nathaniel. He couldn't say because he didn't know; he just reacted.

As he released his fist and the composite plates fanned back inside the greave on his arm, the Chairman regarded him with such awe that he felt instantly embarrassed.

Turning back to watch the fight, Stanley saw that, in a matter of seconds, half of their force was down or dead and the slick wash of blood on the shiny floor threatened to make the battlefield yet more treacherous. No sooner had these thoughts entered his head, than the two intruders began to retreat down the corridor. He fell in step beside Nathaniel automatically to follow.

———

Mouse stepped gingerly as though counting his paces. Creeping his awkward progress down the hallway he heard faint sounds echoing from the floor above and feared for the others.

He feared for their capture more than their death, as well as for his own, because he knew the likelihood of leaving this facility alive was close to zero. He stopped pacing and turned right, placing his thumb on the reader which allowed the door to pop open after the anticipated flash of the small green light he was becoming accustomed to, and stepped inside to find a sight which boiled an instant rage in him.

The girl, Georgina, was strapped to a bed which had been moved to make it seem as though she stood. Her hands were restrained, her ankles pinned to the lower corner, and her head and body were strapped down tightly. A metal contraption was on her face, forcing her eyelids open and her red face didn't register Mouse as he entered, because her full attention was on the man in front of her.

Mouse could see from the back and his body position that his left hand was reached out to her, and his right hand was moving rhythmically in front of himself.

As naïve as he was about the ways of the people above ground, Mouse knew what was happening wasn't something that she wanted, and he felt in every fibre of his body that it was wrong.

Acting on sheer impulse, his right hand snatched up the handle of the baton on his waist and his arms flicked in an exaggerated movement to extend the weapon, rewarding him instantly with the fizzing quality that the air took on when the tip of the baton crackled electrically.

Both the girl and the man in front of her noticed him then. The girl's eyes were already as wide as they could possibly be, but the look she gave him was one mixed of relief and fear; fear for Mouse. He knew why in the next second, as the man turned to stare at him with such a malevolent hatred through his small, penetrative eyes, that Mouse felt that fear tenfold.

In panic, he stabbed forwards with the baton.

In Du Bois' shock at the interruption, he had no fore-thought to put away the thing in his right hand. He turned to see the thin, dirty, bedraggled interloper standing before him, still with his dick held firmly in his right hand.

As soon as he saw the baton coming forwards, he tried to twist and bend to avoid the inevitable contact.

He failed.

As the two tips connected, the sixty thousand volts of electricity tickling the end of the baton found somewhere to escape and earthed itself through Du Bois.

He shuddered on the spot, muscles bursting with the effort of contraction and a strangled noise escaped the man's mouth as the spit bubbled to fleck the rust-coloured beard. The fingers of his right hand were clenched so hard that the contents of his hand swelled and instantly turned purple as the blood vessels were crushed, before he toppled forwards to crunch his nose sickeningly into the hard ground.

Mouse froze for a second, staring at the horrible beauty of what he had just done, before a voice dragged his mind back to the present.

"Get me out of this thing" Georgina wailed. Mouse tried to undo the straps holding the wire frame on her face, but to do so meant looking at her naked body and his embarrassment was too much. He struggled with the fittings as he tried to free her, making the whole thing last uncomfortably long. Finally, when he had unclasped one hand, she started to free the other and waved him down to her feet. Kneeling down, given the ridiculously dangerous situation they were in, he found his head so close to a part of a woman's body that he had never seen before, that he blushed bright red and fumbled with the restraints again.

The man at the centre of the growing puddle of blood moaned, making Georgina flap her hands at him. Mouse finally undid one of the ankle restraints and turned to deliver another strong dose of electricity to the side of the man's neck to incapacitate him again. The same strange, high-pitched gargling noise came from his mouth again, making the welling blood bubble from his broken nose.

As Georgina freed herself and dropped to the ground, Mouse turned back to help her up before feeling self-conscious for her nakedness again.

She walked unsteadily to a man lumped in the corner of the room, and he watched as she stripped him of his lab coat and trousers; the man being so small and thin that they fit her almost as well as they did him.

Mouse watched her as he tried to avert his gaze, and not once did he think to question the presence of a half-conscious man in a white coat. She turned to look at him and held her hands out wide. Coupled with her wide eyes and open-mouthed expression of annoyance, he understood that it was time for him to get them both out of there. He poked his head out of the door and saw no activity on their level. Returning as an afterthought to deliver another shock to the soldier who shrieked pitifully through the blood in his throat, and then to the half-naked scientist who made a noise like a wounded animal.

Both sounds made Georgina giggle. He led her behind him, her right hand in his left, and his right still gripping the crackling baton with a new-found respect for its beauty.

As he ran, he glanced upwards to see his two fellow intruders running. Adam stopped, skidding to a stop as he glanced between Mouse and the girl below, and Eve still running to his right.

His face registered a decision. A choice. An impasse.

With a final glance to Eve's retreating back, he sheathed the knife in his left hand, placed it on the railing, and vaulted over to drop the twenty feet to the level they were on. Mouse stopped, confused, as Adam ran towards them drawing the other blade. A glance behind him told him the information he didn't have, and he turned back to run harder and drag the girl behind him with her bare feet flapping loudly on the polished floor.

Adam ran past, dropping to slide on the shiny surface and propel him into the dozen guards who were pursuing the people he had consciously chosen to protect. His reasoning, even if he didn't know it at the time, was that Eve could defend herself against most things, whereas Mouse was vulnerable enough on his own, not counting the handicap of protecting the girl he had rescued.

The cries and sounds of furious conflict behind him faded as they made distance, leaving Adam to his own devices as he carved his way through the small army.

————

Eve had outstripped her pursuers easily for pace; they were lumbering and heavy whereas she was lithe and agile. She found the door she needed, pressed her thumb to the reader and huffed in frustrated anger as the red light blinked with a small, angry buzz.

She wiped her hand desperately on her black suit, trying to scrub away the wet blood obscuring her thumbprint, before trying again with agonisingly slow success which made the door slide into the wall and open her way to the room behind. She stepped inside, expecting to see Cohen, but instead finding nothing.

The cell was empty.

She did not hear the approaching footsteps from behind, but she felt the sudden and violent shove in the base of her back which propelled her forwards to impact the far wall of the small concrete box with her hands. Spinning and drawing the two blades she started to advance but froze, seeing the two dead-eyed killers blocking her exit.

Where is Adam? She thought desperately, suddenly feeling like the child that she was.

"Hold!" said a clear, deep voice from behind the pair. Before she could comprehend this, the door slid shut with a terrifying noise of finality.

Eve didn't move for a second, then bellowed in fear and rage to scream and beat the blades against the heavy steel of the door. She raged, seeing the man on the other side of the small slit of glass regard her with curiosity.

"Let me out," she screamed at him, "I'll kill you!"

"Some other time," he said with amusement before looking to the side and nodding. At once the vents in the wall of the cell began to fill with a thin smoke.

Eve tried to cover her mouth but there was no escape from the gas which filled the chamber, seeking out every gap of clear air relentlessly. She coughed, inhaling more of the gas as she breathed in after the coughing stopped. It felt cold, and at once her head began to swim. Dizzy, she fell back to the empty cot and her hand dropped from her mouth slackly.

"Where is Adam?" she slurred aloud, just before her eyes rolled up into her skull and her world went black.

Adam dripped with the spilled blood of the soldiers he had cut his path through. He had slid through the majority of the squad, slicing tendons and arteries as he went, before rising to his feet and cutting his bloody path to the furthest troops. Those at the back of any advance were most likely to be the weakest, the most cowardly, he thought.

He had, however, found the fight at the rear to be just as intense as those at the front he had worked his way through. When all of them lay dead at his feet, flooding the whole area with dark, red blood, his chest heaved and his arms hung tired at his sides. The knives in his hands, and the hands themselves, were drenched with so much blood that he looked more of a victim than the slain bodies around him did.

His delaying tactics had worked, because he had seen Mouse and the girl disappear from view around the corner, away from the pursuit.

He slipped on the blood as he set off to follow them, stumbling forwards to land heavily on the chest of a soldier whose neck was laid open and still pulsed weak amounts of red liquid from the deep wound.

The random chance of the fall saved his life.

As he pitched forwards, arms flailing for purchase and to cushion his fall without landing on either of the long blades in his hands, a shot rang out and the answering ricochet sounded loudly down the corridor behind him. Adam's eyes snapped directly towards the source of the sound, and he threw the knife in his right hand by pure reaction. The blades sang as it flew, the sound stopping suddenly as the point buried itself deeply into the visor of a soldier. The helmeted head rocked backwards, the brain inside instantly dead, and dropped to the ground messily just as another sound caught his attention.

It was the sound of boots—lots of boots—coming from the direction of the last squad he had dispatched.

He ran.

Forced to abandon Eve, at least for now, he went after Mouse and the girl.

Rounding a corner, he saw them ahead; detained at gunpoint and forced to their knees with their hands on their heads by two soldiers. Unthinking again, Adam threw the remaining knife in his left hand on the run. The moving start made for a less accurate throw, but the blade hit the soldier in the shoulder and speared through to puncture the chest.

The soldier staggered, dropped to one knee, and pulled the trigger of the rifle it held.

A burst of automatic gunfire erupted from the muzzle, hitting the other soldier fully in the chest. Both black uniforms hit the ground at the same time, but there was a cost. One stray bullet had scored a deep gash through Mouse's hair, and blood flowed out of his head at an unfathomable rate. The girl screamed, then pulled off the white lab coat she wore over a hastily buttoned shirt a size too big and pressed the material onto Mouse's wound hard, making him cry out in pain. Adam hurried them to the door just as twin sounds thumped in stereo behind him. He turned away from the escaping air and regarded the sight before him. Feeling as though he looked on his own death, he regarded the two dead-eyed killers in front of him. Feeling down his right leg for the one remaining weapon he carried, he pulled the wide-bladed knife from the sheath on his calf, spun the hilt so that the knife blade ran the length of his right forearm, and took a fighting stance.

Two men appeared over the railing above, and one ordered the two killers to capture him.

"Keep him alive," he added, the threat of capture steeling Adam to seek death before a short existence of torture and enforced betrayal.

Taking a breath to steady himself, he stepped forward.

CHAPTER FORTY-ONE

THE ENEMY WITHIN

Adam fought with a bravery and intensity dictated by the high stakes of the game. The two rested, highly capable fighters he faced toyed with him. Neither even drew a weapon to begin with, relying on their superior fitness over his blood-soaked exhaustion to evade his clumsy attempts to cut them open.

Both shot occasional glances upwards to their master, but Adam was concentrating too hard on remaining alive to pay the man much attention.

In the end, his own desperation defeated him.

As soon as he deflected a tentative attack from the woman on his right, the man on his left swooped in to hit him with a stinging blow only to recoil out of the way of any retaliatory blow. As she stepped towards him again and he responded by closing the gap between them to use the knife, the other one spun in to deliver a kick to his left thigh which forced his knee to drop to the ground. Remembering in time the proximity of the female, he slashed wildly at her. She stood still, pushing out her chest to allow the vest she wore to absorb the slice as the material covering the protective plate tore wide open. She slapped a small blow at him as the weapon passed, rapping her knuckles on the pronounced bones on the back of his hand.

The blow was sufficient and accurate enough to make the nerves in his hand go dead momentarily, letting the blade slip from his grasp.

He cried out as he felt the heavy weapon fall away from him, just as another blow from behind threw him forwards.

He tried to get up, but another single, disciplined blow to the back of his head put him down, and another switched off the lights.

Adam had the sense to keep his eyes lightly closed and his breathing shallow as he regained his senses. He had to rely on sound mainly for clues. He was still, he thought, in the same position as when he was downed, but he felt that he had shifted slightly.

Probably checking for weapons, he thought.

He heard voices, faintly at first but as he regained more focus he could make out the words.

"Yes," said a gruff voice, "transport to The Citadel sub-levels."

A one-sided conversation, he thought, *radio?*

"For three," the voice confirmed.

Shit. They must have caught Mouse and the girl, he reckoned as he fought to control his face and show no reaction to the news. *There was no way they would be separated,* he tried to reason logically, *unless they had caught Eve and Mouse or the girl was dead? Or Eve was dead?*

The concept hurt him deep inside, that any of them had died and that he could have made different decisions.

He sensed the two people standing over him. He felt the small shimmers in the air current which told a person of the presence of another human in their vicinity, if they cared to listen and interpret the small signs. They weren't the still, brooding and emotionless killers he had faced alone; these two fidgeted and looked around.

Regular guards, he told himself, *at least I have a hope there, even without weapons.*

Somewhere behind his head fingers were snapped and the two guards reached down to haul him to his feet. He let his head flop painfully, the stiffness in his neck from resisting the heavy blows to his skull already aching. His body weight was substantial when he wasn't holding himself upright; even though he was lean, he was made mostly of muscle.

His feet scraped as he was carried along the squeaking, shiny surface of the polished floor inside the holding facility, before his toes bumped down a series of steps and the air grew cooler.

Someone else there, he thought, *holding the door open for them.* He daren't open one eye even a crack for fear of his consciousness being discovered. Better to attempt an escape in transit.

He was bundled into the rear of a dull, grey troop transport and sensed the presence of other people. One cried gently to herself and the other gasped in pain. The copper smell of blood reached Adam's nostrils, and it wasn't from the red liquid drying over his own body.

Has to be Mouse and the girl, he thought as he tried to understand where the soldiers were. He sensed two of them there, probably the two who had carried him, and then the sound of a door sliding shut before two hollow, metallic thumps sounded loudly. With only the slightest of whines, the van started forwards and bumped him around as he still played dead, despite the pain of a guard's boots resting on his stomach.

Before he could summon the energy to attempt a move

to overpower the guards, the van slewed to a stop and angry voices came through muffled by the visors.

The guard resting his feet on Adam was spilled forwards slightly, and leaned back in his chair to shout at the driver for the sudden stop.

"What are you doing?" he called, "Idiot, The Citadel is left here."

"I know," said the driver, "idiot."

With that, he drew a pistol with his left hand, the one taken from the unwitting guard at the front of the holding facility as soon as everyone had gone inside.

Firing a single round into the visors of both soldiers and prompting a scream from the girl, Adam opened his eyes to see the two lifeless forms slumped where they sat. Shoving the boots off him he clambered upright as he felt the van move off again.

"Who are you?" he demanded of the driver, "What's happening?"

"Patience, *boy*," the visor said as it turned back to the road ahead, "now get your head down"

With that, the van slowed and the driver wound down the window to give another solider a verification code. The code evidently matched the records, because the soldier ordered the gates open and the van set off again.

The road became bumpier almost instantly, and Adam tried again to talk to the driver, who was rummaging in the glove compartment of the van and passing back a green plastic box.

"Patch his head up," the visor said, "we've got a long way to go and I don't want Mouse bleeding to death."

Adam paused.

"Mark?" he asked incredulously.

"Yes," the visor answered with a small nod of reward.

"Where are we going? What happened to Eve?"

Mark held up a hand to stop him talking.

"They have Eve," he said, "there's nothing we can do about that. And we are going to the Frontier."

Adam slumped back, his brain awash with too much information as Georgina gently took the medical kit out of his unresisting hands.

Adam raised his head to speak again but was cut off by the faceless Mark.

"No, we can't go back for her," he said with sad finality.

Adam remained silent for a long time before asking a simple question.

"How?"

———

She wiped the keys of the keyboard with a clean cloth before tucking it into a fold of her tightly fitted uniform. She had received her activation code and her instructions, and had luckily found the Chairman out of his office on an operation at the time.

She was no fool, far from it in fact, and she knew that the assembly of Special Operations personnel and the Chairman's absence was linked to her sudden and unplanned activation. For the Resistance to burn such a valuably placed asset in active terrorism must have been worth the risk; she had to trust that.

She had activated and amended the security status of a specific identity chip, granting the user access to weapons and vehicles clearance, then constructed the orders for the transport to be marked as a routine convoy to the Frontier.

Whoever it was in that van was on their own from there, but that didn't mean she had to go down in martyrdom herself. She had fabricated her own orders, changing her identity to another name and wiping clean the trail of evidence. That was the benefit of using the Chairman's own terminal; nobody had a higher authority to be able to analyse what she had done. She had no idea how they had got the encrypted password for her, but it had worked.

Now, clearing the physical evidence along with the electronic, Corporal Samaira Nadeem left the office of the Chairman of the Party and simply ceased to exist.

Her official reassignment had her sent to the Frontier on the transport which was already well clear of The Citadel, and she left to travel north to the mining colonies under an assumed name which had an entire service record fabricated behind it. She could hardly return to The Citadel, as she knew that her personal appearance was noteworthy if not unique, and she couldn't risk discovery under a new name.

No, she thought, *I've got to go. People will recognise me if I stay in The Citadel*

The farming colonies to the west had more frequent contact with The Citadel due to the weekly deliveries of food, and the Frontier held no pull for her, as the purpose of the counterfeit reassignment was to stay alive. She had selected a position from the outgoing personnel transfer lists, deciding that a promotion was in order.

She chose modestly, making herself a full Lieutenant as a Captaincy at her age would potentially raise questions which might make enquiring minds reach out to The Citadel for her history.

She had scrubbed her biometric records from the security profile of Nadeem, transferring them permanently to her new identity, before erasing the computer log of her tampering.

Finally, printing out her requisition orders for the new

uniform and equipment she would need, she folded the paper and left the office.

She paused in the doorway and allowed herself a small smirk of satisfaction; men were so simple to manipulate it was almost disappointing to her.

———

"What do we do with her?" Stanley asked the Chairman as they both looked down through the thick glass floor into the holding cell below. It was a white cube, with a bed which was part of the wall and a toilet constructed similarly. No fixture or fitting in the box could be removed, adapted or used as a weapon, by careful design, but then again it was designed to house things which could be classified as weapons themselves.

"Not sure yet," Nathaniel answered slowly. The girl was still unconscious since breathing the heavy dose of the sedative gas used in the holding facility. She had been restrained and returned to The Citadel under heavy guard, which Nathaniel had overseen himself.

He had Barclay working on deciphering the information to allow an explanation as to how, exactly, the others had escaped and disappeared from The Citadel's territory without a trace.

He didn't like words like 'suddenly' and 'without any warning' or 'simply vanished' appearing in official reports, yet he had seen all of those poor excuses for ineptitude used already.

If something was sudden and unexpected to a soldier, then that soldier was unprepared.

If a solider was attacked without warning, then they had simply failed to read the situation and expect the attack.

And nobody, in the history of the world, had ever simply vanished.

Those failings he would deal with in good time, preferably when he had the full facts with which to properly discipline those at fault, but for now his focus was on the prize he had.

Or, more appropriately, prizes. Plural.

Looking through the heavy, toughened glass floor at the small girl twenty feet below, he could probably forgive himself for thinking that she looked sweet. Her wide eyes had been wiped clean of the sooty substance she had smeared across them; her body had been washed and a drip inserted into her arm to replenish the fluids and nutrients that her thin frame lacked. Her hair, now washed, hung damply off the side of the mattress she had been laid on.

Curiously, her fingernails were still a glossy red. Nathaniel allowed a small smirk at that eccentricity. It showed that she had desires. That she liked something. He knew how to exploit a person who wanted something.

"How long until she wakes?" Nathaniel asked, not taking his eyes away from the girl.

"The lab coats think it will be any time after about an hour," Stanley told him. "She had a big dose and is quite small so they aren't sure. It seems like this is one of the few things they haven't tested on children. Yet."

The Chairman huffed, although whether it was in humour or annoyance or disappointment, Stanley could not tell. The only way the girl could be accessed was by the secured trap door in the heavy glass they stood on, and Nathaniel had no desire to put anyone within striking distance of the girl just yet.

He guessed that she was used to hiding in cramped spaces for her entire life, the evidence of a freshly-inserted chip told him that much, but he doubted whether she was accustomed to the light. He had ordered that the lights be kept on day and night; part of the opening process in breaking her down and chipping away at the layers of her psyche.

Disappointed that she was still sleeping, Nathaniel turned away and strode away from the bright prison pit deep in the bowels of The Citadel and walked along the dull corridors to find the man he was looking for.

Professor Winslow, wearing the permanent expression of a child who had been caught out and punished, sat sullenly at his desk and resolutely ignored the uniformed guard beside him. On the Chairman's orders, a uniformed officer—a junior rank who could be spared, as they were mostly of little use in his opinion—stood guard over the scientist in an obvious display that he was no longer trusted.

"Good morning, Professor," exclaimed Stanley ebulliently, wearing a smile of genuine glee which was for the man's predicament and not his company.

Nathaniel stifled a smirk and sat down uninvited, waving away the second Lieutenant who marched from the room smartly.

"Sir," began Winslow petulantly in his whine of a voice, "I must protest…"

"The last person to protest my orders found himself *retired*," Nathaniel said in gentle interruption and menacing inflection. He left the rest of the threat unsaid, letting Winslow's imagination conjure up what his retirement might look like.

"Do your job and crack the woman for me," he said, rising from the chair as he realised he did not want to spend any more time in the company of the man the other scientists so appropriately called Professor Weasel. As that subject was on his mind, Nathaniel led Stanley the short distance to another holding cell, although this one far less extravagant and reinforced than the last.

"Just a stroke of dumb luck that she was being processed through medical at the time and not in her cell," Stanley mused unnecessarily.

"I don't believe in luck," Nathaniel responded, silencing the young Major. He peered through the glass and met eyes with the small woman. She sat on the cot, body still and hands folded neatly in her lap, but her eyes burned back at the man regarding her with a fiery intensity that made him smile.

"She'll be hard to crack," Stanley said, not quite a question but not a confident statement either.

"I'd be disappointed if she wasn't," Nathaniel answered, turning away to leave Cohen to her own fate.

EPILOGUE

Hundreds of miles away, over wild terrain and deep into inhospitable territory, another prisoner sat in a deep hole of a prison cell.

Shaw's situation was a total mirror of Eve's.

He was shut in the dark, scared of the inky blackness and disorientated with being alone. He lost all track of time and could no longer tell minutes from hours, or hours from days. He was filthy, uncomfortable, and in pain.

In contrast, Eve was disoriented by the permanent, bright lights of her new surroundings. She had raged at the walls initially, issued threats to the constant stream of white-coated people who stopped to watch her and write notes on the boards they carried before walking away. They never left her alone, and all she craved was a dark corner to secret herself away in and not be watched.

She was well fed, had never enjoyed so much clean, cool, fresh water, and had experienced the most glorious thing she had ever dreamed possible. The powerful jets of hot water which washed her body and hair were far superior to the makeshift shower that had been rigged up in her dusty hideout.

It was far superior to anything topside that a citizen could access, and that was all part of the plan to turn her. Within days she had become accustomed to the scores of people stopping to peer down through the high glass ceiling at her. Within a week she had even grown used to the lights, after being unable to sleep for three whole days and exhaustion finally lending a hand.

She knew day and night by the activity above her, and knew the start of the day when the food was lowered into her bright cell. She ate hungrily with her fingers, she knew they would be foolish to provide her with anything sharp that could be thrown, and she began to anticipate the three times daily when the hatch opened under armed guard and the gifts descended.

She knew that the interrogation would start eventually, but for the moment she was happy to eat their food and gather her strength.

———

Shaw was almost delirious through dehydration. He had been starved of food and water intentionally, just to make the meagre offerings seem like the god's own ambrosia when they deigned to throw him a stale crust of bread and a bottle of lukewarm water.

He had grown accustomed to the slightly lighter patch of dark appearing high above his head at random intervals, and had even tried to decipher some of the hissed words that the monsters used when they spoke about him.

One word made a reappearance over and over; Keth.

He was a Keth. Or *the* Keth, he couldn't be sure, but the word was definitely used in reference to him. As he was muttering to himself, sitting back against the smooth mud wall with his right arm clamped hard against his body to stop the pain in his shoulder, he splayed the finger of his left hand and wiggled the fingers in front of his face. He could feel the small disturbance in the still air, but could see nothing.

As he stared into the blackness, the creeping wash of ambient light gave the moving air a shape, and he could see his fingers before his face.

He held his breath, as though the slightest move could chase away the source. His head inched upwards, mouth wide and eyes wider, to see the hole above him glow dully. A shape spilled over the edge and dropped lightly to the earth in front of him just as the gap high above his head shone brighter. He automatically shielded his eyes away from the weak light as it had been so long since his eyes had seen anything but blackness.

He recoiled and tried to shove himself deeper into the hard-packed wall behind him as the shape that had landed softly in the centre of the chamber began to creep towards him. A gasp escaped his lips as the shape reared up and the hooded head was silhouetted against the light above.

"Shhh," the hood hissed as it reached out to him, "*en kosel, keth, en kosel.*"

Shaw froze in terror, half confused and half disbelieving that what he was experiencing was indeed real and not his brain tricking him.

A hand reached out from under the hooded cloak to stroke his face, and the pale fingertips were smooth and soft. Shaw let out a sob at the touch.

The simple act of contact, even if it was with a monster, broke him. The shape recoiled as the light grew slightly brighter.

"Calm, *keth*" the hooded figure said uncertainly, in a

curious accent. Shaw stifled his sobbing and held his breath again, looking at the creature with shock and awe in recognition of a word he knew. His addled brain tried to recover and replay the sound in case he had misheard it.

"Be calm, Shaw," the soft, echoing voice said again. It pronounced his name as *Shaow*, but it was unmistakably his name.

He babbled, his voice croaking in his throat as he muttered, "How?"

In response, the figure in front of him only cocked its head, then darted a small, pale hand out of the folds of its cloak holding the dirty name tape cut from his uniform. The shape recoiled then, startling Shaw with a sudden movement, and sat back on its haunches to raise both hands. Slowly, directly under the shaft of soft light from above, the hands carefully pulled back the hood exposing the face beneath.

Shaw gasped again, and the finger of his left hand fluttered at his mouth as his lips babbled involuntarily.

If he had ever had cause to use the term terrible beauty before in his life, it was ill-conceived. The oxymoron bounced around his brain until it hurt.

His eyes, adjusted now to the illuminated gloom, stared hard at the slim creature, unquestionably female, with jet-black hair trimmed short and eyes that looked through him.

Those eyes were wide-set, large and feline, which gave her a pixie-ish look.

She smiled, exposing small, white teeth, and extended a hand to him.

"Ray-lee," she said, still smiling.

Mesmerised, Shaw slowly extended his left hand as his right was useless. Touching the smooth, warm skin made him sob again. The creature moved closer to him, patting him gently but insistently.

"No, *kosel*-calm, *Shaow*," she said reassuringly, "you talk to me now?"

The End of Book One. The story concludes in Defiance: Erebus.

FROM THE PUBLISHER

Thank you for reading *Genesis,* the first book in Defiance.

We hope you enjoyed it as much as we enjoyed bringing it to you. We just wanted to take a moment to encourage you to review the book on Amazon and Goodreads. Every review helps further the author's reach and, ultimately, helps them continue writing fantastic books for us all to enjoy.

If you liked this book, check out the rest of our catalogue at www.aethonbooks.com. To sign up to receive a FREE collection from some of our best authors as well as updates regarding all new releases, visit www.aethonbooks.com/sign-up

SPECIAL THANKS TO:

ADAWIA E. ASAD	EDDIE HALLAHAN	KYLE OATHOUT
JENNY AVERY	JOSH HAYES	LILY OMIDI
BARDE PRESS	PAT HAYES	TROY OSGOOD
CALUM BEAULIEU	BILL HENDERSON	GEOFF PARKER
BEN	JEFF HOFFMAN	NICHOLAS (BUZ) PENNEY
BECKY BEWERSDORF	GODFREY HUEN	JASON PENNOCK
BHAM	JOAN QUERALTÓ IBÁÑEZ	THOMAS PETSCHAUER
TANNER BLOTTER	JONATHAN JOHNSON	JENNIFER PRIESTER
ALFRED JOSEPH BOHNE IV	MARCEL DE JONG	RHEL
CHAD BOWDEN	KABRINA	JODY ROBERTS
ERREL BRAUDE	PETRI KANERVA	JOHN BEAR ROSS
DAMIEN BROUSSARD	ROBERT KARALASH	DONNA SANDERS
CATHERINE BULLINER	VIKTOR KASPERSSON	FABIAN SARAVIA
JUSTIN BURGESS	TESLAN KIERINHAWK	TERRY SCHOTT
MATT BURNS	ALEXANDER KIMBALL	SCOTT
BERNIE CINKOSKE	JIM KOSMICKI	ALLEN SIMMONS
MARTIN COOK	FRANKLIN KUZENSKI	KEVIN MICHAEL STEPHENS
ALISTAIR DILWORTH	MEENAZ LODHI	MICHAEL J. SULLIVAN
JAN DRAKE	DAVID MACFARLANE	PAUL SUMMERHAYES
BRET DULEY	JAMIE MCFARLANE	JOHN TREADWELL
RAY DUNN	HENRY MARIN	CHRISTOPHER J. VALIN
ROB EDWARDS	CRAIG MARTELLE	PHILIP VAN ITALLIE
RICHARD EYRES	THOMAS MARTIN	JAAP VAN POELGEEST
MARK FERNANDEZ	ALAN D. MCDONALD	FRANCK VAQUIER
CHARLES T FINCHER	JAMES MCGLINCHEY	VORTEX
SYLVIA FOIL	MICHAEL MCMURRAY	DAVID WALTERS JR
GAZELLE OF CAERBANNOG	CHRISTIAN MEYER	MIKE A. WEBER
DAVID GEARY	SEBASTIAN MÜLLER	PAMELA WICKERT
MICHEAL GREEN	MARK NEWMAN	JON WOODALL
BRIAN GRIFFIN	JULIAN NORTH	BRUCE YOUNG

Lightning Source UK Ltd.
Milton Keynes UK
UKHW010652310321
381306UK00002B/334